This is a work of fiction. Names, characters, places, and incidents are
the products of the author's imagination or are used fictitiously.
Any resemblance to actual events, locales, or persons,
living or dead, is coincidental.

Jacket design: Jeanne Elizabeth Whyte
Jacket images: Jeanne Elizabeth Whyte

whytehouses@aol.com

for William

Watercolors

jeanne elizabeth whyte

ISBN: 1502480840
ISBN 13: 9781502480842

Chapter 1

Was there someone at the door? Quinn looked up from the journal in her lap thinking she heard a slight tapping noise, maybe at the back door. Instantly she thought of how awkward it was going to be to go to the door in her nightgown when it was just barely dark outside. She just couldn't help changing into it as soon as the evening light began to fade.

She got up and leaned forward to peek around the corner of the massive stone fireplace, where a lively fire was burning brightly. There was indeed someone standing out there. She could see through the kitchen to the door where his face was illuminated in the glass by a flashlight he held under his chin. The sight was eerie but she guessed that he was making himself visible so she could see who it was without opening the door, frightened by an unexpected visitor after dark. With a sigh she slipped back a few steps to grab her silk robe lying over the edge of a chair, and pulled it on quickly. Then she braced herself to approach the door.

It was Will, the elusive contractor she had been trying to get in touch with about working with her. Why couldn't he call during the daytime?

She pulled the door open towards her, and he stepped in, turning off the small red enamel flashlight and lowering it into the back pocket of his jeans.

"I was in the neighborhood," he said tentatively, tilting his head to the side and moving toward the cook stove that warmed the kitchen.

"I've been waiting to hear from you, so it's good you stopped by," she offered, stepping back from him. Her bare feet and nightclothes were a striking contrast to his sturdy work jacket, jeans and heavy boots. His hat and shoulders were sprinkled with a light dusting of snow.

"We've been slammed. No time for anything these days...you know, I'm almost booked for the summer already and there's so much to do before that even happens..." Will referred to the onslaught of work local contractors faced early every spring as people pressured them take on the myriad things they had been waiting all winter to get done, or to make room on their summer schedule for one more project while the warm building season lasted.

"Have you had a chance to take a look at the plans?" she asked.

"Not really. I mean I've looked at them but haven't really had a chance to get into them. I just wanted to let you know I haven't forgotten about you. I'm gonna get to it and get back to you as soon as I can," he said, shaking his head as if he really didn't know when that would happen.

Quinn waited.

"Is everything alright over here? I mean, I know you're alone and I just wondered if everything was going okay for you."

Will had done a lot of work on the old camp over the years and knew it well – its quirks and every problematic detail. He had turned on the water for her before she had arrived a week ago, and made sure the place was unlocked and lights were on when he found out she'd be coming in after dark. They had known each other a long time, but only in passing.

"Yeah, everything's okay..." she said, looking up at him with interest. She'd never taken the time to really notice much about him, except that he was good at his craftsman's skill of carpentry and log joinery, and dependable as the day was long. Her family had counted on him for years to take care of their old Adirondack camp and know what it needed, even when they didn't. Now she was hoping he would fulfill his promise to do the carpentry work she needed to rebuild the old boathouse that sat at the edge of the water. It had been a tough sell because he was always so busy, sometimes with a long waiting list of projects, but the autumn before he had agreed to fit the project into his schedule in the early spring.

He looked around the old kitchen, checking it out, and she looked too, to see what he might find out of order, out of place.

"Okay then," he said, tipping his chin down with a nod as if to indicate the conversation was over. "I'll be in touch..." he added, looking at her with a smile, and then turning to take his leave. The door snapped shut behind him.

Quinn moved into the center of the kitchen so she could see the red tail-lights of his truck through the window as it crept slowly up the hill of the driveway. She felt like a gust of air had blown through the old camp.

The water had always been her refuge. Even as a small child she would seek its protection and release when things went wrong, submerging down with her eyes open, looking around as if the answers might be there among the slowly moving fish, or along the rocky bottom. Now at 64, Quinn Harvey had decided to literally live with water around her all the time, as if to become some new kind of creature who could breathe air while inhaling the transforming power of water simultaneously. She longed to be infused with its soothing, healing powers of resurrection every minute of the day and night. Here at the old camp where that had been a part of her all of her life, she was already becoming more and more accustomed to the nourishment of the wilderness and water. She felt increasingly dependent on it, yet at the same time rejuvenated.

The ancient Adirondack camp that had been passed through the family for several generations now belonged to her and her sisters, Megan and Lily. They had all spent every summer of their growing years there, along with extended family and many friends. But in the years since her parents had been gone, the old camp had been practically abandoned, with nobody willing to spend their vacation time, not to mention their entire summer there anymore, except for Quinn. She had come up to spend every possible moment she could, and now she was ready to live here, even if it was going to be alone.

When she and her sisters were kids, their dad, like many New York businessmen, sweated out the hot summers in the city alone while the rest of the family camped upstate in the wilderness. When school let out in early June, they packed up whatever they needed for their stay over the three months, and made the trip to open up camp for the summer. The car was always stuffed with their things, but most of the basics were already there in the place their great grandfather had built.

When they first arrived, memories would flood into them when they opened the back door and took in the familiar smell of past summers in the old place. The deep green two-story framed wood camp stood like a tall sturdy tree in the woods that edged a pristine Adirondack lake where they would live a little on the rough all summer long. They'd run in and dash through the rooms just to see if anything had changed. Everything would look just like they'd left it after Labor Day weekend, except for the signs of little critters who always managed to invade the place and make it their own home for the winter.

The whole camp would need a thorough cleaning, and they would not be allowed to run off and play until all the chores were done. The girls dreaded picking up the dead birds who had been trapped inside – probably having come down the cold chimney, and the occasional animal nest brazenly erected on a sofa or in an old comfy chair in the front room where everything seemed to happen. A huge stone fireplace with a high log mantle across the front and wrapping its sides anchored the big room that was the center of all activities, and that was always where they got started dusting. There were so many things sitting up on the mantle that it took forever to look at each one that they had made or collected in years past, dust its space and set it back in place.

There were lots of soft old cushioned chairs, tables with antique lamps for playing games or reading, and a long dining table with a sparkly chandelier above it to eat by. They choked on the dust, wiped all the wood surfaces with rags dipped in furniture polish, and took turns with the vacuum cleaner and broom till everything was tidied, including the huge covered porch overlooking the densely wooded hill that descended to the water below. The heavy wooden doors and wavy glassed window sashes were opened to let the breezes come in through the screens, and before long the musty dampness of the long winter would give way to the sweet smell of Old English and early summer.

Upstairs there were seven bedrooms of varying sizes set beneath the open pine raftered roof. Their parents' room was the nearest to the bathroom, with its old white claw-footed tub. It too had been a bedroom before indoor plumbing had been added. The girls each had their favorite room, and after clearing the dust and vacuuming up there they made up the beds from piles of old quilts, aging wool blankets and paper thin flannel sheets which were stowed in the tin room, whose shiny walls kept the mice from breaking in. They knew that their belongings, as well as those for their parents' room, must be set up and stowed away before they were finally allowed to run down to the lake to cool off.

Mom would handle the kitchen, wiping down all the surfaces after the winter's accumulation of dust, grime, and mouse droppings. A big black wood burning cook stove took center stage, though a more modern gas range had been added so the heat wouldn't get too intense in there on hot summer days. A full sized refrigerator had taken the place of the original oak icebox, and a long white porcelain sink had replaced the water pump that had been there when the house was built. The pine walls were outfitted with oil cloth covered shelves of old blue willow dishes and jelly glasses, brightly colored bowls and wood handled utensils, all of which had to be washed and put back in their places before the food stores they brought with them could be carried in. Red rimmed white enamel pots and cast iron skillets hung on the walls near the stoves and a modest pine table with ladder back chairs sat against one wall for quick breakfasts or light lunches on rainy days. Otherwise they ate in the front room or out on the porch.

Since Daddy would be taking the car back to the city, they had to try to think of everything they'd need from the store before he left on Sunday. It was a long hot walk to the little village that was really just the store itself, and a tiny post office. Since they had hardly any money to spend, they usually reserved the trip up there for ice cream when Daddy was there to treat them. Mom didn't have any money either, so she charged supplies she needed to their account, and Daddy settled it when he was there. When he left, it would be just the girls and their mother between weekends, except when relatives or company came, the more the better.

The hustling activity of opening camp in the old days was a distant but sweet memory. Quinn almost always had to open and close camp herself now, because she was usually the only one there. Everyone lived so far away, and their days were busy from morning till night with the things they felt driven to do, and all the time spent on technical devices that kept them connected to their world, a world they never seemed to want to be separated from. Quinn didn't even have a cell phone anymore, because there was no reception at camp and she was grateful for that. She was relieved to let the landline take her calls and messages, so she didn't have to be bothered with constant interruptions.

She was never burdened by caring for the camp. Readying it for another summer season was a chore she lovingly offered as part of what she considered her duty to preserve the precious treasure it was to her. Now that no one seemed to want the responsibility of it anymore, she had decided to take that on herself, and had come to live there for the summers, visits from siblings, kids and grandkids notwithstanding. She would welcome all of them.

This year Quinn had decided to coincide her arrival at the old house with the time the ice was supposed to go out on the lakes, marking the appearance of the loons and the emergence of sleepy wildlife. She had known it would be cold when she got there, but it actually had seemed like it was still winter! The fireplace barely took the chill off the front room, so she had to get the fire in the cook stove going early each morning to warm the house enough to even sit down in one place. Snowfall was still happening occasionally and you never knew when spring might decide to come for good. There were a couple of electric space heaters she could use for emergencies, but she just hated to turn them on, preferring to use the old ways to heat the camp. There was always the concern that the pipes might freeze, since the water had already been turned on, but the temperatures had not stayed extremely low for any length of time and she kept the cabinet doors open to the relative warmth of the rooms, just in case.

After practicing architecture for most of her life, Quinn was ready to decrease the amount of work she would take on. She would still work, and was already known in the area for her diligent commitment to the natural environment and use of natural local materials that would be fitting to the pristine Adirondack setting. But she was ready for something new.

Now that her kids were grown and off struggling to make their own way with degrees in hand, she had finally begun to make a plan that would be just for her, something that would provide the creative challenge she would need for this period of her life where she might be alone for her remaining years. She wanted to explore her old love of painting in watercolor.

In order to feel the sense of peace she needed in her life, she knew she would need to live by the water - by the lake – and camp was the logical place. The old house could still be shared by the whole family, as it always had been; she would never want to take that away from them. She wanted everyone to have the opportunity to create their own precious memories there like she had, now and after she was gone. But the old boathouse down by the water was another matter. It was dying for a new breath of life. Quite seriously, if not attended to, it would die of neglect. Although the stone cribbing which held it up from the floor of the lake was stable and strong, the above water elements were severely deteriorating. The walls were rotting and leaning, in danger of collapse, and the roof leaked despite numerous layers of shingles applied over the original wooden ones over time.

Because of its age and the fact that it had once housed a little kitchen and bathroom, the Adirondack Park Agency, a ruling board that had jurisdiction over almost all building in the Adirondacks, had seen fit to allow those features to be a part of its new life too. Quinn had taken extreme pains and years of patience to obtain permission to replace the original structure with a new one that would be almost a replica of what was there before. She would keep the original cribbing foundation, shape, size and roof shape, but everything else would be replaced as necessary to completely restore the building.

The bottom level, which was right on the water, had two large boat slips with wood decking around and between them to provide access to boats which could be docked inside. Quinn's father had adored boating and had poured quite a bit of money into the collection he'd had over the years. They had handmade guide boats, and motor boats for skiing, fishing and general fooling around on the water, until they began to get run down. Then it seemed that no one wanted to spend their own money to make needed repairs, and no one wanted to invest in new motor boats. For the time being, the two slips were empty and the remaining boats were kayaks and canoes stacked neatly along the interior sidewalls. Of course there were paddles and fishing gear hanging everywhere along with life jackets, skis and floats for the kids when they came.

On the second level the original interior walls had been gutted away, so it was now a wide-open room just begging for a great design, replete with breathtaking panoramic views of the lake. It was here that Quinn wanted to create a year around studio. She wanted her empty nest home floating above the beloved water all around it. So here she was, on the brink of a life changing experience that brought her to her knees with excitement and anticipation. Who cared about a little cold she might have to put up with in the mornings when there were so many plans to be made and dreams to come true?

Chapter 2

Quinn could set a clock by the rhythm of her body, which responded consistently with the patterns of the sun. Every morning her eyes flashed open just as the dawn began to break over the far side of the lake, and she would edge up on her elbow to see the twinkling light break through the trees. To her it was the prettiest sight in the world. Thus awakened she would settle onto her back into *Savasana*, to stretch and relax fully, taking some deep cleansing breaths. When she felt completely relaxed and comfortable she sat up and moved back until she could press her lower back against pillows in front of the headboard, pulling her soft quilt up around her to stay warm. From there she could determine what the morning would bring, but it was always something good. A morning veiled with fog and mist was as nice as one that was bright and glowing, just different.

She would sit for twenty or thirty minutes of meditation, maybe more if there was something prickling her mind that she needed to calm and quiet. These moments devoted to meditation created a balanced space within her that she could draw from for the rest of the day, come what may. Her years of practice had taught her that to be present for everything was the key to just about anything. Sometimes it just came naturally to her now, but there was no way to avoid life's ups and downs and she wanted to be completely ready for all of it.

There was nothing like a cup of hot milky tea to start the day, so Quinn went down to the kitchen and set the water to boil in the red kettle on the gas stove while she started a fire in the cook stove. There was plenty of kindling in the tattered and chewed wood box beside the stove, along with a stack of newspapers and some fatwood to get the fire going, so she arranged it quickly in the fire box and lit the paper.

Just as the whistle on the kettle went off, she noticed the back end of Will's black truck through the window, parked in the driveway. Was he here again, at this hour? She poured the hot water over the tea bags in her little hand painted teapot, added some milk and topped it with the lid to let it brew. Then she looked out of each window, trying to catch a glimpse of where Will might be, and what he was up to. She couldn't see him anywhere. The fire began to pop and crackle in the woodstove, a sound she had grown to love. She added a couple of larger pieces of wood to keep it going, and replaced the iron lids. Then she went into the freezing front room.

From each of the windows she looked through the woods for him until she finally located him down at the water's edge, gazing at the leaning boathouse. While she watched, he stepped out from the shore onto a big rock that protruded from the freezing water and looked around and up at the boathouse from there. He must be evaluating the thing, she thought, though it was awfully early in the morning for that – and cold too. He had on a brown unbuttoned work jacket, his usual cap, but no gloves. She wondered if he would come up to the door to question her, but decided to trust that he knew what he was doing and returned to the kitchen to see if the tea was ready.

With her favorite white mug in hand, she ascended the creaky wooden stairs and went to her room for a little additional quiet time reading. Currently it was an old book by Pema Chodran that she had had in her library for years, and had turned back to, to reread. Her morning routine was something she cherished as a sort of daily gift to herself and almost nothing could keep her from it. She found that it was a wonderful way of incorporating spiritual study and meditation practice into every day without having to set aside time and plan around it.

However, Quinn was a curious woman, so she looked down at the lakefront from the big square window that faced the lake from the far end of the upstairs hall to see what Will was doing now. He was gone.

Quinn had chosen her childhood bedroom to sleep in, a tiny room that barely fit the bed but was right at the front of the house where she could be closest to the lake. With the window open she would be able to hear the first calls of the loons when they arrived, a sound that thrilled her. It was a bit of a hike from there to the bathroom at the very back of the house but the sacrifice was worth giving up that late evening cup of tea so she could hopefully sleep through the night without having to make the trip.

She set her tea down on the old oak ice chest she had brought up to use as a night table. The tin lined cabinet that used to hold a big block of ice was the perfect place to store her books, journals, writing pens and pencils. She had topped it with a wood carved bear lamp with a faded white shade that made a soft glowing light for the room at night.

The square little four paned window facing the lake was polished clean and hung with crystals that sparkled in the morning sunlight, casting rainbows of color all the way across the room, bringing their energy in. An old oval rag rug of pinks and yellows brightened the dark wood floors, and a soft Indian cotton quilt with vintage cased pillows softened the ancient iron bed, which had been painted white years ago. A thick vintage wool blanket lie folded at the foot of the bed for when the nights got really cold. Some of Quinn's childhood drawings were still tacked to the bare stud walls, along with those her kids had proudly brought to her so long ago. Whenever she had needed solace, the cozy little room was her get-away sanctuary, and was still her favorite place in the house.

When she was done with the morning's reading, Quinn closed the book with a beaded twine marker and sighed as she sat back thinking about the message she had just read. Pema was the expert teacher when it came to learning how to be with what is, in every moment. Quinn was determined to maintain that sense of pervasively calm mindfulness in her life, knowing full well that it took practice that was never ending. But once you were on the path, you had to stay on it. There seemed to be no other choice. It was never easy, but supposedly even life's difficulties served as lessons for the practice. If you could see the wisdom those lessons brought, perhaps it would not be necessary for them to be repeated.

She reached for her sketchbook and opened it to the early pencil drawings she had done for the design of the boathouse. As soon as the weather warmed up a little it would be time to get started right away if she wanted to be in it before another season of cold descended in the fall. It gave her great pleasure to look at the drawings and imagine the details she would incorporate to make the little home uniquely her own. She made some small sketches at the margins of the pages to remind her of these ideas when the time came. The very thought of getting started brought a warm excited hum to her whole body. There were calls to be made to confirm the participation and readiness of her favorite sub-contractors, some who had already agreed to work on the project. She knew she needed to touch base with each of them to confirm their agreements and make sure they were still available.

Setting the drawings aside, Quinn rose and started down the long center hall to the bath for a shower. With every step, she practiced perfect posture as if she had learned it in charm school, her ticking striped gown and robe flowing around her. She turned on the shower and waited for the warm water to come through the cold pipes, setting her towel nearby so she could grab it quickly when she was ready to get out. There was nothing like the clear water of the Adirondacks to warm her from the morning chill in the air, refreshing and readying her for the day.

Shivering as she rubbed herself dry, she dressed in a worn flannel shirt and lose black yoga pants, to be comfortable. She dried her hair and left it as natural looking as she could, then dusted her face with some mineral powder to even out the blotchy color.

Barefooted, she went down to the kitchen again to check on the fire and get something to eat. The kitchen was already warming, and smelled like all the mornings she had spent there with her family in summers past - a mixture of old musty things and seasoned firewood burning in the cook stove. Even the stove itself had a comforting scent as the iron heated up. She opened the lid with the silver lever handle, added some wood to the crackling fire and closed it again, pleased with the way the fire was going. She sliced up half a grapefruit, added a dollop of yogurt and sat down with her bowl at the table, wondering when the phone might start ringing to disturb her morning reverie.

It was so good to have things to do, but on her very own schedule - if ever there was one. For years that had seemed like her whole life, she had had to start early with the care of the kids, getting them off to school with breakfast and sometimes lunches before she would start as soon as she could, working at the drawing board. Sometimes she had even gotten up at 5 am to work for a couple of hours before the kids had to get up, if there was a deadline to be met. Then she would work all day with a short break for lunch, right through the moment the boys peeked in to say hi when they came in from school, and on till dinner which had been prepared with intermittent trips to the kitchen during the afternoon. There had been so many soccer practices to drive to, and so many games, it seemed like she had played soccer herself for a dozen years.

Those days were over and her time was her own now. That was a blessing and a challenge too. Living alone she had no one to care for but herself, and there were many hours available in a day. Here in the Adirondacks, things would be different. It was time to arrange her life in a new way that would not be centered around the boys anymore. Time to let them go forward on their own and focus a little more on what she needed to do for herself now. But although that might seem like a wonderful idea, she still struggled with it.

Quinn rinsed her bowl, spoon and teacup, and set them in the drainer. She went through the front room and stepped out onto the big porch, looking down at the water to get a pulse on the day. Was it going to be a good one for walking? Yes indeed.

Just at that moment the phone rang and the voice of her friend Lisbet was asking if she was ready to get going outside for a hike. Yup, that was just the thing. She headed for the mudroom off the kitchen, throwing a couple of small logs in as she passed the stove. Her thick cotton socks and hiking boots were there waiting, along with a heavy flannel shirt she would wear as a jacket, allowing her body to breath when they walked uphill and began to heat up with exertion. By the time she was ready her friend would be there to pick her up and they would hike the trail to Moth Lake.

Lisbet pulled up in her 4-wheel drive truck, and Quinn stepped out of the camp and joined her in it with a grin. They both knew what a treat they were in for, having made this trek many times before. As familiar as it was though, there would always be sweet surprises. The woods never remained the same. They pulled up the steep driveway, looking into the deep woods on either side for wild friends that might be watching from their many hiding places.

The two women had been close friends all their lives. Their mothers had been best friends, and had been coming up to camp for the summers in the Adirondacks together since they had been little girls, continuing to do so whenever they could even after they married and had children of their own. Lisbet and Quinn had been thrown together when their two families had merged, often sleeping in the same bed when camp was full of relatives and kids. In the old days, there were no modern conveniences and everything had to be done in the simplest of ways, creating precious fond memories and traditions that the women were constantly including in their everyday lives to keep them alive for their own kids and grandkids. They both felt that the prevalence of technological devices was too pervasive, having cut people off from their connection with the natural world, and were determined not to let that happen to them.

They drove in animated conversation down the familiar winding road to the trailhead. Dew was still sparkling on the tips of the pine-needled trees as the sun began to warm the woods. Birdsong was in the air that caressed Quinn's face through the open window — cold but so refreshing. There was no better scent than that of balsam pine awakening in the early spring. As they passed over creeks and inlets they could hear the rush of overflowing waters tumbling over rocks and smashing into boulders, bringing the snow melt down into the lakes and filling them back up again after the long winter period when they were kept lower so that the ice would do less damage to docks and boathouses.

When they reached the trailhead parking lot it was abandoned and quiet. Later in the summer this lot would be filled with the cars, trailers and trucks of families camping along the lake, but for now it was still empty. Lisbet parked and they climbed out, helping each other collect the gear they wanted to take and to strap on their small lightweight backpacks. Being prepared was something they had learned the hard way, so they wanted to be sure to carry water, snacks and matches, just in case.

They crossed a planked wooden bridge over a channel that separated two lakes, and started up the gentle grade looking about them for what might be new since the last time they had been there before the long winter.

The Moth Lake trail was their favorite in spring because you could still see things through the deep forest that were invisible in summer, and there was a tumbling creek that crossed the trail about halfway up, where a hand built bridge was the perfect place to watch the rushing spring water roll and splash its way down the gorge. It was loud and wild, and took your breath away. Lisbet could never resist taking pictures, even though she had taken hundreds of everything already. Somehow though, each new one seemed more perfect than the last. There was always something unique and miraculous to discover and examine in the wilderness.

The two friends were fascinated by moss. There were so many varieties, and they were all so beautiful. It was a wonder how they would be the first green to pop up, before anything else was in bloom, and it was an amazing bright green that just seemed unbelievably lush in early spring. They would be forever stopping to stare at the furry mats of it lining the floor of the woods, blanketing logs and even covering huge rocks.

There was an off trail path that they always traveled up to a very special spot that not everyone knew about, so they headed for that, taking their time and breathing in the newness of the bright spring air. For them, walking was so much more than an exercise. It was an opportunity to listen to the sounds of the natural world, communing with its music and its messages. When the trail became steep and they needed to catch their breath, one of them would call for a "conversation", and they would stop for a moment, just long enough to regulate their breathing before they went on. No need to explain!

The first hike to Moth Lake was a ritual to them that meant winter was finally over. It was the long awaited new beginning of yet another season. Sometimes they wondered how many more they would have left – so many of their friends had been lost to cancer, heart attacks and all the dreaded plagues of old age. Quinn and Lisbet felt so young at heart it was hard to believe the older woman they each found looking back at them in the mirror. They had both been married, raised kids, divorced, and not necessarily in that order. They had been through it all.

It would seem that life would be winding down, but to them it seemed to be just starting! They felt they had all the vibrancy of a twenty or thirty something year old, and wanted to experience the joy of everything that might still come their way now that they had all the time in the world to do what they wanted to do and the energy to give to someone else. Love in their lives was something they cherished, for their families, for men they wanted to have opportunities to share with, and for each other. Their conversations constantly drifted between the concepts they were learning on their respective spiritual journeys and their loved ones. Sharing these experiences and listening to each other with patience and carefully thought out suggestions had become a way of putting the teachings they had learned into practice.

When the two hikers had come through the woods to the highest part of the trail, they came upon the old familiar fire pit, a circle of big rocks that had been created years ago by hikers who looked forward as much as they did to getting to the top of the trail and taking a rest. Just beyond was a magnificent isolated lake that was such a surprise to see so high up on the edge of the mountain. It was like being at the top of the world, a magical place where the water seemed to flow into the sky.

Without a word they wandered separately around the edges of the clearing that emerged deep in the woods, picking up twigs, some brush and pine needles, and bringing them back to build a fire to sit beside on the long log that always awaited them. Lisbet arranged the brush and small sticks because she was the expert fire maker, pulled her matches from her pocket and lit the dry leaves in the pile while Quinn continued to circle around for a little more kindling and a couple of long sticks.

They drank from their water bottles, and when the fire seemed perfect, they roasted hot dogs that Lisbet had remembered, her favorite for a campfire lunch. Quinn didn't think she was hungry until she tasted the first bite. How could a silly hot dog taste so good?

They both stared at the little fire till the food was gone — it was too good to bother with talking. Though they were both avidly healthy eaters, a hot dog grilled over an open fire was the perfect thing for the season's first real hike. It hit the spot! They sat smiling quietly, looking out at the shimmering flat lake, both wondering if loons would come to nest there this year. The place was so quiet and secluded it was as if no one had ever come there, and no one ever would. It was a wild place only inhabited by the creatures of the woods, and them. Lisbet stirred the fire, turning it over so that all the kindling would have a chance to burn before they had to put it out. Quinn dug into her pack for some dark chocolate, and they let that melt in their mouths as the tranquility of the magnificent place sank into their souls.

They both tamped down the coals of the fire, and poured water from the lake over them to make sure there would be no sparks left to worry about. They left the remaining kindling they had collected for the next visitors, as was the habit of everyone who knew about this special place. One year, someone had even constructed a little table against a big tree, with one leg beneath it, but that had disintegrated and was now gone. Still, it was interesting to imagine the many people who had come to this place, as they had, sharing it and then leaving it better for the next ones to come.

As they descended the long trail downhill toward home they drank in the glory of the sun sparkling through the mint green mist that was the sprouting of tiny new leaves getting ready to burst open. Quinn searched for a few miniature flowers to bring back to her kitchen table.

They inhaled the fresh air deeply – something that they had longed to do for so long while the snow had persisted and cold had prevailed. It was finally over and they smiled at each other without having to speak of their heart's desire – the first spring kayak trip.

The ice had finally gone out on the lakes, but it was always a good idea to let the water warm up to something tolerable, though not in any way warm of course, before setting off on the first kayak paddle of the season. The weather bounced back and forth between freezing cold with great big snowflakes falling, sometimes even when the sun was out, to pouring rain and thunderstorms with temperatures in the 60's. The creeks were full and threatening to overtake the roads – flood warnings were in place all over the North Country. Quinn and Lisbet's boats were still stowed away in their boathouses and basements, but they were dying to release them from winter bondage.

An early kayak trip where they had misjudged the bitter cold and difficult conditions in a channel between two lakes was still fresh in their minds and they did not want to repeat that debacle. They had gone out one sunny spring day, but a fierce wind had sprung up just at the same moment they pushed off into the water. They had considered returning to shore again and waiting a few more days, but their excitement getting on the water got the better of them and they had gone ahead with their ill conceived plan. The wind did not let up, and the presence of numerous beaver dams they had not foreseen and had to portage around and over made the adventure go sour to the point that they had considered abandoning the water altogether and carrying their boats on a long hike back to the truck. Although they had braved the weather and the obstacle course to continue on and return the way they had come, they vowed not to make that kind of mistake again. It had not been fun, and they were both chilled to the bone when they finally got back into the truck with relief and turned on the heat to warm up and dry off.

Planning for the first paddle trip was exciting but took a lot of thought and consideration. The loons were in the cold waters somewhere, but when they first arrived it was sometimes hard to observe them from a distance. The idea of getting out to be with them on the smooth clear water after looking at hard white ice for so many months was really enticing. The thought of it made you want to drop everything, grab your boat and go. But the women knew better. They held their desires in check and kept right on planning.

As they drove along route 28 there was a great view of all the lakes from the windows of the truck, and they chattered and smiled at the sight of so much clear water, with just a few large patches of transparent floating ice that looked as thin as a sheet of black tissue paper. They determined that the first warm, sunny day that arrived would be their day to go.

Chapter 3

Quinn came in the back door, shed her outdoor gear and went to stoke the kitchen fire. It was just about out so she added small kindling sticks to get it to catch again. She sat down with a big glass of water and pulled off her hiking boots, then slid her planning book into view so she could see about making the calls she had promised herself to attend to, so that the progress of organizing her boathouse project would continue going forward. She made a few calls and left messages, but did not get a single answer.

The most important connection she needed was with Will, but she didn't want to rush him. Because he had always seemed to be a man who liked to be in control of his work and his life, she knew that bugging him or interfering with whatever process he had of making his own mind up about something would be a mistake. So she looked at his cell number, but did not make use of it. She couldn't help but wonder though, what he was thinking — if he would follow through to do the work with her, and at what price. She didn't want to call anyone else, as she usually did when helping clients obtain bids on construction, because she was so sure that he would be perfect. He was fussy and sometimes bossy, but those traits came with perfectionism, and that was what she was really after. She herself would be very particular about every little thing, every detail, and she needed someone who would understand that and go with it without resentment or the temptation to cut corners.

Sometimes there was nothing to do but wait.

Quinn did not think of waiting as being in nowhere land with nothing to do — a negative space. She believed that a cosmic plan was in place for her, and that by stepping back she would allow positive energies to pull things into place without her interference. Trusting in what would come of its own accord rather than pushing for a desired outcome was the way she wanted to live every aspect of her life now. God knows she had made a mess of enough things in her past by making the kind of mistakes one is bound to make by trying to get what she thought she wanted rather than being led to what was really right for her. She was done with that kind of behavior and decision-making.

Deep inside she had a powerful confidence that everything would evolve just exactly as it should. The challenge was to trust that intuition and not allow impatience to interfere and cause her to make a hurried mistake.

So she threw an old indian blanket over her shoulders, grabbed her carving kit and went to the porch to work on a wooden deer she had started. From there she could look over the lake, listen to a loon that might be calling to her, and keep her hands busy. She slid into her favorite rocker with her work, looked down to the wavy lake below and took a long deep breath. As she gazed at the ice cold lapping water she relaxed with the confirmation that it was indeed too cold to try to kayak just yet.

Carving was the perfect exercise in letting go of what was not needed, and leaving what was. She liked the feel of the knife in her hand, and the soft pale wood in the other. Yes, there was a direction you were going, and you had to make an effort to get there, but the end result could be somewhat of a pleasant surprise if you allowed yourself to be led. The sharp knife would pull the away the soft wood wherever she directed it to, so she had to be careful. Once the wood was gone, it could not be put back into place for a do-over.

She recalled what the I Ching said about waiting. Of course you could be just a human being waiting for something to happen, but you could also ask for help for something that needed to happen or to change. Sometimes you didn't even know what you needed, but there was an energy that was always wiser than you. Your desires could be firmly in place, but you had to find the strength within to check those desires so that cosmic help could come to you when you were receptive. It was never a good idea to act at the whim of your controlling ego - a hard habit to break.

Learning these miraculous aspects of life was one thing. Having the strength and determination to practice them all the time was another. Quinn had been working with the I Ching, meditation, and spiritual practice for thirty years, but she still thought of herself as a learner, ever a student searching for new ideas and ways to be more in tune with the universal laws of the cosmos.

She rocked and carved for a long time, letting a myriad of thoughts roll through her mind. She remembered that she had decided to try her hand at watercolor painting again after a 30 year hiatus, and reminded herself to make a plan to visit the huge art store she had heard about. It would be an all day trip, going there and back, but the thought of looking at all the new paints, papers, brushes and other gear that would be all new to her was something she looked forward to, and at the same time seemed to be avoiding. If she bought all the things she needed, then she would have to use them.

After so many years away from it, she didn't know how to start. It would be just like starting from the beginning again — as if she had never painted a thing in her life. She was dying to approach painting again, but yet she was also avoiding it like the plague, wasn't she? A very interesting state of mind — wanting something so much and at the same time trying one's best not to initiate it.

She knew that she was in the precarious space between working so hard for so many years to make a success of herself and her career, raising her kids, and the brand new time ahead of her where she could do whatever she wanted as long as she could get by financially. There would be lots of choices now, and she wasn't used it that. It was more familiar to have to struggle all the time with what had to be done, putting off things that she actually looked forward to doing into the distant future. Now that future time was right here in the present, and she was just learning how to manage. It was difficult not to feel guilty for every moment she was not working. Work was such a huge part of her life that she didn't know quite what to do without an abundance of it demanding all her time and effort. Free time was something entirely new.

When the chill of the evening air began to set in, Quinn put her carving things into her bag and headed into the kitchen to warm up some barley vegetable soup and put a slice of her oat bread into the toaster. The coolness of the evening put her in the mood for something warm and comforting. She ate at the little table, realizing that she had gotten tired from the busy day and the brisk air, and was ready for a good book in the comfort of her wonderful bed upstairs.

She cleaned up in the kitchen, hating any dirty dishes she might have to face in the morning, and checked the internet for messages or pictures posted by the kids, or notes from her clients. There was nothing. So she closed the computer and the camp down, and headed up to her perfect little room under the eves, lighting lamps along the way.

Her legs ached a little from the long hike, but that was nothing new. At least her hip was not aching with every step as it had last spring. She thanked the stars that the painful hip was not the start of a long-standing condition due to aging, as she had feared it might be. The pain still came and went, and she hoped she could keep it at bay with lots of reasonable exercise. It seemed like hip and knee replacements were now an everyday thing for people her age, something she desperately wanted to avoid.

It was barely dark, but Quinn changed into her gown and robe, so that she could creep into the solace of her soft bed and its warm welcoming covers to read. The camp was cooling off and would get cold, but her bed would be warm and cozy. There was no TV, but she had given that up long ago anyway. She was a voracious reader with no apologies. A good book was something she so looked forward to, every night.

She turned down the cottony quilt and creamy flannel sheets and sat back against the many soft pillows she needed to be comfortable to read. The book she was reading was at her side, the rest piled on a shelf nearby. She had made elegant book place markers with waxed cord threaded through unique beads, and they swung gently from the knob of her lamp when she turned it on. With the novel resting in her lap she sat and thought for a moment about how good it would be to share this place and this moment with someone.

To have someone there in bed with her, some one to touch and hold, to share these beautiful moments, would be so good. Desire was something that could cause you to make mistakes - she knew that. Besides, there was no one she really desired that she could think of. She hoped that one of these days someone would come to love her. There was never any lack of someone she could love, oh she could love lots of people. But at this stage in her life, she wanted to share herself with a person who would want her for exactly who she was. Someone who would choose her, not the other way around, which had never worked.

Every single person she had chosen had been terribly wrong. Yes, she had her precious children, and she was grateful for the connections that had brought them to her, but that was a long time ago. Would it always be this way? Would she be able to find happiness in the moment knowing that she would always be living alone?

She pushed her thoughts aside and began reading, sinking down into the comforting softness. Soon she was into the world of the story, mesmerized by the craft of the writer.

Suddenly Quinn startled at a noise coming from downstairs in the kitchen. Instinctively wrapping her robe close about her, she tossed the book aside and jumped up to see what was going on. Thank goodness lights were still on so she could hurry down the old steep stairs that led right into the kitchen.

There behind the glass in the door was face of Will, lit again by the flashlight below his chin. Why in the world did he always have to stop by when she least expected him?

She took a deep breath of relief that it was nothing worse than an inconvenience, and opened the door.

"I just had a few questions…" he said, holding up the rolled plans.

Quinn was so glad that he was working on them that she forgot to express her frustration with the lateness of the hour, and no notice that he was planning to come by.

"Come on in then," she said, stepping back to let him pass into the dimly lit kitchen, which was already losing the heat it had accumulated from the stove all day. She headed over to the little table to sit down, turned on the lamp and looked up at him expectantly.

He unrolled the plans on the table and looked at them, obviously gathering his thoughts while standing there pensively.

"I see you want to conventionally frame the roof," he said. "Why not use trusses? It will save time and might cost about the same when you consider the cost of labor."

"I don't want to use manufactured lumber. I'd rather use local wood and stick build it so we can have the flexibility of ceilings vaulted all the way up. That will give the room a sense of volume and space that we couldn't get with flat or scissor trusses," she answered. "Why don't you sit down for a minute? You must have had a long day."

"Thanks, I'm fine," he said. Maybe he thought that sitting down would make this an actual meeting.

"I have a place that could manufacture these walls, with all the windows and doors in place, in a warehouse. They could be shipped to the site and we could install them in a day. I've done that many times and it works out well."

"No, I want to buy all the materials myself and do the labor on site. That way I can obtain the savings of charging the costs to my own accounts, and get a discount on the windows from people I have been buying them from for years for my clients," said Quinn. "Plus, I want to be there for the framing so decisions won't be made by strangers in another place who may not know how I want to do things. For me it's an artistry I want to be part of. I can't turn that over to someone else."

Will tilted his head and looked at her skeptically. Most likely he was used to handling all aspects of a project himself, so this one would be very different for him – having her input on everything. He sighed deeply as if to indicate that he didn't want to argue the point. It was probably hopeless.

Quinn sat patiently and said nothing further, giving Will a chance to take in her unwanted opinion and mull it over a bit, but she did smile.

"It will be a piece of cake to build this, Will," she offered. "It's such a simple little building, we can frame it up in a week anyway, because some of the walls are salvageable."

"Oh right! A piece of cake…" he mocked. "You don't know all the complications that come up. It's way harder than you think." He was beginning to sound somewhat annoyed.

"Well I don't mean to belittle the work. I just don't think this job is that difficult to do. It's just a basic box – how can that be so complicated?"

Quinn realized she had better guard herself against making this man feel that they were on two opposite sides of the same question. She needed him to be on her side. She wanted him to see that they could do this together as she worked in partnership with him, not as a distant client he had to please, who showed up on weekends expecting miracles to have occurred. She had built plenty of houses over the years but it would do no good to mention that right now. She needed Will to feel that his many years of experience trumped hers, and that he would ultimately be in charge if he agreed to take this project on.

So she looked down at the plans and waited for his next objection. When the silence continued, she looked up and watched him for a moment. He was a tall handsome man with a ruddy look that was the result of years working outdoors. She thought he was about her age, possibly a few years younger. His hair must have been very dark brown to black, but now it was shot with silver. There was quite a lot of it, but he seemed to always keep his head covered for warmth. His face was strongly defined and his piercing blue grey eyes studied the drawings as he considered them a moment more, then he rolled them up again and stood there stubbornly looking back at her. It appeared that he wanted to get out of there as soon as he could. His visit had probably been reluctant, and apparently he wanted to make it as brief as possible.

Quinn stood up so he could leave.

"Okay then, I'll get back to you," he told her, heading for the door. Just as he got there he turned back. "Is everything going all right? You got enough wood to keep you warm in this place?"

"Oh yeah," she said. "Everything's fine. You okay too?"

"Just tired, is all…" he said, finally letting a little smile appear. It made his eyes sparkle, and that made Quinn lighten up too.

He opened the door, turned and left her with "Gotta go…" walking head down towards his truck with the plans tucked under his arm.

Quinn turned out the light on the table, went to the door and stood looking out as his truck ascended the hill. When he turned onto the main road and the lights disappeared she stared through the big pane of glass into the darkness for a moment more, slowly shaking her head from side to side. She felt baffled as to what had just happened.

She slowly headed for the old wooden steps to go up. It seemed like a gust of air had blown in from the woods, and she shivered. Why did he always have to catch her off guard? He must know that she was basically waiting to hear back from him, with nothing else important she had to do right now all day long. The boathouse project was her priority, and she was filling time, at his mercy as far as being able to take the next step, unless she was willing to settle for working with someone else. To her that would mean depriving herself of getting the best, and that was something she was unwilling to do.

There was no choice but to bare with Will's unpredictability and hope he would commit to taking this thing on with her. Right now it was going to take some more patient waiting, she thought, until he gave her a definite positive answer. She had no idea if she had handled herself well with him, but it was hard to think on your feet when he showed up like that at the oddest hours.

She felt like pacing the creaking floors upstairs to settle her energy, so she walked down the long center hall and went to the big square window at the end to look out at the woods. The wood sash gave with a groan when she pulled it towards her, opening the window wide to take a deep breath of the cold night air. It filled her chest and felt as if it penetrated her whole body with the coming spring. There were stars twinkling, and the glow of the moon softly lit the night sky. Rustling leaves could be heard in the distance, but it was probably just the wind ruffling the tress. The window snapped shut with a satisfying click when she turned the lever to pull it tight.

Quinn shuffled slowly back down the hall toward the bathroom, and ran water from the left tap into the chipped porcelain basin until it warmed. With both hands cupped together she splashed it onto her face without any soap and patted it dry gently, leaving some of the moisture to sink into her skin. She didn't look up into the mirror.

She hung the damp towel, turned off the light and headed back down the hall to the golden glow coming from the door of her room. It was cozy and welcoming there and her soft bed felt like a cloud to land on, comforting her. Her book was waiting where she left it, and she picked it up and looked for the place where she'd left off.

Instead of reading though, she returned it to the chest beside her, clicked out the light and found herself staring off into the moonlit night until she finally drifted off to sleep.

Chapter 4

The next morning Quinn woke with a mission to get everything she possibly could organized and ready for the building process, whether Will would be a part of it or not. Sitting in the kitchen by the stove, which was cranking up to take the chill off the morning air, she called her construction rep at the local building supplier. She faxed him her window and door list, but he already had a set of her plans and was working on a take-off and estimate for the all the materials and supplies needed, down to the last nail. He promised to have it ready by the end of the day.

She checked in with the roofer, leaving him another message reminding him to get her a price for the new metal roof. She found that with most contractors it was like pulling teeth to get answers. They all seemed to have an aversion to the phone, even though it was their lifeline to new work.

Then she went online and specified all the plumbing fixtures and fittings she already knew she wanted to use, so they could be ordered with a click when the proper time came for them to be delivered. She checked out the availability and pricing for the few light fixtures and appliances she already had in mind, so those would be at hand too. Because the boathouse was small in comparison to a house, it was not a huge task, but nevertheless it took most of the morning. There was no use in getting any of these items too soon, because they would be shipped out immediately and then have to be stored somewhere out of the way until the project was ready for them.

Thank goodness the day had emerged as a cloudy one, threatening rain, so there was no need to think she was missing out on a nice hike. Just to make sure she'd thought of everything she needed to order, she went down to the water and climbed the old stairs up to take a long look at the space waiting for her attention. Although it was already swept out, she swept it again to get rid of cobwebs and the droppings from mice that had probably enjoyed the place as their personal playroom all winter.

Sweeping was meditative for her — she could lose herself in the rhythm of the broom going back and forth, and make the place clean at the same time. When the worn out bare floor looked smooth and clean again, she propped the tattered broom against a wall and lowered herself down onto it near an old window that was open to the floor, to look out at the lake. She leaned against the jamb and dangled her legs out of the opening just like she'd done when she was a kid on the dock.

There's nothing as soothing as being on the water, she thought as she looked out. Her mind eased and she felt absolutely no anxiety about the project at hand. If this was to be her home, she wanted it to be smart and comfortable in every way — she wanted to think of everything one might need in a tiny house. It would be like living on a boat. Everything should be compact, efficient, and beautiful.

There would be a place for all her equipment, clothes, food and supplies, but everything had to be minimalized to make it work. There would be just one room except for the bathroom and a small walk-in closet, which would be placed on the shore side so everything else would have the panoramic view of the water on all three other sides.

She looked around the empty space, imagining herself at home there so she could picture everything she would need. She wanted to assure herself that she had thought of everything. Her bed would be in the back corner, near windows facing east up the lake so she could see the sun rise every morning. Then there would be a sitting area with a fireplace facing the water on the front wall, and a small kitchen workspace off to the sunset side, with appliances hidden beneath one expanse of countertop and lots of drawers below it for storage. The vaulted ceiling would be new, but would make use of old log rafters that had been set into place 100 years ago, and would expand the sense of volume and light in the modest living area.

She determined that all the old logs were sound enough to save because they were dry and appeared to be as strong as ever, but they would be used on the inside of the new roof. The immense amount of support now required by building codes for snow loads would be handled by new deep rafters, and the insulation required would be encased within the roof cavity. The original logs would then go on the underside of the ceiling, where they could easily be seen beneath the pine board interior finish.

As she gazed out at the beauty of the setting, Quinn felt a sense of wellbeing, and knew in her heart that she would be happy here. The afternoon sun slanted across the wide floorboards, creating a pretty pattern and confirming that it would travel through the space all day long when the space was finished. Light was so important to her — she seemed to need it to breathe. The interaction of the sunlight and the water surrounding her felt like heaven on earth. It might be that she would be alone, but who could ask for a better place to live in harmony with the natural world and all the cosmic energies. The thought of it was uplifting.

Quinn pulled herself up to her feet with a moan. Sitting for any length of time anywhere made her legs feel weak when she needed them to stand on again. Moving around the room to stretch herself out again, she glanced briefly out each of the window openings as if to check the view from each of them, then headed for the stairs to go down. It was time to go in.

As she walked up the hill back to camp she felt a sense of peace float down upon her like a cloak. It was the perfect time for a walking meditation, so she pulled off her slip-ons, cleared her thoughts away and allowed herself to be brought into alignment with the earth, the old pine needles at her feet, and the piney woods around her. A slight smile came to her face and she walked as slowly as she could to linger in the moment of pure contentment.

The old fireplace in the main room wasn't something she used every day, because the wood stove in the kitchen provided better heat for the house. But there was nothing like it for atmosphere so Quinn laid a fire there, lit it, and went to the kitchen for a glass of wine. It would be the perfect ending to her effective but contemplative day, to sit by the fire, listen to some of her favorite music, and make some notes in her journal.

Just as she had everything set, and had just sat down in her favorite of the tattered cushioned chairs, the back door creaked and Will walked in though the kitchen. He called out "hello?" but he didn't wait for an answer and came slowly around the corner of the fireplace before she could even get up and see who it was. Maybe he had seen the smoke outside drifting up from the stone chimney as the fire struggled to get itself going.

She looked up at him and had to smile as she shook her head in wonderment over Will's sense of timing. At least she had her clothes on...

"Well, you caught me relaxing. Would you like a beer?" she asked.

"Yeah, I could take a beer," he answered her. "Don't get up... I think I know where it is."

Quinn was glad she kept good beer in the fridge for visitors but she didn't know what kind he liked. He came back with one in his hand and headed for a chair, sitting down a little uneasily, as though he didn't quite know where it would be okay to sit...

"What are you doing?" he asked her.

It was then that she remembered she had her journal on a pillow in her lap, pen in hand.

"Oh, I'm just writing...I like to put down my thoughts once in awhile...it helps me consolidate my feelings a little and see where I am. It's not like diary writing or anything. I just write about where I am in my mind with a few notes on what's been happening," she said. "How was your day?"

She didn't think it would be a good idea to tell him right then that she would also often use these journal entries to consult the I Ching. No need to scare him off now when she just might be making some progress.

"It was okay," he answered, talking a pull on the beer. "I'm so busy right now it makes my head spin. Everybody wants everything done during the season, and it all has to be started now."

Quinn could feel the pressure that would create on him. It must be hard to endure a long fairly quiet winter, and then have everything hit the fan at the same time, needing answers. She didn't want to be one of those pressures on Will, but she too wanted to get her project started, so she was one of them whether she liked it or not. She knew that patience was the only key to putting Will at ease, no matter how she felt. So she didn't ask him for answers or commitments. She just waited to see what he had on his mind, observing him as he looked into the crackling fire.

They talked about the little things, the weather, and he commented on the music she had playing, Joni Mitchell's "Blue". The old album was one of her favorites, and she never tired of listening to it.

When Will finally spoke he offered to do the carpentry on the boathouse for her. Instead of giving her a price though, he started to list the things that should be done first, and then the following steps. Quinn smiled inside and out while she listened to him describe the job the way he saw it.

She knew it was important to let him have control over how he wanted to manage it. She would be his help-mate, not the boss. She offered to get all the building materials onto the site right before he needed them. That shouldn't be too hard, she thought, because Will used the same building materials company she was planning to order from, and when they found out he would be doing the project they would be glad to get him whatever he needed, on time, to keep his business coming their way. She told him she would let him review the take-off list before making the first order so he could see if he had any problems with it, or anything more to add. Of course, she would pay the bills.

"I can't tell you how glad I am that you decided to squeeze me into your schedule," she said, trying not to act too happy. "I know this is going the be a great project for both of us and I am so grateful you are giving it a chance."

He got up to tend to the fire, prodding it skillfully with the iron poker so that the flames began to rise. Quinn sensed that he was getting uncomfortable so she knew she had to pop the question now before he might take off for the door.

"So, how much is this going to cost me?" she asked.

He didn't look up or answer. He just continued to watch the fire as it livened. Quinn was afraid he didn't hear her, or just wasn't going to answer, but still she waited for what seemed like forever until he finally turned and gave her the figure he had in mind. It was a little more than Quinn wanted to pay, but she knew she was getting what she wanted in craftsmanship, and that another builder might charge her less, but then charge over and over for extras for the whole duration of the job. It would work.

"Alright then," she said smiling. "We have a deal."

They both looked into the now blazing fire, without a word. He set the fire iron on the hearth against the stone of the big fireplace.

"Do you want another beer?" she asked.

"Oh no, I gotta be going," he answered her softly, looking at the door and moving towards it.

"Well, what's your favorite kind? I'd like to have that here for you if you're going to be here working. It will be right in the fridge and you can help yourself whenever you want."

"I like Stella," he offered, with a slight smile.

"Okay, Stella it is…I'll get some tomorrow," said Quinn.

They both went into the kitchen and headed towards the door. It was dark already, and Will stopped just outside the door to gaze at the night sky.

"Come here," he directed, tilting his head toward the darkness.

She didn't know just what he meant, but she edged out the doorway toward him anyway.

"Look up," he told her. He was looking up himself.

Quinn looked up and saw a vibrant array of stars twinkling everywhere. The sky was completely clear, making the stars all the more bright. She gazed at the beauty of it, and then looked at Will. He was just staring at the glorious scene above him, as if he had nothing else on his mind – in a world of his own – and what a magnificent world it was.

She knew at that moment that there was something more to this man that perhaps she had overlooked. She sensed his strong connection and love for the natural world. That was something she could identify with – it was a big thing to have in common. He also knew when words were not necessary to convey a feeling…

"Gotta go," he said as he slipped his hat on and ambled over to his truck. Just before he got in, he looked back at her and smiled.

That smile was disarming, no doubt about it, and she smiled back.

Quinn went slowly back into the house, snapping the heavy back door closed behind her, leaning against it for a moment to take in what had just happened.

She took a calming breath and went back to her chair, tucking her now chilled feet under her to warm them up again.

She took a slow sip of wine, gazing into the animated fire. Well, she thought, I have finally gotten what I've wanted, the chance to work with someone who will put as much attention and care into this new little house as I will. She reached for her pen to make some notes in her journal about the significance of that big step and how she felt about it, and paused again to let it sink in. It was the best news she had gotten since she'd arrived at camp.

Now, the future summer had the direction she'd so hoped it would. The team of people she felt she needed to make this unique house on the water was coming into place, and she hadn't had to do anything special to make that happen. She had waited patiently, even when she had wanted to take action in the worst way, to push things along. When she'd prayed at night, she'd asked that the pieces come together in just the way the cosmos had in mind for her, and amazingly it appeared that those invisible angelic forces had been behind her all along, magically bringing together this special combination of creative energies.

The thought of it made a quivering little shudder of excitement stir inside her, a feeling she always seemed to have when something of inner truth approached her or was made clear to her. So at that moment she knew with certainty that she was on the right path, the correct way that she was meant to be going. There was nothing more comforting than this realization, whenever it came to her. All she needed to do was to stay true to this path that was being laid out before her — stay true to herself. And with that realization she also knew that building her boathouse home was going to be one of the most precious experiences of her life.

Chapter 5

Quinn had been married a couple of times, but in the eyes of the world these marriages had "failed". After enduring the agony of divorce, and for many years afterwards contemplating her marriages, she no longer saw those relationships as failures. Even though she realized she did not really know what true love was when she had been married, there was a kind of love there, even if it had been brief and fraught with difficulties - and, she had her children, the real loves of her life.

But she felt she had never experienced what she now saw as an interconnection with a loved one on the spiritual level of inner truth, where the ego was subdued. She wondered what it would be like to share that kind of mutual respect and oneness with someone, now that she was aware of this concept of what love really was. It would be difficult to impossible to be lucky enough to find a partner who wanted that same thing, but it was the only way she would ever consider undertaking on a partnership again, as much as she wanted to have one. She knew too, that desire for someone would lead down a wrong path. She had to be with her life as it was in every moment, and just see what it would bring.

Oddly, she had even gotten to the point of not looking for anyone anymore. She looked at men observationally and objectively, she thought, because she trusted that if she was in the right place to have a loved one appear for her, the cosmic energies would provide for that. There was nothing she needed to do. Sometimes there was a little bell ringing in her head for some reason when she encountered someone, so she just acknowledged it – sometimes gave it some thought – and let it go. She was happy, and at ease with her aloneness at last after struggling with how to accept and understand it for so long.

Lisbet had struggled with the same ideas for years too. After a long marriage with five children, she too divorced and had lived alone for years. The Adirondacks was not a place where there was a tremendous selection of potential partners - that was for sure. There were local men who had been born and raised here, and most of them were married – some divorced. It was not easy to meet new people, especially if you had no interest in hanging out at the bars – and they didn't. Then there was the age factor.

Quinn and Lisbet were in their sixties. It might be said they were too old for love, but they didn't think they were meant to keep the love and beauty they had accumulated all this time to themselves. It was meant to be shared.

The problem was it would not be a good idea to risk the level of personal growth they had both attained, only to throw it away on a relationship that very likely would not be in their best interest. So it was the source of endless conversation for them – analyzing the occasional relationship that might come up, and what to do about it. The two friends were a great support for each other, because they could take any concern at all to the table and talk about it, knowing that it would be met with deep listening, understanding, and a thoughtful response.

One morning broke bright and sunny, with the water as still as a mirror. It looked so beautiful and inviting that Quinn could hardly stand it. She knew that would probably change as soon as the first breeze drifted over the lake, but she called Lisbet anyway. Maybe this would be the day for their first kayak trip.

"I'll be down there within the hour, put my boat in and meet you at your dock,'" Lisbet told her. She had stored her own boat in her family camp just down the lake, and would drive there to embark.

So Quinn put any other thoughts of things she might need to do aside, and quickly made a couple of egg sandwiches with her homemade bread and hardboiled eggs she always kept in the fridge. She bagged and sealed them up, grabbed some water and collected her gear to go down to the lake. She smoothed some sunblock on her face, especially over her nose, slipped on a pair of silky black long johns and a top, and pulled a flannel shirt over it.

She found her ragged flip-flops from last year, a life jacket stowed on a top shelf, and her trusty boat hat, which had a terrifically wide soft brim and a cord that tightened under her chin to keep it secure when the wind blew up. Grabbing her good graphite paddle from its safe corner against the hallway wall, she made her way down to the water to retrieve her pond boat from the boathouse.

It was a little buggy, but not too bad if she kept moving. She pushed the wooden door forcefully and it popped open with a waft of the familiar pungent smell of the water, wood, and old boats. Her own favorite was perched overturned on top of a rack, so she lifted it up with one hand, keeping it balanced with the other, and brought it to the water's edge, slipping it into the lake gently. She put the paddle and sandwich bag in, pulled her pant legs up over her calves to keep them dry, then stepped tentatively into the freezing water. Clear as a bell, cold, but bearable, she thought. She slid one leg into the boat, and followed by sitting carefully down onto the hard black foam seat, pulling her other leg in with her.

This was the moment she had waited for all winter - the day she could get back out on the water! The boat drifted out from the shore slightly, and she let it, sitting still so she could just take a moment to look around from the vantage point she so loved, from the seat of her boat. Lisbet was not yet in sight, so there was time to just sit afloat in the silence of the beautiful day.

Out slightly in the distance, Quinn saw the black head and sharply pointed beak of a loon pop up, and then a second one. There was a pair fishing together. She watched them delightedly for a few moments while they watched her too, and then she spoke to them.

"Hello my friends…" she said quietly. "I'm so glad to see you!"

One of the loons answered her with a little cry, a shake of his head and then dove down again. The other followed and they disappeared for a few minutes.

Lisbet came paddling slowly down around the shoreline into view and the two women greeted each other silently by pointing to the loon pair, all smiles. It was just what they were hoping to see that morning.

The sun was shining brightly and a slight breeze had shown up as expected - a good thing, because they did not want to be attacked by blackflies. They knew that the key would be to paddle where they would be just at the edge of the breeze, but yet protected by the sunny warmth of the coves they knew so well. They would head down to the Forever Wild end of the lake and see how far they could go. On the first outing it was not a matter of endurance, but being able to tolerate a cold wind that might overtake them, or the lack of wind, which would bring out the flies. So they set out, happy as larks.

The water was so clear it seemed transparent. It was still freezing cold but the air felt comfortably warmed by the sun shining on their faces. It was gorgeous out on the water – the place they had both longed to be for months. They kept fairly close to the shoreline, ducking beneath fragrant overhanging pines and hemlocks, taking in their piney scent, looking at the familiar old empty camps for changes or damage that might have occurred over winter. There were blow downs in some of the coves where rushing streams were feeding the lake, creating an obstacle course to maneuver, but that was fun to do too. All the while they looked keenly around them for possible new loon nest sites, taking in the scent of the fresh clean waters infused with new spring growth.

Almost no one was in camp yet anywhere. It always amazed Quinn that the lakes were so underused – quiet and abandoned for most of every year. Everything was still shut up and silent. There was no activity at all, though the summer season was really only a few short weeks away. Most people only came for a brief vacation, rather than for the entire summer like they used to. So, they had just about the whole lake to themselves.

They kept watch for the loon pair, and any others that might show up, and after awhile they noticed another pair come into view a distance away. That was good news. Chances were that one of these pairs would have an egg or two to nest on, and there might be some babies to look after all summer. This was something the women loved to do, follow the development and activities of the baby loons. They would come to feel that the loon families actually belonged to them like relatives, compelling them to paddle out and check on them every few days.

They fell into easy conversations, catching up each other on any news of the last day or two. Quinn told Lisbet about Will's surprise evening visits, and that he had agreed to work with her on the boathouse renovation. Lisbet knew full well that this was what Quinn had been waiting and hoping for.

"Don't fall in love with him like you do with all the carpenters you work with," Lisbet told her with a grin.

No doubt she was right. There was something about a man with a hammer that Quinn had always been drawn to. Maybe it was the rough and tumble look, or devil may care attitude, who knows, but she always claimed it was their "creativity."

"Oh don't worry," she said, rolling her eyes. "He's not my type."

Quinn had always been attracted to the tall, dark, handsome but perhaps sullen type of man who was on the quiet side. This preference had gotten her into deep trouble numerous times. Tall and dark were attributes men might have had in her younger life, but not now. Now that she was older, all the men near her age she encountered were gray or bald, barely her own height, and there didn't seem to be a choice anymore of whom she might find appealing. There weren't enough available men out there to even have a choice! You were lucky to find even one or maybe two men in the whole area who might be single and still have teeth, for god's sake. The situation was practically hopeless, and the women both knew it, so they loved to tease each other about the rare occasion that a man crossed either of their paths.

You could never tell when the situation might change, though. Lisbet had a friend she had been seeing for quite some time, and it seemed that the relationship was destined to remain in the friendship category, as much as Lisbet wished otherwise. She could always think of new ways to get together with this man, but he never seemed to be the one to make a move. Oh he was friendly and definitely fond of Lisbet, but who knew if it would ever be more than that. He consistently accepted her gracious dinner invitations, but never offered one himself.

Quinn often recommended that Lisbet endure an endless amount of patience, to be in the moment with exactly what was being brought to her, and to resist the urge to push things forward. She believed that coaxing a man into a relationship would only drive him into an attitude of resistance. It had to be his idea, she thought, and if a woman remained receptive, the man would come forward towards her if he were interested. Otherwise, being the one to initiate everything was a recipe for disaster, she knew from her own experience. Making it easy, being a pushover, and worse, being the aggressor, would emasculate a man and make him resent you forever, even if it was in silence. That kind of silence was a tough punishment, and she never wanted to experience it again.

She knew that her ideas were not at all consistent with what Lisbet's other friends thought. They thought she should dump Ben and move on. If a man didn't try to get you into bed within a certain amount of time, and who knew how long that was supposed to be, he just wasn't into you and you might as well hang it up. No use wasting your energy on a dud when there were so many other guys out there. But at their age, there weren't that many to begin with, and wasn't it the friendship you needed to develop first anyway?

Quinn's attitude of patient waiting did not go over well with her friends or her kids either. They all thought she herself should "get out" more – make more of an effort to meet someone and stop living alone in quiet acceptance. They told her that in today's world it was fine for women to make the first move, to call and invite a guy out. But that was not her, and she couldn't do it. She felt that if a man was meant to come into her life, he would show up at the perfect time, without her needing to do anything.

She had never been able to trust in the energies of the cosmos where love was concerned in her earlier life, but she was determined to do so now. She would let heaven decide for her, and if nothing happened, so be it, she would go on living alone. The most important thing for her to do was to be her true self. The process of getting to that place inside her had been so difficult, but increasingly rewarding to her as time went by. She felt that she was truly beginning to identify with who she really was, and this identity was opening her up further all the time to cosmic harmony. She could feel it embracing her, especially on a day like this.

"Have you heard from Ben?" Quinn asked.

"Oh yes," Lisbet answered. "He's been texting me. His retirement's about to happen and he's really wondering about what will come next for him. I told him to just take some time to relax with his new free time for a while, and then see what comes up. I just hope he doesn't decide to leave the area for a new career."

Ben had been working for years with the New York Department of Environmental Control, taking care of trails and wilderness reserves in the Adirondacks. After years of service that were finally over he would be able to retire with full benefits and go on to something else if he wanted to – his working years were definitely not over. His familiarity with the forest and everything in the natural world was something that deeply attracted Lisbet to him. She could talk of fishing, birding, and flower identification with him endlessly without either of them becoming bored. They both loved cooking too.

Lisbet had graduated from the French Culinary in New York City after taking a long course there that was similar to the one Julia Child had taken in France. It had been demanding and even grueling, but Lisbet had loved it and had shared her experience in a way that had even improved Quinn's cooking skills. They had especially loved trying new bread-baking techniques and were both devoted to making all their own bread. Store bought was just too boring and tasteless, not to mention full of preservatives and other useless ingredients, they both agreed. Making their own was now part of normal routine – no trouble, and rewarding in every way.

Lisbet and Ben were a part of a community based group of people who liked to cook for each other and met once a month for a shared dinner. They all participated regularly in volunteering for services in the area, and the dinner get-togethers were a sort of reward for their work. It had been a perfect way for the two to see each other regularly. Lisbet had enhanced the idea by inviting Ben to her house to cook special meals for the two of them. They had both really enjoyed that, but Lisbet couldn't help holding more intimate ideas about him, and she was hoping that he would feel that way too at some point. She just couldn't tell what was holding him back. Was it the painful divorce he had experienced? Or was it her - that he just wasn't attracted to her? She didn't know, but the question was always on her mind, though she tried her best to let go of hopes and expectations. She wanted to be closer to Ben, but she was always afraid of scaring him away. It wasn't like it was when she was younger – there was so much to risk now. She had found a person she thought was perfect for her, and she didn't want to lose the opportunity she had with him by being too anxious for forward progress. She agreed that she had to be patient, but sometimes it seemed impossibly difficult. Waiting was not her strong suit.

They talked on pleasantly about the recent communications between Lisbet and Ben, evaluating everything, but they were unable, as usual, to come up with any conclusions. It was a tough case that didn't come with obvious answers. They both figured this thing would just take time, and they would have to wait it out. What other choice was there? Lisbet was unwilling to let Ben go, but yet he wasn't acting like he was ready to pursue things further with her. At least their talking it over diffused Lisbet's anxiety over what might happen next, temporarily.

The two friends paddled on until they felt the bugs had found them and weren't going to be willing to let them go, swarming them until it wasn't fun anymore. They tried moving into the open water where the stronger breezes were, but the flies seemed to follow them.

"Okay, time to go in," called Lisbet.

"Not a moment too soon either," returned Quinn.

They sat up straighter in their boats and paddled quickly back to the old camp, leaving exploration of the rest of the lake to another day. The hardest part was always rising up out of their boats with stiff knees and joints, coming to a stand without tipping the boat or taking on water at the last minute. It could be embarrassing and at the very least, "not pretty." They accomplished the task fairly easily with a breath of relief, pulled the boats out, and climbed up the hill to camp to eat the lunch they had hoped to have on the water.

The day was still beautiful, so they brought their egg sandwiches out to the big porch with a pot of hot tea and stoneware cups. A heavy long wooden bench acted as a combination table and a footrest, as they sat in two rickety old rocking chairs with their plates on their laps. Lisbet loved cookies, so Quinn always kept a bag of her favorites in the bottom drawer of the freezer, out of sight and temptation. She did not want to eat cookies herself, and the habit of hiding them worked most of the time. Lisbet knew right where to find them, and she could enjoy them with her tea whenever she wanted, so she went to get the bag of her favorite fig newtons.

"When are the boys coming?" she asked when she had made herself comfortable back in the rocker.

"In just few weeks," answered Quinn. "They can never get away at the same time, but Kole has a wedding to attend. It seems that so many of their friends are getting married now, and it's an obligation they cannot avoid despite of the cost of airfare and trying to get the time off. Thank goodness neither of them has had the expense of participating in a wedding till now though. It costs a fortune to rent a tux!"

Both of Quinn's sons were in their twenties, Kole working jobs to get by as he began to build a career in the healing arts while his older brother Jackson suffered his way through medical school. Quinn had always encouraged them to follow their passions and allow things to evolve, and they were doing exactly that. She was pleased and a little surprised that they had both chosen paths in healing and medicine.

They had worked many summers in the Adirondacks during high school and college as wait staff in almost all of the local restaurants and bars, so they knew what it was like to do whatever you had to do. Lisbet's kids had done the same thing. The women had great sympathy for the plights of their grown children who were not kids anymore. They were adults struggling in an economy that did not offer the instant job and career for college graduates as in the past when they were recruited before graduation, and had a great position waiting for them as soon as they received their diploma. Those days were gone now and everyone had to compromise, taking work they never planned to do without much confidence that their desired work would ever materialize.

They all had sweet memories of their summer times in the Adirondacks, and were always coming back to the lake to reclaim them.

It was a dilemma to cherish and yet to dread in a way when the kids came home. Seeing the kids was a joy, spending time with them, touching and just being with them. But then there was the chaos in the house, the chore of providing meals everyday, and even ideas for activities for the friends they brought along with them, the laundry, the noise, and the late nights. When the visits were over, it was a relief to experience solitude once again, even though the pain of missing them was acute at first.

Quinn was more relaxed with her kids though, than with her siblings. There was never a criticism or questioning with her sons – just a chance for them to relax, enjoy the lakehouse and the friends they missed. With her sisters there was the underlying question of what would happen to the camp. Would they always share it and the expenses that went with it? What if one of them got sick of that, tired of coming up, and wanted out? What would happen then? Then there was the issue of Quinn coming to live there. Her sisters were still skeptical of that idea, and maybe even a little jealous that she was now staying full time and enjoying it more than they were.

Quinn and Lisbet could discuss these things endlessly together, because they both understood the dilemma. They each faced essentially the same problems, but in Lisbet's case she owned her camp outright and could leave it to her kids as she wished. She shared ownership with her own siblings in another small camp right down the lake from Quinn, but it was a seasonal place and the family had seemingly worked out the times each of them would be able to spend time there. They had to share the expenses of it too, but that was working out all right as well so there were no ongoing family arguments for now. That could change if any major repairs were necessary though.

They sat back in their rockers companionably for a while, enjoying the woods before them and the beautiful water beyond, through the trees. Lisbet got ready to leave and took her plate in to the sink. She knew that Quinn loved doing dishes so she left it for her. It was part of her meditation, she said, but Lisbet never fully understood that. Washing dishes was a chore, so why in the world didn't a person want a dishwasher?

"Thanks for the paddle and the lunch!" she called as she slipped out the old screened door and it slammed behind her.

Quinn nodded as she approached the sink with her own plate and the cold teapot, turning on the warm water and soaping the sponge to do the dishes. As she dried the plates and touched up the kitchen, Quinn began to think again about the watercolor painting she wanted to do and devised a tentative plan to visit the big art store some of her friends had told her about. Evidently the store had everything an artist could ever want or need, so she determined to go there to get all of the paints, brushes and paper she would need to start painting again, as much as it frightened her to even think about it.

It was intriguing to imagine wandering around the big art store at her leisure, looking at everything without hurrying, and with no pressure, because it had been so long she didn't even know what she needed anymore. She had made a list of the colors she had favored in the past, remembering most of them, but she wanted to use some new tints this time around too, and would have to see what was available.

Drawing was never a problem. Unlike when she was younger and afraid to approach drawing, she now felt confidence with drawing just about anything. There was even a time when she had been afraid that she could never design another new house - that every idea in her head was already presented, used, and there was nothing left in her imagination to draw from. However, that fear had been totally unwarranted and she had gone on to design hundreds of house projects over the countless years of her architectural practice.

Now she knew that she still had lots of ideas to bring to fruition, because she didn't have to invent them, they came to her on their own when she evaluated a client's program and house site. Her head was full of them. She didn't use CAD in her work. She still drew every line herself, and believed her work illustrated a uniqueness of design expression. She did not think the computer offered that for young designers. She felt that the rigid lines and format of the computer itself were limiting, whereas she was unlimited when she conceptualized something – her imagination and fluid hand sketching could take her anywhere.

She wanted to get back to the blessed freedom of watercolor painting that she had experienced years ago before she even began to do architecture, because it too had a mind of its own, and the idea that the medium would lead you instead of the other way around fascinated her. You couldn't direct it exactly where you wanted unless you used the dry brush, which she now wanted to avoid. The impossible unpredictability and fluidity of watercolor itself was what drew her towards it, just as the ever changing water of the lake also called her. She wanted to be the instrument of the watercolor, as she had been for the houses and camp designs she had always done for others, making their dreams come true. She wanted to let watercolor dreams come through her, but she still had no idea how this would work.

Quinn went to the front room and took the top from the rigid white palette she had dragged around with her from place to place for so long. Dry cracked paint was still clinging to the little square pots around the perimeter and in the center where she had mixed colors long ago. It seemed to be preserved exactly the way it was the last time she had used it, though she could not remember when or under what circumstance that was. The hinged metal case that stored her brushes and other gear still held stiff tubes of paint, a selection of old brushes and other small items that had not been used for so many years. There was even an old rag spattered with colors. The brushes were of a high quality then and still seemed usable but she would not be able to tell till she tried them. The paint might be okay too, but it made sense that paint not used for decades would not be too good even if you could get the cap off the tube. She didn't even try, not wanting to be disappointed. She put everything back where it had been and snapped the case shut, leaving it where she could see it on the table.

Quinn did not know what would inspire her, if anything, but somewhere deep in her heart she wanted to try her hand again. Somehow, the little gray metal case encouraged her. She felt a longing toward it. She wanted to use it like she used to with ease and familiarity, and she knew she needed to find a way to put her longing into action.

The paintings Quinn wanted to do now would be nothing like the painting she had done earlier in her life, nor like the houses she had designed. For some reason, many of the watercolors she had done in her early years were of abandoned houses. Whenever she saw one in a field or a copse of trees just off the road she would stop to sketch and photograph it, and even try to get into it to explore. Stepping carefully through the derelict rooms she could feel an affinity with whoever might have lived there when the house had life, and she could feel its loneliness as if it were speaking to her. She would later paint it from her photos and thumbnail sketches. At the time, she had no idea that she would work with houses as a career for much of her life.

But she did not need to do houses anymore. She felt that her watercolors now would reflect her emerging feelings about the natural world. They might be very abstract, loose and soft, but they would be about light, its effect on everything, and the dark negative space behind it. That was the direction she wanted to go in, but she had no idea where it might lead her, as she had never tried such a technique before. She felt unready.

She went out to the big porch with her carving bag and sat down to work again on the little deer, looking out at the lake wondering. The carving took her mind off it somewhat, but never completely. As the wooden deer began to come to life in her hands, she thought of the project ahead, the watercolor painting she very much wanted to do, and of what might happen next.

Chapter 6

A quote for the boathouse materials take-off was resting in the fax tray the next morning when Quinn came down to make tea. She scanned it quickly at the kitchen table while she waited for the kettle to whistle. The supplier was one she had made orders from many times, so she trusted the contractor's rep who had done the work. It wouldn't hurt though, to check a few of the quantities with those she had already arrived at herself, such as the number of plywood sheets needed – just to make sure it was based on calculation and not guesswork. She looked in her notebook at her own figures to see if hers matched those shown on the order, checking them line by line. The list met with her approval.

She knew that she should show it to Will so he could check it for any missing items or things he wanted to add before finalizing the order, so she picked up the phone and called him, hoping that wherever he was would have service so he could receive her message. It was still pretty early, so there was a chance she could reach his cell phone before he disappeared onto one of his projects where there might not be service.

"Hey," he answered.

"Oh, you're there," she said. "I didn't expect to be able to get you. Just wanted to let you know the take-off came in, if you want to take a look at it before I make the order."

"Yeah, I do," he answered. "I'm not too far from you so I'll stop by there shortly."

Oh God, she thought. Here I am still in my robe again and he's coming over right now. There was no time to run up and get dressed. Should I have waited to call him later? Oh well, too late now – she ruffled her hair a little in a useless attempt to make it more presentable, and poured her tea.

Within minutes Will came through the door with a big paper cup of coffee, and headed for the microwave to heat it up. It was a machine Quinn had no use for, but had to go along with, outvoted as she was with everyone else who came to camp. After a minute the thing pinged, and Will grabbed the cup to take a sip. She was surprised he felt comfortable enough to just come right in with his cold coffee to heat it up without asking. He must have seen the microwave there before and known he could make use of it, so she made no comment.

She handed the materials list to him. He took his glasses out of his pocket and stood reading through it silently for what seemed like a long time with a very serious look. It was the first time Quinn had seen him use glasses, and it comforted her a little to know that she wasn't the only one who couldn't see to read anymore. And he looked good in them. They lent a sort of bookish sophistication to his otherwise rugged demeanor, and the contrasting combination was appealing.

Her gown and robe made her feel vulnerable, and of course underdressed, but she leaned back against the old kitchen counter trying to appear relaxed. What was there to be nervous about anyway? She didn't think he would even sit down in a chair to review the order - he always seemed to be more comfortable standing. Maybe all the better for a quick and easy escape whenever he was ready to leave. She watched him as he looked it over attentively.

"It looks okay," he said. "Anyway, we can add to it if anything is missing. These guys are glad to pick up anything we decide we don't need when they make their next delivery out here."

"Great then, I'll call and get it scheduled for delivery as soon as they can do it," she said.

Will handed her the list and turned toward the door.

"Let me know when it gets here then – gotta go," he said as he headed out into the cool morning.

Before she knew it he had disappeared and Quinn was standing there alone in the kitchen again with the order in her hand. Wow, that man was like a gust of wind sometimes, she thought — he blew in and before you knew it he blew right back out again.

The morning had broken warmer than recent ones, so Quinn decided against a fire in the cook stove. Spring was finally settling into place, but it would be short. Winter seemed to turn directly into summer in the Adirondacks. You had to look quickly in the woods for the little spring flowers before they disappeared and left you wondering how you'd missed them after waiting so long.

She picked up the phone and called the building supplier to give him the go ahead for an as soon as possible delivery of the materials. He told her it would be soon, maybe even the next day.

It was still very quiet on the lake though. The summer people wouldn't be coming until school let out, and Quinn remembered back when she was one of them and couldn't wait until the day her mother would tell them to start packing up to go to camp. That was the best day of the year.

Filled with the memories of arriving at camp as a child, she took her tea out to the chilly porch, grabbing a tattered indian blanket to throw over her as she went through the screen door. The sun was gorgeous, making all kinds of sparkling reflections on the water and even on the shifting pine branches with their wet dewy surfaces. As she slid into one of the old rush seated rockers she felt in her bones the deep blessing it was to be in this precious place, and now to live here for good was going to be a dream come true. No matter what came next, she knew that she had made the right decision. She tucked the blanket around her bare feet and let the hot tea warm her.

Suddenly Quinn raised her head and looked up. She knew in that moment that today was the day she would go to the big art store and get the supplies she needed to paint. Her rocker stilled, and she sat for a moment stunned with that realization, before standing up and turning back into the front room with her tea cup in her hand, the blanket trailing behind her. The door smacked shut but she was already on her way upstairs to change.

Within moments Quinn was dressed, running down the stairs to grab her list from the kitchen table and out the door to her car. It was a beautiful day for a road trip.

She stopped for a small cup of coffee and a freshly made cinnamon doughnut from the local convenience shop as a treat, and headed out through the familiar village, the local town, and on down the long road between the lakes on a route she knew well because it was the same one she always took to the airport. She hated the thought of having to navigate the streets of a city, but she had hand written directions to follow from the internet when she'd searched to see where the store was, and was used to finding her way to unusual or hidden destinations because of all the out of the way places she had had to locate to evaluate projects for clients.

After two hours, she found herself in the almost empty parking lot of the art store in an old section of the city. She locked up the car and approached the front door.

The place was huge. There was apparently everything one would need to do any sort of artwork — even furniture and a selection of drawing tables lined up on a high wide shelf around the perimeter of the retail space. Not knowing which way to go, she strolled slowly down one of the nearest aisles taking it all in, while casually looking for the watercolor section.

When she found it, there were many brands to choose from, with racks of paints for each, and all kinds of accessories. Her old favorite, Windsor Newton was there, but there were also new brands she had never heard of, so she had to take a look at those too. The tubes were expensive, and smaller than they used to be, but she gradually began to collect the ones she thought she would need from her list. She chose several yellows, three blues, payne's gray, the umbers and siennas, and two reds. There would be no greens from a tube — she had learned to mix all greens herself. She picked up a fresh jar of masking liquid and a new soft eraser.

A saleswoman came to her and asked if she needed help, so Quinn confessed that she had not painted in many years. She still needed paper and a rigid board to tape it to. On the way to finding paper, the woman showed Quinn another aisle of the many new products now available to use or mix with paint to create innumerable tints, textures and finishes. It was amazing how many choices there were, but Quinn decided that if she could just lay down the very first sheet of color, just get some paint on paper, she'd be happy, so she avoided all the new products and stuck to the basics. No need to get ahead of herself...

She asked about brushes, and was told that red sable wasn't used as much anymore — many brushes were now synthetic. The thought that she still had a couple of sables in her tin box pleased her - they used to cost so much. She picked up one of the new ones in a medium size and was allowed to wet it and try it with some paint from a palette that was sitting on top of the front counter for customers to experiment with. It felt great in her hand as she pulled it along, turning and drawing it across the heavy sample paper, making calligraphic shapes and narrow lines, which came easily to her. It had been so long since she had held a brush loaded with paint, and it felt great. Why had she been so determined to avoid this? She decided to buy the brush.

Watercolor paper was even more expensive than ever, so she picked up a pack of several large single sheets of 140lb cold pressed Arches to get started with. She remembered she had a watercolor tablet somewhere, but she wasn't sure of the weight of the paper. Certainly the tablet would suffice for the practicing she was going to have to start with before moving on to the beautiful big white sheets. Her first exercises would be no works of art.

The painting boards were all foam core, not heavy solid wood like the one she had screwed a handle to and dragged with her everywhere years ago. An improvement, she guessed, and she picked one up that would be big enough for a half sheet of the good paper. It was light as a feather.

Armed with all her purchases, Quinn paid at checkout and took everything to her car. Other than the big sheets of paper and the foam board, she was surprised at what a small quantity of things she was coming away with — it all fit in a little brown paper bag. She set it on the seat and sat for a moment to think before she started off for the long trip home. It was a long way to come for such a tiny package.

It was at least something, getting those materials. A step forward on the road to making herself drum up the courage to do this thing that she had sheltered herself from for several dozen years - a small lifetime!

There'd been no fear in her heart the first time she had tried to paint, just excitement and wonder. Her teacher was such an inspiration; the way she spoke to the students in the class Quinn had been a part of in the woman's unfinished basement, after school. It had been a place where you felt you could do just about anything — there were paints of all kinds - jars and cans of brushes, easels and stools, canvasses, spotlights, palettes, bell jars of murky water, paint rags stained in rainbows of color, still life arrangements and enthusiastic faces everywhere. The place was a wonderful mess, and Quinn had loved just being in the room with it all, treasuring the time she spent there once a week. It was the highlight of her life then.

She had continued to experiment with watercolors even into her twenties, garnering a couple of "one woman" shows at banks and libraries, selling paintings before she had even gotten them hung on the walls. But any of the work that was any good was gone. There was nothing to reflect back on as a good example - nothing to show for those years except for the few pieces she had given her family members, and she now saw that those very early pieces were flat, boring, and devoid of life. Quinn had begged them to let her throw them out but she was never able to convince them they were worthless but for the frames they were in.

Now she would have to conjure inspiration and courage on her own to start again from the beginning. There was nobody around to push her forward, encouraging her to let her fear drop away and just take the first step. The dilemma of how to do it was something she hadn't solved yet, but she figured it would resolve itself somehow when she was ready.

When she pulled back into the camp driveway several hours later, she was tired from the long drive but just a little bit excited. She carried all the new things inside and stowed them safely away in the closet.

Chapter 7

Early the next morning Quinn heard the beeping of a truck backing down the driveway, and instantly knew that the materials delivery for the boathouse had arrived. There was nothing she needed to do but maybe sign off on the order, so she didn't have to rush through her morning routine. It was time to put the kettle on though, so she ambled downstairs to the kitchen and ignited the light beneath it on the gas stove. By the time the kettle whistled, the big truck was already crawling nosily back up the driveway, its big wheels sputtering gravel as it went.

Relieved that she wouldn't have to meet and greet anyone at the door that early, she selected some black pekoe to brew, poured hot water and some cream into her teapot and placed the cover on top. It seemed to be warm enough to go without a fire again but she headed out to the porch to make sure. Oh, what a beautiful morning! The air was sweet with spring dew and the water of the lake was sparkling bright in the rising sun and flat as a mirror.

Quinn had heard somewhere that Will went swimming in the lake every single morning from when the ice went out until it froze over again. She wondered if he was doing that right then, entering that freezing cold water to refresh himself for a new day just as she looked forward to the warm soothing shower she was about to step into. What would make a person want to subject himself to that kind of punishing temperature first thing every morning? She could imagine how nice it would be in the heat of the summer, but never in the brisk chill of an early spring day like this one. Still, she admired the strength of spirit one would have to possess to take on such an invigorating commitment.

She shook her head slowly just thinking about it and returned to the kitchen to pour tea and take it back upstairs with her. The old wooden steps creaked amicably as she made her way up, trying to keep the cup level so tea would not go all over her, though her step was lively and quick in anticipation of a good day that she wanted to get started.

She took the hot cup straight to the bathroom and started the shower, taking a tentative sip while the water warmed as it came through the freezing cold pipes. After testing it she hung her gown on the hook behind the door and stepped in carefully, minding the slippery curvature of the bottom of the old claw foot tub and pulling the curtain around it. There was nothing like the feeling of hot water streaming over your head on a cool morning, and a long sudsy shampoo. Why would anyone want to trade this in for freezing lake water? That man must be crazy as a loon, she thought. And with that thought she remembered that she had heard the loons calling in the night. Maybe they were getting ready to nest.

As she toweled her hair dry Quinn wondered if Lisbet had heard any loons yet over at her lake. Their excitement would indeed be shared over the anticipation of seeing the fascinating birds appear regularly again, and all the tasks they would take on together to see where the nesting places would be - later counting the days while the loon pair took turns sitting on the egg. They wouldn't be able to resist paddling down into the quiet places to protectively check on them as often as they could.

Quinn combed through her own tangled nest. Her hair had always been thick and especially tangled when it was wet, but now it was getting ridiculous. The soft brown color was as close as she could get it to her lifelong natural color, but she knew it would be completely gray if she stopped coloring it now. Both her sisters had let theirs go gray, but she dreaded doing that, though she would have to face it sooner or later. She observed that women with gray hair did look older, though she had to admit that her sisters' hair was healthy, not dead and dull like that of so many gray haired women. She was afraid to find out what hers would be like when she made that transition, if she lasted long enough to make it. She pulled the comb through gently, so as not to pull out any more hair than necessary. That was the other problem, thinning hair, and the awful bald or thinned spot on the top or back of your head that seemed to be inevitable.

The horrors of aging. Then there was your neck — she didn't even want to get started thinking about that nightmare.

Lisbet had always been blond, and Quinn thought that made it easier for an aging woman because blond was closer to gray. You could always slowly introduce gray into blond. Doing that with brown was substantially more challenging — okay, let's face it - you couldn't fool anybody going suddenly from brown to gray. But Lisbet had kept her hair blond and it looked wonderful. Not the least bit inappropriate to her age. It was shiny and natural on her.

Quinn wondered how long she could get away with keeping her color. She felt her hair still looked natural, because it took color unevenly, and had many colorful streaks and highlights just as it had when she was younger. She had to be careful not to bleach it out or dry it in the sun on the many paddles and unavoidable hours in the sun, but a soft, very wide brimmed hat took care of that most of the time. It was increasingly dry though, and always tangled, like her grandmother's had been. At least the color formula moisturized it and gave it some shine.

She finished combing out and went to the bright bathroom mirror and its light for makeup. She dotted on and softly blended in a rose cream moisturizer that was of all natural ingredients and smelled like heaven. Next came some under eye concealer she had needed all her life for the dark patches under her eyes that apparently were hereditary, and then a very light dusting of translucent face powder and a bit of blusher from the same natural source. It had been a blessing to be able to find these great all natural products on the internet, because she would have never been able to get them locally.

When she was about 13, Quinn had tried eyeliner and mascara, and from that day forward she had used it every day — it made such a difference. She wouldn't have been seen without it. Now, she left it off on most days, adding it for meetings and the rare evening out. She knew that she looked better in it. Even her boys told her so, but she was beginning to hesitate because she didn't think it was necessary when she was at home, on the water, or even in town. Older women looked garish when they made themselves up too much, she thought, and she didn't want to become one of them.

Her lips turned red if she used lipstick, so she applied a neutral glaze, then a touch of light color on her bottom lip. That would have to do it for today, she thought.

When she dried her shoulder length hair she lifted it with a brush to give it body, and then bent over and dried it upside down for the last minute or so. She hated flat, long limp hair – always had. Brushing it out was another tough task – she did that upside down too with a natural bristle brush and then another one that would leave it with more body, finishing with a toss of her head and some light hairspray so it wouldn't fall in her face all day or require pinning back. She couldn't bear to cut it short, but loved to clip it up to get it out of her way on hot days, or when she just needed it away from her neck for a change.

The trials and decisions of aging were tremendous. Quinn wondered if there was a woman out there who just didn't care – who could face all these changes unwavering and confident. She didn't think so. Still, it didn't make her predicaments any easier. Women mostly didn't talk about such things, seeming to make myriad decisions on their own, in private, hoping to present the best possible face to the world that they could, for as long as they could.

In her spiritual practice, Quinn had learned to be in the moment. But what if you didn't feel like you were in the moment you were actually in? What if you felt like you were 20 or 30 years younger in your own heart, not an aging 65 year old grandmother who rightfully had experienced everything exciting, ful-filling, frightening, earth shaking, and should be satisfied with that, gracefully embracing the older years. What if you wanted to fall in love again, to experi-ence the thrill and ecstasy of a life with another being you could relate to fully, to share everything with, knowing you now finally knew how to do it? Why didn't God see fit to provide us with this knowledge to begin with, instead of waiting until it was too late? Was it all about reproducing the species? Why was it not about fulfilling the happiness of the species?

This was on the minds of so many of Quinn's friends now in their older years as she was. They had learned about meditation, solitude, being with what is, finding meaning in ones life – even if you couldn't. But the troubling idea that seemed to remain for each one of them was that they would like to share it all with someone. And Quinn was no exception. She too had longed for a companion to share herself with for years on end - for too many years to count, or admit to.

Had she hidden herself away, studying the teachers and finding out the vast store of what she needed to know for too long? Had she sheltered herself too carefully from the pain that had inevitably come from every relationship she had ever had? That seemed indeed likely to her. But now that she was ready to grab energetically onto these mature years, to experience once and for all a good, healthy mature relationship with all that came with it, and all she had to give it, was it too late?

Quinn knew that the person she needed would have to choose her for who she was. He would have to see her inner beauty, and an outer beauty too, even if she couldn't see it herself. He would have to foster and encourage her spiritual growth, and she his. That was the biggest hurdle, for many men didn't even know what spiritual growth was, or care. It was scary to think of the offerings. It would be impossible to teach your loved one what you needed from them before they could give it to you, so where in the world would you encounter that person who would intuitively know? It was pretty much hopeless.

Quinn had given up the bar scene for years. It was okay when she was in her 20's and loved to drink and dance herself silly, but those days were long gone. Her kids thought there might be very few other ways to meet a man, so she should try it. But Quinn would not give in to going back to bars. So, there were not too many other outlets. In writing and poetry groups, they mostly came in couples or it was all women – no single men.

Some people had had success on the internet, but Quinn would not trust it because of her belief in magnetism, or chemistry. She believed that people had a magnetic field or aura around them, and sometimes these spheres of magnetism overlapped, causing the two to be attracted to each other through the magnetic forces. She believed that was the way the cosmos was able to bring people together who needed to be together. Though in her own life she had been intensely attracted to men that had eventually caused her great pain and trauma, she also thought that these relationships were perfect for her own path, and that they were necessary for her growth. When she looked back on them, she could not see how she would have become what and where she was without the experiences of these people in her life.

Feeling refreshed, Quinn put on one of her sports bras, a long, soft, buttoned cotton shirt, and black yoga pants, her day-to-day outfit. She loved to be comfortable, and was always barefooted. She never wore shoes in the house or anywhere else, unless they were needed for walking outside. As she dressed, she looked out the window to see what the lake was doing, and was surprised to see Will below, looking over the delivery of materials that had just come that very morning. She surmised that the rep had let him know when the delivery was due to arrive, and that was the right thing for him to have done, but the amazing thing was that Will was already there, looking it over and checking it. It had just gotten there! She stood watching him through the window.

He moved about the huge pile of wood knowingly, lowering his head to check or to count boards, stepping about with care and agility. He was very slim, and his movements were quick, but graceful and effortless. He wore no jacket, just a dark cotton shirt tucked neatly into jeans, his usual cap, and sturdy boots. He made no written notes, seeming to keep all the information he needed in his head.

Quinn decided to go down to greet and talk to him about the delivery. She headed for the stairs and almost skipped down them, excited as she was. She opened the door at the bottom and was ready to go out when she saw that Will's truck was already gone. How had he disappeared so quickly? She looked around, unbelieving, almost as if she had imagined him right there walking around. Where had he gone?

Oh well, she thought. At least he knows everything's here. But the thought lingered, where did he go so fast when I just saw him right here?

The phone was ringing in camp so Quinn ran to catch it. Sure enough it was Lisbet, wanting to paddle on the fine, smooth lake. Of course she wanted to go, so the two made plans to meet on the water and the beautiful day began.

Chapter 8

The very next morning Quinn was startled in her early meditation by the sounds of doors slamming, men talking, and general noise. She arose and looked out the window from one of the side bedrooms to see that two guys had arrived in the yard below and were taking materials down to the lakeside near the boathouse. The project was starting!

She was not concerned about the disturbance, just delighted that it was happening. Her meditation now over, she pulled on her long silky robe and breathlessly descended the stairs to the kitchen. While she waited for the tea water to boil, she paced back and forth from the stove to the porch, looking around outside and watching the men, wondering if these guys who were sorting and moving materials downhill into place by the old boathouse would be the same ones who would do the carpentry work. She felt like a bit of a nosy spy. Maybe it was not her business how these guys did their work but it sure was interesting.

Well, they were early for one thing. Their boss was not with them, so they obviously knew what they were supposed to do, and they were doing it efficiently. She could not keep her eyes off them.

When the kettle called, she attended to it and prepared tea to brew for a few minutes, giving her yet a little more time to watch what was going on outside. Then she added cream and had no excuse but to get upstairs and prepare for her day. Just as she started for the stairs the back door swung open and in came Will, heading for the microwave with his paper coffee cup.

"Mornin," he said as he passed her on his way, putting his cup in, touching numbers and turning to her as he prepared to wait.

Her robe swirled around her as she turned to him.

"Morning?" she answered, her eyebrows raised at the surprise of his presence in the kitchen, unexpected and uninvited...but nice.

He looked around the room surveying it quickly, till the bell of the microwave rang, when he turned back to it, took his cup out, and began to take his leave. "Gotta go," he said.

Quinn nodded, but she knew he didn't even see her as he left in a whirl of his own energy, clicking the door shut behind him in a quick, silent action. Trying to gather herself together, she moved toward the window to see where he had gone, but there were only the two same guys, steadily working to get the material down the hill to the boathouse. What had she missed?

She moved slowly towards the stairs as if slightly in a daze. She took the stairs step by step, thinking it over and feeling a strange stirring of her whole interior as she went. She was so excited about the brand new day but something strange and new had been added to it. What?

Quinn was fascinated by the idea of cosmic energy, and what it could do. Where her original family came from in Ireland, the invisible world had tremendous significance. Its unseen power could be intense – and you could definitely feel it even if you couldn't see it. For some reason, there seemed to be an uncanny presence of inexplicable energy in the atmosphere whenever Will blew in and out, and she couldn't identify it. It was almost as if he was like a spirit floating just out of the corners of her eyes, never quite right in front of her. When she tried to catch up and get a good look at him, he would disappear. She shook her head to clear it.

With activity going on outside the camp, Quinn was unsure what to do. Should she stay close by in case she was needed, or leave these men alone to do as they were obviously being instructed to do? She decided on the latter, got dressed in an old flannel shirt and cotton pants that she could feel warm enough in to go in and out as needed all day, and went back down to the kitchen. It wasn't going to be a day she could sit and contemplate in her quiet room while there was so much going on down there.

As she washed and pared strawberries, she saw that the men were constructing a sort of flat thin wooden platform on the ground, with a lip along each side, and she wondered if it was to keep the materials off the wet ground.

Usually lumber came with a rough palette to keep it dry. But when she looked again from the window she saw that it was to slide the heavy lumber down the hill to the jobsite below. How clever! How much better was that than trudging up and down the steep hill with a ton of weight on your shoulders…

She put a couple of spoonfuls of yogurt on the berries and savored them in her mouth as she walked out the porch door, letting it slam behind her. The sound always reminded her of summer and more than anything she was ready for it to begin. She sat in a rocker and let the perfect blend of sweet and sour melt in her mouth. The taste seemed to whet her sense of energy.

The idea of the ingenuity of these guys, and the excitement she felt stirring up inside her was distracting. She would never get anything done on a day like this, so she decided to sweep. Yes, the kitchen and the front room could use a good sweeping this morning, and the big porch too. She dragged the broom out and quickly put it to the use it was made for — calming her down and helping her regain her inner balance. They were working on her very own brand new home and the thought of it brought her to the brink of insane delight!

By the time Quinn finished the inside the sun had risen higher and the day was beginning to warm. Down at the lakeshore, the men had downed a couple of small saplings so that they could make a clear pathway right onto the dock to the old structure with their materials and tools. They cut and stacked the cut logs neatly between a couple of small trees. Quinn was dying to go down the hill so she could watch from up close, but she knew that wouldn't be well received so she started the chore of moving furniture, dusting and sweeping the big porch. At least it provided a not so far away view of the goings on. Nothing like a little nearby construction to get the camp clean…

When she finished the porch Quinn grabbed her laptop and slumped into a rocker to rest for a few minutes, and checked for email messages from the kids. There was an invitation there from a local group of individual painters - who like to get together once a week to paint outside - for her to come and paint with them that very morning. The thought of getting out and painting this soon after getting her new supplies had never occurred to her — she had assumed a few months would slip by before she would ever be ready. However, what better way would there be to get out of the way today, when she was too churned up to concentrate on anything anyway?

She rose from the chair, took her computer inside and went to the table that held her tin paint kit, opening it to look at the old tubes and brushes. She would never know if the paints were any good till she tried them. Slowly, she made her way to the closet where she had conveniently stored away her new things, and brought them to the table. She separated all the old tubes into a divided section of the old tin box, not that she wouldn't be able to tell which ones they were, but to begin the process of organizing herself for some possible action. She felt the silkiness of the old brushes between her fingers, and pulled the sticky tag off the new one, adding it to the stack. There were even some old thin clean rags in there, ready to blot paint with. She shook them out, refolded them on top of everything else, and snapped the box shut.

The tablet of watercolor paper lay on top of her palette and she remembered that she wanted to check its weight. It was 140 lb Arches — a real surprise to her. That would be heavy enough not to buckle too badly if it was secured tightly around the edges of the tablet with masking tape. The new large sheets could wait till later, after she'd had some practice runs. Well, all she needed was water.

There was a large bell jar with a lid in the kitchen — perfect for the job, so she grabbed it and filled it with water. She picked up her camera and tucked all of these things into a plastic coated grocery sack with strong red handles. Without overthinking it any further, she picked up the bag, went to her car and headed out for the location at a nearby old hotel in the village where the group was to meet. As she drove, she thought it the perfect way to kill two birds with a single stone — get herself out of the way, and on her way to something she had been dying to do. It was as simple as that.

When she arrived at the parking lot she realized she didn't know any of the people she was to meet, nor where they would gather. She'd never met any of them. She pulled into a spot in the almost empty lot. Just as she did, she saw another woman doing the same thing, so she waited to see if she might be a member of the group. Sure enough, the woman lugged painting gear with her as she got out of the car, trying to get organized so that she could carry it all. Quinn grabbed her bag of gear and keys and went over to her.

"Are you part of the Plein Air painting group?" she asked.

"Yes, yes I am! Hi, I'm so glad to meet you. Are you Quinn? We have heard that you wanted to come paint with us and we're always so happy to have someone new. I'm Montana. Welcome!"

Moments later Quinn found herself on her way down to the front of the hotel, loaded with her own bag and helping Montana with some of her gear. As they rounded the corner of the tall building the big lake sprawled before them. There were a few men there who were obviously getting ready to paint, wandering slowly about looking for a good place to set up with a perfect scene of subject matter. Quinn was introduced to them with more welcoming greetings. Every one of them was very friendly and seemed to be really happy that she had decided to come. They all had kits of supplies, easels, portable chairs and various mediums of paint. They really appeared to know just what they were doing.

As she slowly walked the grounds, Quinn searched for a place where she would be able to see not only something interesting to paint, but where the morning light played upon it, casting light and shadows that would enliven the subject. The wide expanse of the lake was just too vast. She needed something where she could contrast the light on an object with the negative space in shadow that defined it. Finally she sat down on a drying log that faced a copse of thin pale trees that were casting long shadows on the light sandy ground, with deep dark pine foliage behind them to bring out their lightly textured trunks and wispy branches.

She opened her box to retrieve the masking tape and taped three sides of the paper down to secure it tightly to the tablet of watercolor paper, then set that on her lap and lifted the flat top from her palette. Seeing the old familiar colors there made her stomach jump with the recognition of something deep in her memory. The paints were very old and dry, but rather than scrape them away she decided to add some new paint in the same color to the individual pans and see what would happen. Maybe the old paint would still be good. Many of the old tubes opened easily and the paint came out in surprisingly good condition, but some of the tubes were too hard to even squeeze at all. The top on the old tube of cerulean blue was so tight she had to strain a bit to get it to twist, at which point it broke off entirely, squirting the sky blue paint all over her hands. She scraped some of it onto the palette, but had to go inside the hotel holding her hands up in front of her to wash them before she could continue to do anything further. How embarrassing!

When she came back to her spot, she knew there was nothing to do but just dig in and get something started. So tentatively, taking a shallow breath, she picked up her pencil from the kit and began to sketch the scene lightly onto the paper, remembering how important it was to identify the center of interest for the work, and to balance the composition so that the viewer's eye would be led right where she wanted it to go. Drawing was never a problem - maybe it was the most comfortable part of making a painting for her, but when the sketch was made, it was time to take the next step.

She picked up a no. 4 brush, wetted it in the jar of water, and pulled it back and forth over a small piece of soap from the tin box to coat it before dipping it into the pink masking liquid she would use to cover the parts of the paper she wanted to remain as pure white when she began to wet the paper with paint. The trunks of the trees and some of the branches got a light coating. Then she waited for this to dry while she put the masking liquid lid back on tightly so it wouldn't spill out into her kit, and rinsed out the brush so she could paint with it later.

The wind was now blowing a little more briskly so it didn't take any time at all for things to dry. It was getting a little chillier, but Quinn barely noticed the temperature dropping. She was completely focused on what she was doing now, and the momentum of her body energy was leading her along as if in a long ago dream. She didn't even have to think about it – her actions came in a natural response to the memory of exactly what she used to do.

With a wide flat sable brush, she wet the entire upper portion and left side of her paper for the sky, and dipped her brush into the cerulean blue with a touch of ultramarine added to it. She tested the color on a blank space of the palette. Satisfied that it was pale enough in tone, she pulled it across the top of the paper, and in several strokes she created the morning sky, with the white of the paper between the strokes becoming soft clouds. As the blue bled into the white, she smiled at the magic that watercolor created. The sky was giving birth to itself as she watched the process take place, and the joy of it spread all through her midsection in a familiar hum. It was a beautiful feeling.

Quinn remembered too that there were many ways to ruin a painting. She had to hold herself back from getting too anxious, and let the medium do its own work. While the sky dried, she planned the dark colors she would use in the background to make the trees come forward, and when the time was right she began to touch the paper with all kinds of intense deep green that she mixed herself. She painted the dark spaces behind the light ones in the foreground.

While those dried, she pulled on her flannel over-shirt, finally noticing how cool it was getting, never taking her eyes off the work. Though her back was beginning to feel the strain of leaning over for so long, she worked on until the lighter washes of forest greens and yellows were added. When they were sufficiently dry, she delicately removed the masking with an eraser, pleased with the blank white spaces that revealed themselves. The white of the trees would become the light bark of the birches that were going to provide the detail in the foreground. She carefully brushed in the texture of the peeling bark, and the long waving blue-gray shadows that the trees cast on the light ground, then she stood up to relieve her back pain, and take a look.

Just then a couple of the other painters gathered behind her to see what she had done, taking their first glances at the very same time she was able to straighten up to look with a critical eye from a distance.

"There is definitely a watercolorist in there…" someone said.

"Yes – it sure looks like you've been there before," added another voice. "How long did you say it's been since you did this?"

Quinn was very surprised and pleased with the little painting exercise, and the comments. A sense of excitement was running all through her body, and though it had gotten colder, she was warm all over. She had expected nothing, but yet she had indeed done something, and that something was almost good. She felt a kind of thrilling anticipation that was blossoming from the very center of her being. It was the blessing of creativity that was filling her to the core, stirring new life and the wonder of just what that new life would bring.

Smiling to herself, she packed up all her things while the little painting continued to dry, and helped Montana carry hers over to a spot where all the painters set their work upright for a review by the group. One by one, each painter explained what they were trying to accomplish, received praise and ideas on how to do it even better next time. For Quinn, their overwhelming consensus was to keep painting - to do what she was doing and much more of it. That was all the encouragement she had needed. Nothing could stop her now – she was on her way.

On the drive back to camp Quinn wondered with amazement what on earth had kept her away from something she loved so much, for so long. She knew it was fear. But why? What had she been so afraid of? The paper, the paint itself – or not being able to remember what to do with it? Now, looking back, it was so hard to understand, but this fear had held her fast in one place, a place of inertness, for nearly 40 years. She had all the excuses for what was keeping her from it neatly piled up and organized in her mind so effectively that she hadn't even questioned their validity.

Now these excuses had been blown to pieces. Gone in just a few short hours after all those long years. Amazed at the truth of this, Quinn suddenly began to wonder how many more areas of her life were trapped in a similar prison of fear.

Chapter 9

Within days there had been amazing progress made on the boathouse project. Lumber was stacked neatly within reach of the crew, organized by when it would be needed, and covered. A big metal dumpster had taken a huge space in the gravel driveway, and the men had begun to load it with old shingles and other discarded pieces from the roof and walls that could not be recycled or used for kindling or campfires. The place was noisy now from morning till about four o'clock each day with the demolition of the old roof and any sections of walls that were questionable, had some actual rot, or were warped such that they were no longer straight enough to keep the building level and plumb. The wonderful antique logs that supported the roof had been numbered on their undersides already, so that when they came down they would be easily recognizable as to what location they had come from in the original roof. A wood pallet was already waiting for them to be stacked on inside the lower level of the boathouse so they would stay dry and out of the weather.

Quinn found that she had to either get up earlier, or miss her morning meditation because she wanted to be dressed and ready in case she was needed to answer questions or go get something from the local lumberyard or hardware store. She had made coffee for the guys a couple of mornings to be hospitable, but when she saw that the cups were usually left half full and set somewhere then forgotten, she gave up on that. The guys were getting their own coffee much earlier either from home or the local convenience store, and obviously didn't need her help.

She wanted to be down by the lake every minute of the day watching what was happening, but she also knew that leaving the crew alone was the better course. So she tried to plan her days pretty much as she had before the project started. In the late afternoons though, she would go down the big hill by herself when everyone was gone and look everything over, sometimes sweeping up and organizing a little just to be able to spend more time there taking it all in. She was surprised at how neat and tidy they were. The jobsite always looked great, and Quinn appreciated that in the same way she loved to come home to her own house looking perfect and welcoming when she opened the door.

Will had constructed a small flat wooden surface in the lower boathouse that acted as a desk where the plans were lying open in case they were needed. That man thought of everything. He was not always on the job with the others, but when he did come he was all business with them and she could tell that their respect for him and what he wanted made them very attentive when he was there. They had their questions at the ready and he always had an answer.

Before she knew it, the old roof was completely gone, and they were framing the new one. The original logs were neatly stacked on the pallet below in a way that air could circulate between them. The existing exterior walls had already been stripped of the old siding, straightened, strengthened, and revised wherever need be for the placement of new windows. It was surprising how quickly the little place was coming together, and it looked wonderful.

Quinn's favorite part of any construction project was the framing stage, so she savored the short amount of time she would be able to wander through the building shell while it was still so open to both the water and sky above. The shimmering lake all around it reflected itself with wavering patterns of light everywhere on the inside. It felt ethereal — like a little cloud of heaven on the water. She loved to look through each of the new window openings, stopping at each one to listen to the birds with their spring activity on the water, imagining how she would feel living right there with the lake around her all the time. Everything smelled deliciously of fresh cut pine as she moved around in the big open room, and she saw that the work was being done exactly as she had hoped, with careful precision.

When she had put her old house on the market the previous fall, it had surprisingly sold within days, so she had had to sort through all her belongings immediately and move what she wanted to keep into storage. Thank goodness she was more of a minimalist than a hoarder. Her plan to come to camp for the summer had already been in place, but she had no idea the house would sell so quickly, so she'd had her hands full making the deadline for settlement in time by getting all her things packed up and out. She had stayed at her sister's house in the meantime, until the ice went out up north and it looked like it might stay consistently warm enough to turn the water on in camp so she could stay there. The whole process had been rushed, and she was not quite sure about exactly which possessions she had decided to keep and move up into the new place. She hoped that she'd planned well.

Because of the early settlement, there was already money available to pay for everything she would need during construction, and to pay Will and the other subcontractors in a timely manner. She hadn't had to get a construction loan, which would have meant that they would have had to apply for a series of bank draws to pay bills. She just had to manage the budget herself, and since she'd done it so many times before, it was fairly easy. The biggest challenge was to stay within the budget parameters she had set for the project, resisting the temptation to spend more on upgraded equipment like costly appliances and fancy countertops. Thank goodness she didn't like them anyway, always having preferred solid wood workspaces and workhorse appliances that didn't tend to break down in the kitchen. The thought of using luxury items did not interest her, and in fact would have embarrassed her.

It would be important to have some money in her account as a buffer for retirement, or for emergencies like a serious illness or accident. Quinn couldn't believe that she was about to receive Medicare instead of having to pay for her own healthcare policy as she had done her whole life as an independent architect. She had paid for her kids too, and what a burden it had been for so long. Now those days were over - the kids had their own inexpensive coverage because of the Affordable Healthcare Act, for as long as it lasted.

She had elected to take her social security benefits at 62 instead of 67, so she was already receiving them and trying her best to keep all her monthly expenses limited to that amount. It was hard but she could do it if she didn't have a mortgage or rent payment. She had eliminated all the extras, even the ones most people considered to be essentials like a cell phone and TV. The biggest problem of course was taxes. She had to be careful to be able to come up with her share of property taxes on the camp she shared with her sisters, and had agreed to pay the increase that would be generated by the boathouse residence, because she would be living there.

Even with all those things in place, her retirement years would be difficult if she didn't continue to work, so she planned to keep her architectural practice going. So far, work had been slow for her in the Adirondacks. Since most people didn't live there year around, projects were few and far between, and nearly non-existent during the winters. If she could just get enough work to supplement her social security and pay the tax bills, she felt she'd be okay for as long as she could work. When she couldn't work anymore, things would really have to take a different track, and she didn't know what would happen then.

All three sisters wanted to keep the camp in the family, and that meant that it would eventually go to Quinn's and Megan's offspring, because Lily had never married and didn't have any children. Thank goodness she didn't seem to resent the fact that the property would go to her nephews – she loved them all. They all had concerns about how these young people would be able to support the camp and pay the ongoing taxes when it was their turn though, because none of them had permanent career jobs, and none of them could live there either. This was a dilemma for all families in a similar position. Most people wanted to save their old camps, but how to do it was a big question. Quinn hoped they could find a way, but she also knew that someday it would be out of her hands, and become someone else's decision. She wanted to do whatever she could to make it possible.

The boathouse would add market value and living space to the entire property because it expanded the one main dwelling to two, and provided more of the most desirable kind of property on the water – year-round living space with breathtaking views. It gave new meaning to the phrase "location, location, location." Knowing all of this gave Quinn confidence in her decision to go ahead with making the vast improvement, and then taking it for herself as a place to live. No one else would or could live there full time, so she wouldn't be asking anyone to sacrifice anything for her benefit. The boathouse had been unusable as a place to stay the way it was, and was even in danger of deteriorating permanently without attention. So Quinn had decided to remedy that to her advantage, knowing that later it would benefit everyone in the family, because she was generously donating her own money to make it happen, but all of them would own it.

In the mornings, Will often came by unexpectedly and let himself into the kitchen to warm his coffee on his way down the hill to the boathouse. Quinn loved to catch him for a moment for a brief conversation if she could, but since she never knew when he would be coming, she could never plan for it. She sensed he liked it that way — coming and going as he chose with no one to answer to. Even if they did run into each other, he was always on his way somewhere else.

Late one afternoon she was upstairs in the boathouse making her usual rounds to see what had been done that day, when the energy in the room changed and she knew without looking that some one was there with her. Without turning she shifted a little and saw through the corner of her eye that Will was standing at the top of the stairs leaning against the door jamb watching her.

"Coming along pretty good, isn't it," he offered, more as a statement than a question.

She turned to him with a huge smile and said, "It looks fantastic." She shook her head with wonder. "The sense of volume and light in here is amazing! I knew it would be great, but I guess the reflections from the water and sky that move through it have made it even more spectacular than I had hoped…you guys are doing a wonderful job."

"Well, it's your design…" Will offered. He pointed to her feet and said, "Where are your boots?"

Quinn looked down, remembering that she had on flip-flops, endangering her feet to the presence of an untoward nail, even though the place was immaculately swept and neat. With a guilty smile, she looked over at Will's well-worn work boots, and had to admit he was right. But she said nothing, knowing that she would never be able to make herself wear boots every time she came down here. At least she had something on her feet, she thought. Most of the time she was barefooted.

"We're done sheathing it in," Will said as he looked up at the big rafters above them. "The roofers will be here any day, maybe even tomorrow, to do the metal roof. Have you heard anything about the window delivery yet?"

"No, but I'll call first thing in the morning and see if we are still on schedule. I don't remember exactly what the date was they gave me, but it's soon. Do you want them up here or downstairs?"

"If the roofers are done we'll want 'em up here for sure, if they'll bring them up. Otherwise we better let them stack them below, just in case of accidents — you know, we don't want anything dropped on them."

Quinn hadn't thought of that precaution, and realized it was an excellent idea since there would be extra people working for a few days while the roof was being done. A broken sash could cost hundreds of dollars, not to mention lost time waiting for another window if one were damaged.

"Okay, I'll find out the exact delivery day and be sure to be here, just to make sure they know what to do," Quinn said. "and I'll let you know too."

"Good," he said. "When do you want to do a walk-through for the electrical? There's no hurry but it might be good to get it out of the way so there are no surprises."

Will walked through the room looking at every joint and connection, as though he were a doctor checking his patient. He used his wide wooden pencil to make marks on the studs where he must have wanted to remember something he wanted to do later. When he passed a window opening, he looked out, pensively listening to the sound of birds chattering in the nearby trees in the woods. He called her over to have a look.

"I never get tired of watching them," he said.

"Me either," she said. "They probably won't come near us while all the racket of building is going on."

"Well they will sooner or later," he answered, gazing over at some playful finches and chickadees hopping from branch to branch.

"It's too late to put out a feeder up at the main camp even if I had one," said Quinn. They both knew that as spring arrived bears could be roaming around looking for any kind of food to quell the huge hunger they had when they woke from their long winter's nap – and birdseed was something they would definitely go after. It was about time for them to be up, too.

"Yep. Too late for that," Will said as he turned back into the room. "I'm assuming you want pine for the ceiling and walls. You want any bead board anywhere?"

"How about in the bathroom," she said, "and I want the wide plank boards everywhere else. Let's get them prefinished before we install them, okay? I just want them to be clear poly."

"Makes it easier on me," he said. "When's the fireplace coming?"

"Next week," she answered, as she looked up the silvery pipe and saw blue sky through the hole above. She had had the triple pipe chimney delivered right away so it would be already installed when the roofers came, and they could flash it while they were doing the roof. It was snugly in place, waiting to be connected later to the fireplace flue.

They both continued to wander around the big room, looking at the work and circling each other at a distance, trying to think of everything that might still need to be discussed while they were there together.

"Everything looks just great, Will," said Quinn. "Thank you for all you are doing. I'm just so happy with everything. I want to give you a check - let's go up the hill so I can get it."

"That sounds good," said Will, and he moved toward the stair to start down.

Quinn took one last look around and then followed him. By the time she'd climbed the long hill up, he was fiddling with something in his truck, so she went inside to get the checkbook for the construction account. She wrote out an amount that was roughly a third of what she owed him for the framing, and logged it in her ledger. Then she went out to bring it to him, grabbing a fresh loaf of bread from the counter to take with her.

The light was already dimming. There was a faint glow of pink in the distance over the lake, but the woods were already pretty dark. Will had his truck running with the lights on, and he sat halfway onto his seat, checking his phone for messages.

Quinn waited quietly by the door of the truck until he was finished, and then handed him the check. Without looking at it he put it inside a notebook on the seat, which was piled with papers and tons of other things.

"And here's some food for you," she said, giving him the loaf which was tied securely with raffia. "It's a multigrain."

"Thanks," he said, looking down at it with a small smile.

"Maybe I'll see you tomorrow," said Quinn, and she stepped back so he could pull the door shut.

He put the truck into gear and it began to slowly roll forward as he looked out the side window and tipped his hat just slightly.

She stood in the cool evening, beginning to feel the cold drop down as night began to fall. The red lights of the truck blinked brightly as it slowed and stopped before entering the main road, and then it went forward and disappeared.

Chapter 10

As the weather warmed, activity in the camp, at the boathouse and in the village began to hum, and everyone's thoughts turned to Memorial Day weekend, the official start of summer. That was when many families came to open their camps and enjoy the holiday even if their kids were still in school and they would have to come back in mid June to begin the real summer break. Local shops were stocking up, preparing to open for the big weekend when hoards of people would be coming up for their first getaway of the season. The quiet time of spring was soon going to give way to the joyful din of summer.

A message was waiting for Quinn one morning that the windows had arrived at the distributor, and would be delivered the following day. Wow, she thought, what perfect timing. The roof was almost done and the windows would arrive just when they needed them. She pressed in Will's number on the phone, wondering if he might answer for a change. But no, it was his message system, so she left him the good news, set the phone back into its dock and started the day's chores.

Quinn was so looking forward to seeing her son Kole, who planned to come to camp for as long as he could while he was on the east coast to participate in a friend's wedding. There was always so much energy in the air, and activity in the camp when he was there. Still, she did not know what his schedule was — when he would arrive and how long he'd be able to stay. So far, it didn't look as though Jack would get enough time off to come up at all.

Since Quinn had brought them to camp all their lives, her kids knew it as a second home that they loved even more than their year-round one. Their very first summer in camp was the year they'd each been born, so being there was like second nature to them. When they were tiny Quinn took them into the lake with her and floated them around endlessly, acclimating them to complete comfort in the water. As toddlers they played all day at the water's edge with little boats and other toys while she sat nearby with her feet always in the water and a book in her lap. As soon as they could stand they were dropping fishing lines into the water off the dock from their tiny poles, and beginning to catch little fish that she had to retrieve reluctantly from the end of a hook and show them how to release back into the lake. They never wanted to go inside, and when they were finally coaxed in for some food they would literally fall over with exhaustion, sometimes into their dinner plates.

She had always let them bring friends with them when they were old enough to need the companionship, and had even let the friends stay with them all summer long. As they grew older and wanted to make money they and their friends all had their fill of waiting tables, landscaping and doing yard work, from high school through college, even when Quinn had to stay home to work and come up when she could. They had eventually begun to come up to stay by themselves almost all summer, and Quinn had to allow it because they were working so hard to pay for the cars she had let them buy, and help cover their school expenses.

Now when they visited, they really enjoyed catching up with their local friends at the familiar old haunts. Colleagues from university were scattered all over the country either still searching for or just entering their new career jobs, but the locals in the Adirondacks had often come right back to the place they had roots, and were still there. It was comforting to be able to connect with them and go hiking, boating and skiing just like in the old days.

Quinn began to plan ahead, making a long list so she could stock up on favorite foods, and ready the upstairs rooms that had stood empty since last summer.

Because of her love of vintage textiles and blankets, she'd been unable to resist the rock bottom prices most of them went for over the years, and had quite a collection. When she'd emptied her house, she brought the whole lot with her rather than pack them away to be subject to the dust and damp of a storage container. She dragged out a selection of softly worn flannel sheets, cotton blankets and comforters for a thorough washing so she could make up the beds, and shook the pillows out over the rail of the porch. The quilts she needed were hung out on the line to air and soak up some sun.

There would always be overnights when the boys were there, so she made up a couple of rooms, starting with the ones the kids had claimed for their own. They had chosen the larger ones, so there would be room up there for their friends to hang out or sleep over, and they had kept coming right back to the same ones since they'd been little, just as she had. Her sisters each had their own rooms too.

Getting camp ready brought back so many fond memories. There had been great adventures for all of them over the years, but also many painful sorrowful times when there had been a breakup, and even the loss of a few of their friends - times when they thought they would never be happy again, and Quinn had had to be there with all the quiet perseverance she could muster, listening and trying to soothe them. Now when they were upset, they were too far away to comfort other than over the phone. Quinn had learned that the best thing she could do was to hear them out and let them know she was with them in her heart, and then just let go and allow them to heal on their own. This was harder for her to do than it had been to actually be right there for them as she had for so many years. Keeping quiet when you would rather give advice was a practice she was still trying to perfect.

She hoped that her sisters would come up too, but she never counted on that. If they came, they would call her at the last minute, and probably only come to stay for a few days. After a very short period of time they would begin to long for home and all the busy activity they were used to. It was much harder for them to give in to the relaxing atmosphere of camp than it had been for her. Since there was no way she could plan ahead for them, she put those thoughts out of her mind to enjoy the anticipation of seeing her sons.

Lisbet was facing the same summer preparations, but on a much larger scale. One of her daughters would be coming to spend the entire summer at their old family camp just down the lake. A son was going to bring his girlfriend and stay for a month, and another son was giving up his two bedroom apartment near the city to come stay at the main house to save money for a house of his own. Then the other grown children would come and go along with all the rest of her extended family who loved to come up, and did so every year. Lisbet took care of them all with loving attention and a huge amount of work. The visitors never seemed to realize what it took to make things presentable and welcoming for them, nor did they have any idea what it was like to clean and do up the bedding after they left.

When the main house was brimming with people, Lisbet didn't feel she could just go and escape at her secluded cabin retreat, as much as she wanted to. Nothing brought her more peace and happiness than waking up in the silence of the woods, a morning skinny dip in the glacial waters of the lake, and a day of fly fishing off the dock in solitude. But with lots of family in the main house, she always felt like they were waiting for her appearance in the big kitchen, and longing for her wonderful home cooking.

So, Lisbet sacrificed her halcyon summer days to stay with them so that the aroma of a fresh pot of coffee and bacon sizzling would awaken them in the mornings. She cooked a big breakfast, staging it so that the early risers as well as the sleep-ins would have something wonderful awaiting them when they came down. She left them to their own devices for lunch, but often found the refrigerator ravaged of things she'd planned to use for the next meal. She made a big dinner too unless plans were for them to go out. There would always be freshly baked bread and homemade pies, cakes and cookies sitting on the counter for anytime they craved something sweet. Everyone at her house really benefitted from Lisbet's love of baking and cooking.

Quinn's kids were both very selective about their food and wanted fruit, salads, steamed or stir-fried vegetables and rice as their staples. She always made bread for them, and they didn't hesitate to toast that up and eat it with raw honey at just about every meal – a treat they always looked forward to. She made cookies for them too, which they could never resist, but they consistently reminded her to go easy on those kinds of things so they could stick to their healthy eating habits. They felt better if they did, and Quinn did too. She just wanted a few opportunities to spoil them. Fortunately both of her sons had somehow developed an interest in food preparation themselves, so she was able to stand aside and let them do the work for some of the meals. She just needed to bring in the staple items she knew they depended on for their main dishes and let them have at them.

Whenever the sun was out in a big way and the weather looked stable, she and Lisbet set aside their preparations for summer to go for a kayak paddle. On one of those beautiful mornings Lisbet called to say she was on her way, so Quinn stuffed some sheets in the washer, switched it on, and went to slip into her bathing suit. It was warm enough to wear that with a big long sleeved shirt over it now instead of long johns, and always the chance of getting a little sun on her legs too.

Within 30 minutes they were on the water floating and gently paddling down toward the wild end of the lake. It was a feeling like no other — like taking a deep cleansing breath of relief from the whole world. The day seemed so promising that they decided to try to go all the way to the back end of the lake where it would be most likely that the loons might nest, in or near the same bog they had used the past couple of years.

As they paddled they caught up on their own news. Lisbet was dying to tell Quinn about a wonderful day she had spent out at her secluded cabin in the deep woods, with Ben. He had asked if he could go fishing out there, and of course she was delighted to agree to that and had quickly gathered the makings for dinner, just in case he got hungry at the end of the day. She managed to arrive before he did, and got the fires started in her cook stove and in the big stone fireplace in the main room of the ancient log cabin to take the winter's chill off the place and set the atmosphere. Years ago the cabin had been built as a hunting camp on a completely private lake in the middle of hundreds of acres of woods. Lisbet had purchased the property from the Nature Conservancy with the idea of preserving it, meanwhile using it as a secluded retreat. It didn't take much to set the stage there — the entire place spoke of its uniquely wild and natural setting. It was one of the most peaceful places in the world.

"He took off right away to hike out to Constance Lake, loaded down with gear," she said. "So I used the whole day to do some spring cleaning and baking. It was just wonderful. I made roasted chicken with wild rice, fresh biscuits, and a big batch of oatmeal cookies. While that was baking I swept, vacuumed and dusted everything."

"I bet the bear and moose were salivating out there in the woods…" laughed Quinn.

"Yeah, it sure smelled good, and of course he was starving when he came back down off the trail exhausted! I couldn't let him go home hungry!"

"Of course not!" said Quinn, shaking her head knowingly from side to side. She was well aware of Lisbet's ways to extend the time spent with Ben.

"So we sat down to eat, and it was great. He went back for seconds, and then we cleaned up the kitchen and went outside to sit by the campfire. He smoked a cigar, and we talked out there till late. We had to add logs a couple of times but we had a beautiful fire. The stars were all over the sky. We felt so relaxed I never wanted to leave but finally we both knew we had to go in and get ready to go – we both had early morning plans for the next day. He gave me a warm gentle kiss, and then I followed his truck out so I could close the gate. It was a perfect day…"

"That's wonderful, Lisbet," Quinn said sincerely. Then she went quiet, because she knew her friend would continue on with her thoughts.

"I've given up on expectations. He's such a good person and a wonderful friend. There's nothing I can do but wait and see if anything further develops, but I really hope it does…I just can't give up on him."

They floated on companionably in the silky water, resting their paddles in their laps, in no hurry to get anywhere, looking all the while for the loon pairs. They could hear them, but not see them.

They talked about the family and friends who were planning to come up, and all the work they both had to do to get ready for them and for the emerging summer with all of its busyness. Despite the immense amount of work, they both really looked forward to seeing everybody in camp. Quinn spoke of the terrific progress being made on the boathouse, and how happy she was with everything. She kept her inner thoughts about Will to herself, because she had no idea what those thoughts really were about or what they meant. She just knew that things felt very different when he was around, and that she was beginning to look forward to those times for some reason. Who knew why. He certainly wasn't interested in her, nor she in him.

She told Lisbet about the new little painting exercise she had done with watercolor when she went out to paint with the Plein Air group – and that she was pleased with it. Just thinking about it made her want to try it again, and she surveyed the tranquil majestic lake around her for ideas of scenes she might use. She didn't want to paint the places, she wanted to paint the feeling of it. So far, she didn't know how she would do it, but she trusted that it would come to her. Maybe that was a metaphor for her life. Just live each day in the fabric of life, working the color of it like watercolor on the fiber of paper. You never knew what would happen, how it would turn out – you just had to trust in the process.

Quinn took a long drink of water and thought about how happy she was. There was nothing more delightful than being out in the middle of the water with the whole world in all of its natural beauty literally surrounding her. She marveled at the mesmerizing diamond-like sparkles the sun was making on the surface before her. Yes, there were things she definitely wanted to do, and she was excited about them, but she was also glad that she was happy right at this moment, and there were now times like this seemingly every day. What more could you ask for in this life? She felt that if she was on the right track, cosmic energies would support her, and she would know. Those energies were now beginning to align in a special way, and she felt a unique sense of balance and wellbeing that she had never experienced before. It was almost like being in love.

Lisbet coasted silently along the shoreline, in her own world too. She was inhaling the sweet scent of the pines, hemlocks and cedars. Long graceful boughs of shad were overhanging the water, the white blossoms reflecting in it as beautifully as a Monet painting. Lisbet gently angled between them, pausing occasionally to capture them in a picture with the camera she always tucked between her long legs in a dry bag. The scene was breathtaking.

When they reached a long expanse of open water they paddled more energetically until they reached the wide shallow channel that would take them through to the silent waters of the Forever Wild end of the lake. They had no need for conversation because they both knew exactly where to go – toward the edge of the wavy green bog where the old nest had been, and might still be. They paddled slowly and noiselessly as they got closer, knowing that one of them would have to look first and the other to follow behind.

Suddenly a big smile spread over Quinn's face and Lisbet knew that she had found it. She nodded a silent "yes" and stretched her neck forward to get a look between the reeds and tangles of bog shrubbery. Sure enough, there was a loon curled down upon herself, nesting. What a beautiful sight!

Quinn took her time watching for a while in complete stillness and silence. Then she carefully backed her boat away so that Lisbet could come in close and see for herself. As she did so, Quinn waited. There was nothing but the clicking of Lisbet's camera and the drip from her paddle settling into the mirror-like water to disturb the scene.

They looked at each other with the tender feeling of privilege for being there. Then they slipped away without a word, leaving the loon with her precious egg to herself. Only when they were far enough away to feel that their presence was negligible, did they speak to each other. But really, words were unnecessary. They both knew that should the egg survive, it would bode for many trips down the lake that summer to check on the baby, and most importantly, that he should survive to carry on the tradition of the loons thriving on their lake. It was a warm feeling to know that at least there was a good chance.

As they approached the channel, another loon appeared in the distance floating and then diving in the deeper waters near the back end of the lake. They hoped that to be the partner of the nesting loon, feeding before it was his or her turn to sit on the egg. He might be attempting to be a decoy so that attention could be focused on where he was rather than on the nest. Another good sign.

Their trip had been such a success already but there was much to see along the shoreline in spring, so they decided to head back around the far side of the big island that loomed in the middle of the main part of the lake. They paddled hard for a bit over open water till they reached the tip of it, then slowed almost to a stop so they could slide in through sheltering branches of the shallow cove along its edge. The kayaks drifted quietly in the sunny water with buttery yellow sand less than a foot below them. Taking care to avoid rocks and boulders scattered here and there, they made their way in and out of the small channels and then slowly on out into the deeper water just beside the island. The view down the lake was magnificently peaceful, with still barely any human activity save the silent appearance of a caretaker checking for winter damage and probably opening a camp for the owners.

They had been on the water much longer than they had planned, and wished they had taken the time to bring lunch. It was probably getting too late for that now though, so they finished their water and finally separated so that Lisbet could head for her old family camp where she kept her boat, and Quinn for her own place. They waved to each other one last time as each of them faded from the other.

Quinn knew that getting out of her boat after such a long trip was not going to be easy. Her back ached with the pain of the extended exercise of sitting in basically the same position, and she tried to relieve it by stretching forward, and from side to side. It would feel better for a moment, but then the pain would reassert itself seemingly even more strongly.

She knew that the men were most likely working at her place, and there would be a great view of everything from the top of the boathouse. She didn't want to be the awkward object of their curiosity, so she decided to direct her boat to a low boat ramp that was to the far side of a boathouse the next property down the lake from her own. It had been built mostly to make access to the water more agreeable for kids and dogs, but Quinn could make good use of it today to get out of her boat. She didn't know if her knees would be strong enough to hold her when she stood up from her boat after so many hours. She remembered fondly how she used to be able to disembark from any boat with ease, and she could still do that in her mind, but the reality was something very different.

Thick pines overhung the shoreline where the wooden ramp was, and as her boat glided into the deep shade and dark glimmering water she considered her options. At least this place was completely hidden from everything, so she could slide out of her boat into the water if she needed to. Looking the ramp over, she could see that it was likely to be extremely slippery underwater, where she would need to step. It would be better to step directly into shallow water where she could get a better footing. She moved the boat closer to shore and relaxed there for a moment. Then she took a deep breath, slid both of her legs one at a time over the side of the boat where the rocky bottom was just below her, and with each hand firmly pushing her up she came to a stand right beside the kayak. She quickly grabbed for a small sapling at the edge of the water to steady her.

What a relief! No mishaps and she was standing right there with her boat upright and still almost dry inside. There had been times when she had had to actually kneel down in the water beside her boat before she could stand up, and she was grateful that had not been the case. She took a moment to stretch, and found her legs feeling shaky, but it felt so good to take the pressure off her back that she smiled to herself and waded over to the ramp pulling her boat along with her.

She could see that the ramp was green with a slime that was definitely not going to be safe to stand on. Holding onto the trunk of a narrow leaning tree, she pulled herself up onto the dry higher slope of the ramp. Before it could slide back out into deeper water, she grabbed the cord tied to the bow of the kayak and pulled it up and onto the dock that surrounded the boathouse. There was no one there in camp yet, so she decided to store her boat in the unlocked boathouse until she was ready to use it again. That would be better than carrying it up the steep hill and across to her place.

She took her paddle, hat and empty water bottle back to camp with her, skirting the jobsite so that she could walk through the woods to the front porch without making an appearance before the crew if they were still there. The hill seemed much steeper than it had been that morning. It was going to be great to get to the bathroom before she did anything else.

Her clothes were waiting where she'd left them on the hook behind the door, and it was good to get her damp suit off and into her dry things. Her face was glowing pink from the sunny day even though she had used her sunblock and worn her hat. She bent forward to brush her hair over her head to get the tangles out, then lightly brushed it back from her face, and used a little powder to even the blotchy color out, and some tinted lip glaze for her parched mouth. Heading back through to the kitchen, she filled a small bowl with grapes and a little handful of almonds, and continued out to the porch to sit for a few minutes while she watched the day end.

Twilight was one of the prettiest times of the day. She rocked gently in her chair as she ate the fruit hungrily and looked out over the calm lake reflecting the evening sun. Suddenly she felt a cool breeze drift over her, so she pulled the indian blanket that was draped over the rocker onto her shoulders. When she looked up again she saw Will standing at the bottom of the steps of the porch in front of her.

"Have a nice paddle?" he asked.

"It was fantastic," she answered thoughtfully, wondering how he knew she had been out. "We saw a loon on the old nest – the same one they used last year."

He leaned slightly forward against the thick porch step post as if he was tired too. "Well the roof is almost finished. It'll be done tomorrow if the weather holds. I got your message about the windows, so I'll try to be here when they come – they're gonna call me when they're on the way."

"That's perfect timing isn't it? We couldn't have done better if we'd tried to plan it that way," said Quinn.

"That's the truth…" he answered. "Everything's coming right along, but that doesn't mean anything. The next glitch is right around the corner."

"I don't think so," Quinn added. "This project is going to go right along, just like it is, till the end. I just know it."

"I wish I had your optimism," he said quietly, looking down. "Well, I gotta be goin'…enjoy your evening…" and with that he slipped around the corner of the porch and was gone in the dim light.

Chapter 11

*L*ater that evening the phone rang and Quinn heard Kole's voice calling with the flight schedule for his upcoming trip. It meant a long drive to the airport and back, but there was nothing to be done but look forward to seeing his handsome face and hearing all the news of his life on the way home. Kole was excited as he always was about coming, a little less so about the wedding he needed to go to. He couldn't wait to get there, sleep in his big old comfortable bed and eat his mom's home cooking. He knew his mother could never turn him down for soft scrambled eggs 'n toast in the mornings, just like the ones he'd had growing up. Home with Mom always somehow made his overall exhaustion catch up with him, and he looked forward to being able to sleep in as long as he wanted, go for a dip in the morning and then go and enjoy the great outdoors.

Quinn smiled contentedly as she set the phone down and started up the stairs to change. The dark had settled already, and she was ready to get into her night clothes.

As she passed by Kole's room she couldn't help but look in, imagining her son there in just a few days time. She wished both of her boys could be there together, that was always such a special treat now that neither of them lived with her and had their own places so far away. But it had become really impossible once Jack had entered med school. Even when he had a little time off he always had huge amounts of studying to do, labs to attend and research papers to finish. He couldn't do any of that if he was away from school so he almost always chose to stay put and do the work, and Quinn was proud of his commitment. She would just have to enjoy them separately, and she remembered how great it could be to give each one the special attention she wanted them to have.

Her kids were everything to her. They were half the reason she was even restoring the boathouse. It was for her, but it was also for them. She wanted them to have the best of her, and her architectural skill was part of that. Her way of making a living space part of its natural place in the environment was a gift, and one that would last for many years. She wanted to give that to them.

She slipped off her pants and felt the chill of the air on her legs. Quickly she finished undressing, pulled the long gown over her head, and grabbed her robe to put over it. She hugged her arms around herself for a moment to take in the warmth, then hung her clothes on a peg for the next day — she had hardly worn them.

With her book in hand, she went down to the kitchen. She lit the kitchen lamps, heated some soup and sliced a crust of bread, taking these to the little table to eat. Without the fire burning in the cookstove, the kitchen cooled off quickly in the evenings, so the hot soup was comforting. She ate her little meal slowly, thinking about how great it would be to have her son there with her, even though it meant she'd have to do some actual cooking. It would be so nice to have someone to eat with.

When she was done she rinsed out the bowl and saucepan, setting them in the dish drainer to dry, and set the kettle to boil. While she waited she went to the front room to get a fire going, crumbling newspaper and spreading sticks of kindling in the big fireplace. In a few moments the tea was ready and the fire was crackling gently, so she added a larger log and settled into her old chair close to the fire. She pulled the worn indian blanket from the back of the chair onto her shoulders and stared pensively at the mesmerizing fire.

Now that summer was right around the corner there would not be many more nights of solitude. The camp would be full of the energy of those coming and going, and Quinn would be on hand to help give things direction. It was a good thing the boathouse had come along as far as it had so that she would be needed mainly for the details. Knowing that Kole would soon be there with her was an immensely satisfying thought, so she opened her book to where she'd left off and immersed herself in the story.

Bright and early the next morning the big truck delivering the boathouse windows backed awkwardly down the long driveway and parked near the mudroom to the old camp. Will's truck was ahead of it and he was already there assisting the driver in the effort. They lost no time raising the huge rear overhead door of the truck and sliding out the metal ramp they would use to wheel the packaged windows out and get them down the long hill that led to the building site.

Quinn had risen a little earlier than usual with the idea that the delivery could happen at any time. She wanted to be dressed and ready to see the whole thing, and provide help if needed.

The morning was beautiful. It was cool but the sun's bright rays were piercing through the thick woods putting everyone in an optimistic mood. The winters were so long that just the anticipation of a warm breezy summer like day was intoxicating.

Quinn opened the kitchen door so the fresh morning air could flow into the house. She raised the heavy window over the sink a bit too, so she could be a part of what was going on but not interfere – the last thing they would want out there was a woman. It was definitely a guy thing to get the heavy but delicate window units out of that truck, down the hill, and safely stacked in the boathouse without mishap. The steep hill would be quite a challenge. Taking small bites from her bowl of grapefruit and yogurt, she stood at the counter where she could see everything. The windows looked beautiful, and there were a lot of them for such a diminutive home.

When the order was unloaded, the driver pulled the ramp back into the truck, closed the door and went to his cab to retrieve the delivery papers. Quinn joined him there and provided her signature.

"Thanks so much for bringing them!" she said cheerfully, "They look wonderful."

"Oh they're great windows," he said, taking the clipboard from her. "Enjoy them and have a great day."

He climbed into his seat and pulled the door shut. In a moment the truck was ambling loudly up the hill.

Quinn went back into the mudroom to slip off her flip-flops to avoid Will's harassment for wearing them. She found some old work boots she knew Will would want her to wear, and pulled them on over her hiking socks but left them partly untied. She grabbed her heavy dark flannel shirt and pulled it on as she began walking cautiously down the hill, minding the slippery pine needles and last fall's leaves on the steep path. She could hear the guys chatting inside as she stepped onto the dock, and it made her smile to hear their animated voices.

"How do they look?" she asked Will as she came through the boathouse door.

"Pretty nice," he said. "I really like the way the screens retract."

"Me too," she answered. "It's one of my favorite features – that and the way they open by just turning the latch and giving a little push out, with no crank. I think that makes them look old fashioned too."

She came over to where Will was standing to look more closely at the units they had lined up against the wall to be used on the first level.

"I think they look kind of campy, don't you?"

"Yep," he said. "Nice choice. I just hope they hold up as well as they look."

"When do you think you'll be able to install them?" Quinn asked.

"They're already starting to put them in upstairs," Will said.

"Oh, that's wonderful!" Quinn said, obviously delighted. She was so pleased that progress would continue at a steady pace.

"Why don't you come on up and go over the electrical with me since you're here," he said, heading for the stairs.

"That sounds great," she said. "You know the electrical is already on the plans though." She picked up the set that was lying on the rough handmade desk and brought it with her so she could look at the drawing in case she forgot what she had been thinking when she did the electrical layout.

"Yeah, I know. I just wanna check everything out one last time before we run the wires cause Jimmy's gonna do the plumbing and heat now too, and I want everything to be right for insulation to follow that right away. It's almost impossible to change anything after the foam goes in."

"True," she said, following him up the steps.

When they got to the top and entered the big room Quinn grinned at the airy space that would soon be her home. It looked so open and full of the light she so loved. The crew was already pulling packaging off the first of the window units and setting up to get them installed. The manufacturer no longer used wasteful corrugated cardboard boxes to ship in – they had changed their ways and now used shrink wrap packaging that the men were crumpling and throwing into a big black trash bag. Rigid cardboard strips went into a big box so all of that could be recycled.

"Let's just start in the kitchen area," said Will as he walked over to where the long countertops would be. Quinn followed.

Referring to the plans, Quinn answered his questions one by one, and watched with interest as Will marked the studs with electrical symbols to indicate the exact position for each thing that was to be wired, sometimes checking with her on the height or the positions she wanted. The outlets were easy because they had to follow code, other than the ones she wanted for special needs like either side of her bed, or for lamps she wanted to locate in a particular place. She liked everything to be symmetrical, so she asked him to place outlets so that they would be balanced on either side of windows, especially in the workspace above countertops.

He teased her about her insistence on symmetry.

"Is that centered enough for ya?" he would ask.

"Well, no, not exactly…let's measure and see just where the center is," she would say, taking his metal measuring tape from him and doing it herself.

"Okay, that's the center there and now let's make it centered the other way too."

Will would sigh deeply and shake his head as if he had never experienced such fussiness, even though she knew he had, many times. He seemed to enjoy trying to make her feel as though she was an extreme pain in the neck.

She persisted because she knew that this kind of nerve-wracking perfectionism would pay off later when everything in the design was carefully thought out and worked in a seemingly flawless rhythm. It was what went behind the scenes that counted. The casual observer would have no idea what had gone into the organization of a small living space like this one, to make it function effortlessly. It was the kind of challenge she loved.

Finally they came to the end of all the electrical questions, and Will moved on to the fireplace.

"Okay, obviously you want this thing centered," he said, making light of all the symmetry they had both been creating for the last hour, "but exactly how wide do you want it, and what's the mantle height gonna be?"

"Well, first, let's set the firebox 16" off the floor," she said, picking up the stapled set of documents that had come with the unit. She flipped through the pages searching for the exact height for the mantle above the firebox that would be required to make the fireplace meet with the manufacturer's specifications.

She found the diagram she was looking for and gave Will the written dimension. Again he made a note of it with his black marker on the stud wall, and looked back at her.

"Okay, let's allow for the trim on these windows," she noted, moving to the window openings at each corner that were already framed facing the water. "That will give us the exact size to make the mass of the fireplace including the stone."

"I guess we should allow for 2-3" for the stone facing," Will offered.

"Yes, that's about right. I cut these things mighty close in the design, so that everything would fit in with just about no room to spare."

"I can see that…" Will said, almost too softly to hear. Everything looked like it was going to fit like a glove. "You want the stone to go all the way up to the ceiling?"

"Oh yes," she answered. "We want it to look like it's a masonry fireplace that's been here a hundred years."

"No problem," he said, rolling his eyes. "Ya got the stone ordered yet?"

"Yes. I've been looking for some hearth-stones too. All I need is the day you want them and they'll be here before then."

"Good," he said, looking down to see if he could think of anything else to ask. "Are the masons scheduled too?"

"They've agreed to squeeze us into their ongoing schedule because a huge job they're working on will take a year, so they can do it any time, they said. I told them about the stone so they could check the quantities we need and they have that all confirmed with the stone people. I just didn't want it to be in your way."

"Sounds like everything's covered then," said Will. "We'll get these windows and doors in, and then we can actually lock up the place. What about the hardware?"

"It's already here," she said. "I picked it up myself but it's stored up at camp for now. As soon as the doors are hung I'll bring the boxes down here for you."

"Suits the heck out of me," he said. "Just makes my job easier."

Quinn looked around one last time at everything. It was so gratifying to see the guys back in there working and everything humming right along. She figured that Will wanted to stay a bit, so she turned to go downstairs.

"Okay then," she said. "I'll be up there if you need me."

He nodded once to her and turned toward the guys who were working.

She grabbed the plans she'd brought up and went down to replace them on the makeshift desk.

Ascending the hill again she thought about what a wonderfully productive morning it had been. The guys were probably starving for their lunch but she had no idea what the time was. She figured they would wait until Will had given his last orders before they would take their break. She was hungry too.

It was a great day for a salad so when Quinn reached the kitchen she drank a big glass of water then threw some kale, spinach and romaine into a bowl, sliced cucumber, onion and celery, and doused this with lemon and a little olive oil. For color, she threw in some craisins and sunflower seeds. Mixing it up with her fingers, she decided it looked pretty good and took the bowl out to the old rocking chair on the porch and sat to eat.

It was quiet down the hill so she figured the boys must be eating too. Will had probably slipped away while her head was turned, as usual. She thought about what she might do for the rest of the afternoon and decided that the day was just splendid enough for a trip to town. Making some notes on a scrap of paper, she put together a haphazard grocery list. The charming little local grocery would probably be open now for the summer, so there was no need to fret about forgetting anything. It was just a minute's drive away.

She rinsed her bowl, picked up the pile of library books that had accumulated on the shelf in the mudroom and went out to her old jeep, which still managed to start on demand, most of the time. Her boys, and actually the rest of her family, had been trying to get her to replace the 15 year old car with something a little newer — something they thought would be more reliable for her - but the car had been so faithful that even after it had passed the 200,000 mile mark she hated to part with it. Its worst defect now was the fact that mice loved to sneak into it, get warm and chew wires. They had eaten through the windshield wiper fluid pump wire, and constantly got into the heating vents, blocking them and having to be dragged out after impaling themselves on the heater fan. Every time Quinn appeared at the local garage they would ask - another mouse? Usually the answer would be yes.

In frustration, Quinn had left the last varmint right where he had died, in the vent, as a deterrent for others who might be tempting a similar fate. So far so good, but with the warmer weather coming it would soon be time to visit the long suffering mechanic who had removed the last half dozen critters. Thankfully he had a sense of humor, but unfortunately he had no solution other than the possible use of mothballs, the scent of which already pervaded the old vehicle.

Quinn set the pile of books on the seat beside her and headed for the post office. She picked up her mail about once a week unless she was expecting a check for payment from a client, but that hadn't happened for a while. Any place of business in the area was good for a pleasant hello, because everyone knew everyone else, and everything they were doing. Quinn opposed gossip for its negative effects, but she still loved to hear the local news, most of which would probably be categorized as gossip, and a trip to town always meant an earful.

The postmistress greeted her with a happy smile and noted that she hadn't been in lately. It was certainly true, and the tightly packed box filled with advertising circulars belied the fact. She opened everything right there at the counter while inquiring of the postmistress's children. Thankfully there was a recycling bin for just about every thing in the box. The only pieces she needed to take with her were a few bills.

On her way once again, Quinn drove at the speed limit and was amazed, as she always was, at the beauty of the Adirondack setting. Tall jagged rock faces rose dramatically on either side of the road, dripping with the freezing water of hidden springs, some with pines standing right on their very tops. These gave way to the dark green of thick woods, penetrated here and there by rumbling rocky streams and magnificent indigo lakes. Then it would all recur again as the road wound its way through the forest, little villages popping up occasionally with just a few ancient buildings to define them. The park was such a treasure, one that relatively few people knew about. Quinn was so grateful that her parents, and those before them, had sought out this place to find relief from the city, had discovered its wonders and passed them on to her.

She went to the biggest local town of Old Forge, a place that didn't even have or need a traffic light. At the local library she brought in her pile of books and picked up the ones that had been on hold waiting for her, greeting the wonderful librarian there and catching up a little on the weather and the kids.

Wandering around the largest local grocery store was something she always enjoyed. They had almost everything you could need, or would order it if they didn't. Taking her time there helped her to come up with ideas for meals she could create that she hadn't planned on, so she took her time, picking up the things that were on sale and avoiding those that weren't. Food was a very expensive part of her budget, especially when the boys were there to feed. It never ceased to amaze her how much they could eat, and then come back to the kitchen for more an hour later.

When the shopping was done she loaded the bags in her car and headed reluctantly back the way she had come, glancing at the marquee above the old movie theater to see what was playing. There was no need to go to the bank, so she had to head home and put the perishables away. It was good to see activity picking up all over the town in preparation for the influx of summer people for the upcoming holiday.

She turned on the radio to NPR and listened as she made her way through the woods again back to camp, looking from side to side at the unbelievably beautiful place that was now her forever home.

Chapter 12

*K*ole stretched his long legs out as best as he could by tucking them under the seat in front of him. Flying was sometimes a necessary thing but he never looked forward to it. A train would have been much more pleasurable but it would have been too long a trip. Time was of the essence because he had to travel further to participate in one of his best friend's wedding right after his visit to camp, all without taking too much time away from work.

The plane would be landing in Syracuse before long. It was such an inconvenient place to fly to. There would be two and a half more hours of driving after he arrived, not to mention the same mount of time it would take Mom to come get him. He knew it was hard on her too but they were both always so happy to see each other that the pain didn't last too long.

It had been almost year since he'd been to camp the previous summer. Gone were the days when he could take his whole summer there, working of course but also having tons of fun at the lake spending practically the entire time outdoors. He had been spending summer time at camp his whole life since he was an infant and couldn't even remember it.

He smiled when he thought of the happiness he felt being outside in the woods following Jack everywhere he went, exploring and feeling free to go anywhere they wanted to. They'd spent hours just fooling around in the water, hanging on to floats until they just about turned blue, then getting out to wrap themselves in a big towel till they warmed up enough to take out their poles. They dug under rocks for worms, and would stay on the dock fishing till their mother called or rang the bell and made them come up for dinner.

It was amazing how much she trusted them by themselves on the water. She had taken them swimming with her from before they could walk, so the water was second nature to them and they had no fear of it. They had obviously inherited her own love of the water from her.

He thought of his room up in the huge attic at camp, where he had slept with Jack for so many years, their beds pushed close together so they wouldn't be scared at night when the roof soared over them. The ceiling was open to the unfinished rafters above, with wooden decking at the roof, and it had sometimes seemed too big a space for a small boy. They brought their many stuffed animals, cars and action figures to bed with them for comfort and played in the light of the nightlight till they dropped off to sleep in sheer exhaustion.

Then one summer Jack decided he was too old to share a room and dragged all his stuff to the next big empty one down the hall leaving Kole alone to make his own way. He'd had his own room at home in their real house but camp was always different. So, he started to fill the emptied places with his favorite collected things from the woods. There were lots of rocks from the lake bottom, fossils, feathers, pieces of stiff fungi he'd carved on, and various other odd objects he'd somehow found fascinating at the time. Lots of his drawings were tacked here and there along with his favorite old toys sitting on shelves that were actually just bare studs turned sideways. Mobiles he'd made from driftwood and fishing line hung from the beams above. These old things were still there and he loved going back and seeing that everything was right where he left it.

He knew that Mom would have already made up the big soft bed that his legs had long ago grown too long for, the linens softly worn but smelling like the sun, balsam and pine. There would be an old quilt and plenty of tattered blankets in case he needed them when the nights got cold. His many books would be stacked on shelves and just about everywhere else - he'd be so glad to see them, like old friends.

He wished like hell that Jack had a more flexible schedule so he could get away and come up. It had been a while since they'd been able to just hang out and catch up on things. A phone call never really worked too well because Jack seemed to always be on rounds or in conference when Kole tried to touch base with him. He seemed to literally live at the hospital now, and that would probably go on until graduation, getting even worse when his residency started. He never had time for email either so communication had really become a challenge. Kole knew that his mother had the same problem and that she missed Jack as much as he did.

There was nothing that could be done for it so Kole hoped some of his old friends would be around for company, though he really didn't mind going for a hike or a paddle by himself. There was something soothing about being alone in the woods. His brother had taught him that. Even though they had been together most of the time they had never hesitated to go off to hidden places that no one else knew about. It made them feel somehow braver when no one knew where they were, and they would die first before letting anyone find out where their special places were.

Kole knew that the childhood experiences he had been blessed with in the wilderness had made him a more balanced and secure person, and he was deeply grateful for them. The hours and days he and Jack had spent roaming the woods exploring everything in them had led to a realization of the connectedness and the sacredness of all living things, and they both wanted to participate in a hands on way to help other people feel safe and receive healing when they needed it. Because he could not bear the idea of literally years locked away studying in medical institutions, he'd decided to create a career for himself that would be a conglomeration of everything that could bring a person into the realm of wholeness, and he was in the process of educating and certifying himself in every one of them. It would be a long process, but he felt it would lead to an expertise in the art of healing that would be unique and very much in demand, if he could only manage to support himself in the meantime.

He saw his mother standing there watching for him as he moved through the security gates into the waiting area. He knew without even a word from her that she was nearly breaking down with the quiet joy of seeing him again. Their reunions were always so touching to both of them, because the time between was always a little too long and the visits too short.

They caught up with the trivial things on the drive back to camp, stopping about half way so he could buy a sandwich — he was starving and there was never any food aboard flights anymore.

When they finally reached the boundary of the park he felt the subtle change in the atmosphere. After visiting a dozen or more countries and hundreds of beautiful places all over the world, this place still had the power to draw him gently into its embrace and make him realize it was his true home. The road curved its way through dense woods, parting the smoothly mirrored lakes on each side, their edges broken intermittently with aged wooden docks and tilting boathouses, all so familiar to him. He could feel his body settle down, his breath slowing and his muscles relaxing minutely but perceptively as the fragrance of balsam floated over him through the open window.

Passing through the quaint villages, some of them with buildings literally falling to the ground in neglect, he saw one by one the landmarks that he and Jack had excitedly recognized in their nervous anticipation of getting to camp every time they came. His body remembered the thumping of his heart he had felt as a child, anxiously chomping at the bit to get there so they could jump from the car and run down to the water, and he found himself feeling the same way now.

When they reached the top of the driveway that led down through the woods to camp, Kole gave up trying to remain cool and started to gather his things together. The peaked metal roof spiked through the canopy of trees below, and then he saw the dark forest green of the siding, the old white trimmed windows, the log porch posts and the worn stone steps leading to the back door. He couldn't wait to step through it and be overwhelmed with the musty pine smell of the place.

Quinn gave her son a wide berth when he came through the wooden back screened door, passed slowly through the mudroom and into the kitchen, so that he could take it all into his senses as she too loved to do. He set his bag down gently and went to the sink for some water, looking around at everything that was essentially the way his grandmother had arranged it. He smiled at her without a word, leaning back against the counter in contentment.

"It's s good to be here," he said finally.

"So good to have you here too," she answered, grinning over at him.

He set the glass down and moved into the front room and through to the screened door that led to the wide front porch. Stepping out onto it was like going back in time to the most beautiful place he could think of. The view was shadowed by 100' towering pines, their needles covering the ground everywhere save the stone steps that were carved into the hill leading down to the dock and boathouse. He could hear the lake lapping gently against the edge of the shore below, and he thought of his fishing pole where it would still be leaning against the inside of the boathouse wall by the door. He turned to see his mother watching him and surveying the scene herself from the jamb of the door, smiling. She knew just what he was feeling.

"I'll go down there in a minute," he said, coming towards her.

She stepped aside as Kole came back through to the front room again. Finding everything just about exactly how he remembered it, he shook his head in wonderment. It was about the only place he could think of where nothing changed, and no one wanted it to.

Taking his bag with him, he started up the old wooden stairs, glancing at the coats, threadbare sweaters and well loved hats hanging on pegs at the landing. He made the turn and ascended the last few steps into the wide attic hallway that ended with a big square window overlooking the lake.

When he started down the hall he almost felt Jack's presence as he used to when they tromped up the steps together as kids, running to throw their stuff on the beds. Back then it seemed like there was no time to do anything – they had to get to the water at breathtaking speed. They would tear their clothes off and grab their suits, pulling them up as they pounded back downstairs and raced out the door, letting it slam loudly as they leapt over the steps and down the hill yelling at each other. The chaos didn't stop until they had jumped from the dock into the water, and that shut them up when the cold hit them.

When he got to the door of his room he stopped and looked in, a little smile appearing on his face to see how small it looked, though exactly the same as he'd left it. He thought wistfully for a moment how good it would be to have Jack next to him right then and there. He set his pack on the dark hickory rattan bench by the door, and opened it to pull out a bathing suit to change into. The water was going to be frightful but he didn't care – it would be the best tonic he knew of to get the dregs of travel from his skin.

Quinn was already paring vegetables in the kitchen for stir-fry. The bread had proofed all day in the oven, and was ready to be formed into two round loaves - the basmati rice was ready to go, in the cooker. From the corner of her eye she saw Kole pass by the door on his way out to the water, a big cotton towel hanging over his shoulder.

She finished chopping the sweet potato in her hand and went to the front door to watch her beautiful son step onto the dock, drop the towel over the back of a chair and slowly pace to the end of the dock where he tilted his long body forward and dove gracefully into the freezing water. How he could stand the cold she could not imagine, yet she had done exactly the same thing when she was a girl. She stepped out to the edge of the porch where she could see him better when he came up, and sure enough he was shaking water from his head as he rose from the water like an otter.

Kole turned toward the shoreline and looked up, knowing that his mother would be up there on the porch watching like she always had.

"Whoa…that's cold!" he called to her, panting to get his breath back.

She grinned widely at him and called out, "Dinner will be ready when you are!"

Kole dove again a few more times to let the feeling of the water fill his heart and soul. After a few minutes the bitter cold began to disappear and he just felt the clean silkiness of it. He looked across the surface to the big island in the middle of the lake with its timelessly familiar dock and steep wood steps up to the handbuilt camp that looked out over the promontory edge of the island where it had perched with grace for so long. Then he swam in a slow breaststroke back to the dock and climbed the ladder. He grabbed his towel and rubbed his face and arms roughly before wrapping it around his back like a shawl. Slipping on his flip-flops he went into the boathouse to have a look around.

The old fishing pole was right there where it always was, by the door, with the tackle box on the shelf above it, but the boathouse had indeed changed. It actually looked as though it was going to survive. The walls were straight, with new studs mixed beside the old ones, many removed. The guys must have moved everything away for their work, and replaced it all carefully, because it looked like it had all been put back just where it was, with the addition of some new shelves and pegs here and there for better storage. The canoe and kayaks were stowed on a refurbished rack, with paddles hung between long nails beside them. The boats looked so great it made Kole anxious to get out on the water in one of them.

He opened the door to the staircase that led to the second floor, and started up. So this was to be his mom's new home. When he got to the top he was amazed at the progress that had already been made after so short a time – it seemed like his mother had just arrived at camp!

The walls here were stabilized and straight, with the windows installed, and a new vaulted roof graced the entire place. Framing was in place for the fireplace, and it looked like the electrical wiring was underway. The space smelled of pungent fresh pine and felt extraordinarily open and filled with the light and airiness he knew his mother loved so much. It was a far cry from the derelict old place he and Jack had spent so many hours playing in – pretending it was their house and even camping out here with their friends as they got older. Well, the boathouse was becoming a really magical and beautiful retreat, literally right on the water. He had seen and even been a part of all his mother's work, all of his life, but this place was truly special.

He walked the perimeter and looked out through the new windows at the captivating view in all directions. You could see all the way up into the Forever Wild end, and all the way down to the bridge that crossed between this and Sixth Lake. The fireplace in the center had long tall windows on each side too, that brought the reflections of the water right into the space. It was mesmerizing.

Kole was proud of the skill his mother had demonstrated in creating this dynamic living space. It was a tiny house, like a boat on the water. And it would be there for him and Jackson now for the rest of their lives.

He slowly made his way back up the hill, stopping to turn and take a look at the boathouse from there. He'd been in such a hurry to get down to the water that he hadn't even noticed it on his way down! The warm color of the new board and batten siding, together with the coppery roof made a very pleasing combination. Windows practically lined the upper story walls, giving them lovely definition. It was quite an improvement over the building that had been ready to fall into the water.

When he climbed the porch steps he could already smell fresh bread baking in the oven, and it made his mouth water to think of how that was going to taste hot, with butter and raw honey. All of a sudden he felt hunger take over and he couldn't wait to get the wet suit off and get down into the kitchen.

"I'm up here Mom, and I'll be there as soon as I get changed," he said as he headed for the stairs. "The boathouse looks fantastic."

"Okay honey, just take your time," she answered, smiling to herself and stirring the vegetables with a big wooden spoon.

She opened a bottle of wine and set a board with Kole's favorite cheese and some olives on the table with two glasses. Then she went in to light the fire in the big stone fireplace.

In moment Kole appeared looking refreshed and happy in a pair of well-worn cotton pants, a long sleeved Henley with a soft indian scarf around his neck and a woven hat on his head. They took their wine in by the fire and sat down to take a few moments together while the bread finished baking. The only thing they could think of to make it perfection would have been having Jackson there with them.

Chapter 13

The next morning Quinn woke to what she thought was the smell of coffee. It smelled so good! Had Will been there already to warm his in the microwave? She didn't think he would have a reason to get there that early though. Both she and Kole usually started the day with tea, unless he was up already and had decided to change it up this morning. Oh well, we'll soon see, she thought as she swung her legs over the edge of the bed and got up to look out the window. The day was barely breaking but it looked like a good one. The sun was just beginning to sparkle like so many crystals through the trees. Perfect for the Memorial Day weekend holiday.

It was exciting to think of all the people who would be arriving this afternoon or in the morning for their first visits to camp this season. Doors and windows would be flung open, flags raised, and pots of flowers would appear all over the place as people turned their cold lonely neglected camps into welcoming summer homes. The lake would hum with boats and even a few hardy water-skiers. She loved to see the transformation, the activity long awaited, and all the people she knew for so many years returning for summer at the lake.

She skipped meditation, pulled on her robe and headed down to get the day started. On the way past Kole's room she saw that he was still curled up asleep. Let the poor baby rest, she thought. But where was that coffee smell coming from?

She brushed her teeth as she went down the stairs, unable to wait at the sink for the two minutes her dentist insisted on. When she turned the corner into the kitchen her heart jumped when she saw that someone was standing there at the counter. He turned towards her and she almost fell to the floor.

"Mornin' Mom," said Jackson, cheerfully. "Coffee's ready."

Quinn's mouth fell open and toothpaste threatened to fall out. She rushed to the sink and spit it, wiping her mouth with the back of her hand.

"My god, how did you get here?" she said, turning back to face him as he came forward with his arms open wide.

They hugged each other tightly and then Quinn backed up to take a good look at her elder son and take him all in. She couldn't stop smiling – God, he was a sight to behold…

"I finished my research paper early, and my advisor was so happy he told me to take off for the weekend - he'd make sure someone covered for me. So I jumped on the red-eye, and here I am!"

"I can't believe it…" whispered Quinn – just about to break into tears.

"What's all the racket down h…" muttered Kole, coming sleepily around the corner.

Jackson looked up from his mother to his brother and immediately stepped over to embrace him. "Hey man…what're you doin' sleepin' so late?"

"What? … oh man I can't believe it's you!" cried Kole, rocking his brother back and forth in a huge bear hug.

When they separated the three of them just stood there in an amazed silence, not knowing what to say, smiling, all of them like Cheshire cats.

"Well, if the two of you have no objections, I'm gonna make breakfast! There's coffee already brewed there so get yourselves a cup and give me a hand," said Jackson with a huge grin all over his face.

Since no one seemed to be able to move, he fetched two more cups from the shelf of blue willow and handed them to his brother. His surprise feat was *au complet*, and now he was hungry.

Finally Kole took both cups to the big coffee pot Jackson must have had to search for, and filled them with the hot fragrant brew. He added half and half to each and handed one to his mother as she brought a pound of bacon and a box of eggs out of the fridge. Seeing that, he spied a big skillet hanging against the wall and placed it on the stove for her. Jackson had already found the locally made maple syrup and was beginning to measure the ingredients for pancakes into a big yellow-ware bowl.

"I'm so excited to be having pancakes with real syrup I can hardly restrain myself," said Jackson.

"Don't get too ahead of yourself till I get this bacon going," Quinn answered. "I know you two like it crispy."

"Well, hurry up then Mom, I can hear a fish out there calling my name," said Jackson, as he and Kole exchanged smiles of appreciation for what the day might hold.

"I just can't believe you're here," said Kole. "What the hell changed to make this miracle happen?"

"Your genius brother wrote a fantastic paper on some lab work I've been doing, and an abstract's already being submitted to a few journals that want to publish it. I might even be asked to present it at a medical conference, that's what," Jackson said. "My advisor is really into it and has supported me big time. He's so thrilled with the outcome he wanted to give me some time with you two for all the extra time I had to spend in the lab this semester. It's really turning out to be a great thing for me, and might even give me some pull to get into a special residency program I'm looking at, and even generate a research grant."

"Wow. That's amazing, Jack," said Kole. "No wonder you never have any time to do anything. Are you a scientist now as well as an emerging physician?"

"'Fraid so, bro," answered Jackson with a sly little smile. "But right now, all I care about is you and me getting out on that there water," he said, pointing with the spatula. "So let's get this show on the road and eat, and then we're gonna play all day till our heads hit the hay..."

Kole was so pleased he could hardly see straight. He grabbed three plates, silverware, salt and pepper, butter and syrup and took it all to one end of the table in the front room. They had to eat there so they could see the water.

Quinn separated bacon in the big cast-iron pan, already beginning to sizzle. Though they rarely ate meat, bacon from the skillet at camp had always been a huge exception. It didn't count, the boys told her, because you had to have bacon with camp pancakes and syrup. She had to agree and was as excited as they were.

Suddenly the door cracked open and Will poked his head in.

"What the hell's goin' on in here?" he said with a little grin.

"Look who's here!" said Quinn.

"You didn't tell me these boys were comin'," said Will as he stepped into the room.

"I didn't even know myself…" answered Quinn. "Isn't it great?" She could hardly contain her joy when she looked at them.

Will stepped over, extending his hand to the young men, and they shook it with obvious pleasure.

"Here," said Jack. "Dump that out and fill it with some fresh." He took Will's paper cup from him and filled it from the pot.

"Thanks man, don't mind if I do," said Will, taking the hot cup.

"You have a full crew today, Will…or are the guys wanting to be off for the weekend?" asked Quinn.

"Hell no, I never give them any time off," said Will. "No, we pretty much make hay while the sun shines here – they want to work as much as they can and I need them. There's so much to do in the season."

Everybody nodded, understanding how busy contractors were when summer approached.

"Well, I hope you can take some time yourself," said Quinn, "though you never seem to stop working for a second."

"We'll knock off a little early today if that makes you feel any better…" he answered, smiling. But he knew the crew would not expect him to come back and check on them after lunch – they'd be free to leave whenever they wanted.

"Why don't you go down and do your thing and come back for some pancakes?" asked Kole. "Jack makes a mean pancake and there's always tons to spare."

Will thought for a second and then said, "You know, that sounds pretty good. See ya in a few then," and with that he turned and went back out, leaving them speechless.

"I can't believe he agreed to eat with us," said Quinn, pensively. "I thought he lived on air."

Kole added another place to the table while the other two finished the bacon, eggs and pancakes. They all sat down, not wanting anything to get cold waiting for Will. As soon as they lifted their forks he stepped in and came right to the table, helping himself, and seeming to enjoy everything mightily.

Kole had made a fire so the room was full of morning light and cozy warmth too. The front door was open to the cool breeze because they had to have the mountain air. They all talked animatedly between bites about the upcoming holiday weekend, how they planned to spend it, and what a great job Will and the crew were doing on the boathouse.

As soon as Will finished, he took his plate to the sink and said, "That was really great, but I gotta go," he said through the doorway. "You guys have a great weekend!" and he slipped out the back door.

"Let me clean up," said Quinn. "You guys go do your thing – you hardly ever get to be here."

"No argument here. Thanks Mom," they said as they stood up and headed upstairs to figure out what would come next.

Quinn was happy to do the dishes sipping coffee and taking a moment to think. She knew that she must step aside and let her two boys just be together. They so needed it. She would be right here for every moment of their visit, but she'd leave them alone, too.

When Will had shown up she'd felt that discomfort of appearing yet again in her gown and robe, but when he came so early what was she to do, run upstairs self-consciously and change? She thought that would be worse than just going ahead and being herself the way she was - it was still early in the morning for god sakes. Besides, he seemed perfectly comfortable himself coming into her kitchen at daybreak...

Before the washing up was done the boys came through in swimsuits, tee shirts, hats and flip-flops.

"Goin' fishin'," one of them said as they continued out through the slamming screened door and down the hill. Quinn could only smile.

A moment later she stood at the door behind the screen and watched as they floated silently from shore in the canoe, paddles in their laps and fishing gear at the ready beside them.

They're already full, no need for a lunch, a little voice said inside her. *Oh, stop trying to mother them*, said another. She was so glad they had been somehow blessed with this precious time together. They were a little family, the three of them, and the last few years she had seen them separate and make their own way. It was hard. She so wanted them to lean on each other for the rest of their lives, when she would no longer be there for them. They would need each other.

So much for dreaming - Quinn headed upstairs to get herself ready for the day. First, she checked Jackson's old room and made sure the linens were fresh and there were plenty of warm blankets and clean towels for him. In her mind she knew she had done this already while never expecting him to come and enjoy them. Now that he was here, she felt unsure that his room was really ready for him. His bag was there and he'd been into it so she knew he had been there, no matter how briefly. He would never complain.

She took a long warm shower and blew her hair dry. She dressed and went back down, considering how Jackson's appearance could change the food supply she'd brought in. The boys might even go out though, so there was no need to overthink the situation.

She slipped on her flip-flops and headed down to the lake. Glancing up at the boathouse, she saw that the men were working, but she didn't need to bother them. Her boat was still over next door stored in the neighbors' boat-house so she needed to retrieve it anyway in case they came up to open camp, which was likely. Walking sideways on the piney hill down to the water, she got to their boathouse and pulled her boat out. It looked so inviting.

She gently pushed it into the water and followed herself by stepping care-fully into the lake onto rocks that looked fairly solid on the lakebed. Pulling the boat up beside her, she placed the paddle in, slid one foot in while dropping into the seat, pulling her other leg in at almost the same time. It was an action long practiced but becoming increasingly delicate. One mistake and you would find yourself overturned and the boat full of water.

The boat floated out into the lake of its own accord like it always did. She sighed deeply and looked about, bringing the paddle into her lap. The little cove she was in was so protected, and the big lake was out there now in all its glory with people, boats and even planes on the water. Was she ready for it? She paddled out slowly.

The loons were probably hiding on such a day, so she didn't look for them. Paddling so softly it was almost like just dipping a knife into the water, she eased along the overhanging shoreline. As she went, she looked in at each camp to see who was there, always finding pleasure when she saw that people had come and were in camp as she was. The great heron she loved could be anywhere, so she was constantly on the lookout for him. He would always appear, standing like a statue, but actually fishing for his dinner. The heron was a sign of good fortune, and Quinn loved the idea that he was near, watching over her. She just knew he was.

After a while, she saw the canoe with her sons leaning back in it, their poles stretched out. It was unlikely they'd catch anything, but she knew that was not the point. They'd look for cold spots, and knew where they were, so they had a better chance than the occasional vacationing fisherman who came to their lake. Though she adored fresh trout, the chances of having it for dinner were slim.

She watched them from a long distance, loving the sight of them and taking in their presence on that precious day that she had them so near. She said a meditative prayer of gratitude for that very gift - that she had had them at all, that she had been given them in her life. She was sorry that their father had neglected them and to this day had no idea what he had missed. Maybe at the point of her death she might understand why he had left them to her, and had left her too. She was sure she had been so drawn to him so that these two might come into her life, bringing their gifts and all that she had learned from them. They were the greatest blessing she'd been given.

The boys came in late that afternoon tired and ravenous. They grazed right through the humus, salsa, raw vegetables, cheese, bread and honey she set out for them, and then ran up to get showered and changed for an evening out to see who of their old friends might be about in the local hangouts. They were both pink and full of energy despite Jackson's obvious lack of sleep. Quinn did not expect them home early, if at all, since they knew better than to drink and drive.

After they'd gone, she called Lisbet to tell her what had happened.

"It was a total shock to see Jackson here in the kitchen this morning!" she exclaimed.

"Jackson came too? You must have been totally surprised!" said Lisbet. "I'm so happy for you though. Just relax and enjoy those boys," she said.

Lisbet had a house full. She wasn't quite sure how much she would enjoy that. The chaos of all the kids, their various schedules and food needs always overwhelmed her, and kept her on edge the whole time they were there.

"Just try to be in each moment," Quinn told her. "Each moment is for you, and is meant to be."

"Okay, my friend," Lisbet answered. "You too…"

Quinn straightened up the kitchen, then went to gather up the wet suits and towels the boys had brought back in after their dip in the water, taking them straight to the washer. No need to hang them up to dry all over the place. At least they weren't thrown on the floor like they used to be when the boys were little and couldn't wait to get to the next adventure they had conjured. She smiled to herself as she thought of those wonderfully busy days when she was lucky to have a moment to herself. It had been all she could do to keep up with those two. Tonight, she treasured the few short moments she would have with them.

When darkness fell she changed and went to her comfortable bed to read, but she was distracted, and when she couldn't read another word, she still couldn't get to sleep. The moon was shining brightly through the window, so she blamed that for keeping her awake but she knew it wasn't so. Her thoughts were running through her head. Even meditation did not still the rambling, though she had no idea where it was going. Her only recourse was to silently bring reiki to calm herself, and to bring healing to herself and her sons, though she had no idea what was ahead for them. Having exhausted reiki too, she lay quietly thinking, and a voice came to her — *this moment is for you, and is meant to be.*

It was a voice that came with the very words she had spoken to Lisbet earlier, but this time they were for her. She resisted the temptation to analyze what special message was there, and just took in the words. *Don't plan ahead. Don't try* to figure out what's going to happen next, or need to know what's in their future. Just be here with them in the now, and love them.

As Quinn meditated on that thought, she felt her body release its tension, her shoulders and back falling heavily back into the comfort of her familiar bed. Her breathing steadied and slowed, and she let sleep take her.

Chapter 14

The morning finally came although Quinn had no idea from where. It seemed that she had finally slept soundly and didn't hear a thing, though her two sons were in their beds sleeping like babies when she padded down the hall, looking in on each of them. She was so relieved.

It was another lovely morning. The guys would not be working on this Saturday of the holiday so she felt relaxed in the camp – it was going to be a quiet time, all her own, with no hammers pounding. In the kitchen she made tea and took it to the porch to sit alone while her precious ones got their rest upstairs. She was careful to be as quiet as a mouse, because they needed it.

She closed the screened door without a sound, headed for her favorite rocking chair with the book she was studying now, Anam Cara by John O'Donohue, and sat with it in her lap, setting the hot tea in front of her on the bench.

Just as she opened the book, she saw Will coming up the hill toward the porch. She was surprised to see him this early, not to mention on a holiday weekend.

"Morning," she whispered. "What are you doing here?"

"I work here, remember?" he answered with a little smile, taking a sip of his coffee.

"But it's Saturday, and it's a holiday. Don't you ever quit?" she asked.

"I had some things I had to check on," he said.

She didn't quite believe it but was willing to go on, because it was Will. "Is everything okay?"

"Yup. Everything's fine." He stood there looking up at her for a moment and then said, "How's it going with the boys?"

"I thought just Kole was coming, and was so excited for that, and then when Jackson showed up I was shocked. So happy but really surprised….so now I have the two of them and I'm not sure what's going to happen, but I'm just so happy to have them both here."

She rocked back and forth in the creaky rocker and sipped from her cup, looking at him. He seemed relaxed, leaning over the porch stair handrail on his elbows, with his coffee between his two hands.

"Your neighbors are coming up this weekend and want some more work done – mostly repairs. I'll have to meet with them while they're here," he said, looking over at their camp.

Quinn remembered that Will had indeed built their camp twenty years ago on the empty wooded lot beside theirs. At first her family had resented another camp so close to theirs, but had gotten used to it and grown to love the new owners and their extended family. It was a good thing she had brought her kayak up from their boathouse yesterday, though she knew they wouldn't mind that she'd stored it over there for a few days.

"Oh. I wasn't sure if they were coming up or not. It'll be good to see them. What are you going to do for them?"

"Their deck is deteriorating in some places," he said. "I have to remove part of it and replace it with new, and build some new stairs."

"That doesn't sound too bad," she said.

"No, just another in a long list of summer projects," he said, looking out at the lake pensively.

"I know what you mean," she said. "I'm asked to do so many little things that may mean so much to people, like restoring their bathroom… I just wish I could get a nice new camp project. That would make my day – make my year for that matter. I need a nice project I can sink my teeth into."

"Well, you never know what the summer's gonna bring," he said.

"The boys are so impressed with everything you've done on the boathouse, Will," she said. "It really looks wonderful."

"Well, wasn't that your doing?" he asked her with his eyebrows raised.

"I gave it a start, but it would have been nothing without your attention to craftsmanship. I'm so glad we've been able to work on it together – that's what makes for the best possible outcome," she said. "I hope we can work on something else together when it's done."

"Yeah, I don't know," said Will thoughtfully. "Seems like everything that comes my way already has a design in place."

He finished his coffee and crushed the cup in one hand. "Have a great weekend with the kids. I have a house full of company myself and I need to get back to them."

He raised his other hand in a gesture of goodbye and disappeared around the side of the porch as he headed up the hill.

A house full of company, and he's here? She wondered. She looked out at the lake and thought what an unusual person Will was — tough and always on his own terms, but sweet and gentle too.

Just then she heard a little rattling from the kitchen. Somebody was up and getting coffee or tea. She bent to her book to wait and see who was up first, and smelled the pungent aroma of coffee percolating — *must be Jack*, she thought.

He came out and dragged another rocker over to her, his cup steaming in the other hand.

"Hi sweetheart," she said softly. "How was last night?"

"It was great," said Jackson. "We saw a few old friends, but there really weren't that many up here yet — mostly just the locals gettin' ready for the season... We took it real easy and paced ourselves so we could drive back home and sleep in our own beds. Man, what a great sleep I had — the fresh air is so refreshing — nothing like sleeping in the hospital or my apartment. I really needed that."

"I hate to think of you having to get such a little bit of rest with all you're doing, Jack," she told him. "I don't know how you do it."

"Sometimes I don't even know myself," he said. "You just have to get everything done somehow, and you keep going. There's no other option if you want to finish the program and go to the next phase."

"Well, I'm so proud of you," she said. "Have you decided on a specialty yet?"

"No, I haven't made a firm commitment to anything, but I'm going to have to soon. We're rotating through all the departments now so we can see what they're all like. I actually like them all, but I guess I've ruled out surgery and gynecology – I do love research, but I want to do something where I can be hands-on with the patients too. I just don't know yet."

"Well, whatever you decide, you'll be good at it, Jack. You always put your all into everything you do – always have."

"That reminds me..." he started. "There's something I've been wanting to tell you."

His mother looked over at him with great interest, tilting her head a little. "Uh oh..." she said. "What is it?"

"Well, I've met some one that I've really come to care about," he said slowly. "Her name is Eilish, and she's in my class – same year, and we became friends. Now we've been spending as much time together as we can with our crazy schedules notwithstanding – I stay at her place when I can and she stays with me when she can. It's hard to find any time together though. It's been a slowly developing thing but that's been good because I didn't want to get involved with anyone, as you know, and this kind of just evolved into something comfortable and it's kind of wonderful, actually."

"I'm so glad to hear that, Jackson," his mother said. She knew full well that Jackson had been reluctant, to say the least, to go anywhere near a relationship since the one he had had in college that had a very painful ending for him. He had shied away from getting close to anyone since then, even with girls who were obviously head over heels for him, and she suspected it was one of the reasons he had decided to enter medical school. That way he would be consumed with a program that was known to be grueling for four years, and he wouldn't have to put himself out there again because there wouldn't be time. She waited to hear more.

"We found ourselves seeking each other out. We have a lot of common interests – obviously medicine, but other things too, and we've become great friends," he went on. "It was just the way you had always said it should be, Mom – that the friendship had to come first so you could get to know each other really well before jumping into the sexual thing that would bond you together before you had the chance to know the person really well, and then it would be too late to go back and do that.

She had come off a painful relationship she'd had in college too, so we had that experience in common — one neither of us wanted to repeat. As tough as med school is, the last thing you want is to have to go through a heartbreak that might really throw you off track. So neither of us wanted to get into anything with anybody. We just started to hang out casually, and then we both at some point realized we had become attached in other ways too and wanted to go further with it. It was so great — she's a beautiful person and gorgeous too. I think I'm in love with her."

"I'm so happy for you honey," said Quinn, placing her hand on his arm and squeezing it gently, "Really happy. So now what are you going to do?"

"We're going to keep it cool for the next year through graduation, because we both have residency ahead of us, and we want to let things emerge in the right direction. She's too brilliant not to take her career to wherever it needs to go, and I can't ask her to do anything otherwise — so we're just gonna wait and see what comes next. If we're meant to be together we'll be together despite even having to go to different locations for the next few years to do our specialty work. We both want what is best for each of us — and I so love that about her. She's not possessive and demanding. She knows what I need and wants that for me, as I do for her."

"Oh God, that's so wonderful!" said his mother. "There's nothing more you could ask for, Jackson. I'm so happy you've found someone who loves you that much. It's rare, you know."

"I know, Mom," he said. "It's like the perfect match — almost too good to be true. I can only hope that it goes forward in the same way it has so far."

"Oh, me too," she answered.

They both took a breath and looked out at the beautiful lake before them. It was wonderful news to know that the long dry spell had finally broken for Jackson. He needed intimacy in his life, and was open to it again at last. He took a long drink of coffee and they rocked in their chairs.

After a moment Quinn got up from her rocker and asked, "So, you want some French toast to get this day started?"

"Oh yeah," smiled Jackson, getting up himself to head upstairs and rouse his little brother.

Quinn smiled broadly and went to the kitchen. By the time the two came down she had the bread slices thoroughly soaked in egg mixture, sizzling on the griddle, with sausage patties grilling and maple syrup warming.

Jackson set the table while Kole sipped his first cup of coffee looking out at the lake from the door to the porch.

"Where we goin' today, Jack?" he asked.

"Wherever your little heart desires," answered Jackson. "I'm in such a relaxed good mood I'll let you do the deciding today."

"Wow, it sounds like you've just unburdened your heart," said Kole.

"Somethin' like that," said Jackson.

He and his mother shared a knowing look.

Chapter 15

On Monday morning, just as the orange sun was rising in all its glory over the far side of the lake, Quinn found herself again out on the big porch cradling her hot tea in her lap. This time she was alone.

Although it was technically still the holiday weekend, the boys had already left for their trip to the airport in Jackson's rental car. They had gotten up painfully early in the dark for flights to their respective cities — Jackson back to school and Kole to the wedding where he would see many friends from his childhood. Quinn had gotten up too, to say goodbye. They hadn't even let her make them breakfast, insisting on picking up coffee and some sort of to-go breakfast sandwich on the way.

Jackson had prudently arranged his return trip to coincide with Kole's flight so that the brothers could drive together and not have to trouble their mother with another five hours of driving to get Kole to the airport. She was grateful for that, but it was always so hard to face the sudden separation from her kids when they left. It was like withdrawal.

In its early stages it always felt like a loss, in the midst of a kind of being lost too. Where to turn? What to do? It was easier to know when they were there — take care of them, of course. When they were gone again, who was there to take care of? She herself didn't need anything…or did she?

Jackson's story of finding his love had reminded Quinn of what it had felt like when she had had that exhilarating experience. New love brought such an astounding rebirth of joy — the mindlessness of being outside of your self and merging willingly with another. It was one of the most astonishing experiences of one's life, and Quinn wanted to feel it again — she admitted that to herself. She'd done a wonderful job of taking care of herself these past couple of years after the boys had left home, finding creativity and a sense of belonging, but why did it have to be alone, and for what might be another twenty years, alone. The thought of that made her sad - it would be such a waste of everything precious she had to give.

She stared at the bright sun as it rose, turning pink like the inside of a shell, then paler, and then lighter and lighter into the twinkling brilliance of a silver star. Rising before her, piercing through the web of trees, she felt its warmth and the promise of a new and magnificent day, and a brimming future. It was messaging her to keep her focus on all the possibilities. She remembered the words she had heard a few nights ago, *this moment is for you.*

She went to the kitchen to pour a second cup of tea from the china pot and picked up her book lying where she had left it on the table. She went back to her rocker and opened it where the beaded cord marked the place she'd left off when Jackson had come to talk to her just yesterday. John O' Donahue wrote,

> *"For love alone can awaken what is divine within you. In love, you grow and come home to yourself. When you learn to love and let yourself be loved, you come home to the hearth of your own spirit."*

She closed her eyes and allowed those perfect words to sink into her tender heart. Her longing for love to be present in her life, and missing it so deeply when she found herself alone again, was nothing more than the natural urge to be at one with who she really was - to be whole, and to identify with the light within her soul. As the sun continued to rise, streams of light touched her face, and she knew at once that she must always remember that she was already loved. She had her sons.

From next door came the muffled sounds of someone letting the dog out, accompanying her on a short meander around the back yard. Quinn opened her eyes and realized the neighbors must have arrived at some point but she'd been so engaged with the boys that she hadn't even noticed them.

The world was awakening so she decided to go in and get the day started. She peeled and sliced a half grapefruit and added a few small raspberries to the bowl, while she silently wished that she could hear bacon popping in the skillet and the boys tromping down for their first cups of coffee – aching for a big hot breakfast. Suddenly she just wasn't hungry so she pushed the bowl back on the counter and headed up for a nice long soothing shower.

When she was done she put on a big white button down gauze shirt over softly woven cotton gray pants that fell from a drawstring, and left her hair a little wild when she dried it. She brushed on a little mineral powder, blush at her cheeks, and fluffed her hair – not minding if it looked a little messy - and took the stairs with a little skip, barefooted.

Since there would be no one down at the boathouse, she decided to brew some hot coffee and take it down there to see how things looked in her emerging new home. It was great to be alone there with her imagination.

When the coffee finished perking she grabbed a big mug, added some cream and held it carefully balanced as she made her way down the steep hill. The pine needles felt cool and spongy on her feet, like a hint of summer.

The aged decking on the dock warmed her feet again as she watched the morning activity on the water, sipping from her cup. There were fishermen out on the far side gliding in the distance, and several kayakers tilting their bright yellow paddles to and fro as their slim red and green boats slid delicately in the flat shining water. It was good to see people out early enjoying the lake. She went to the stairs to go up.

At the top, when she stepped into the room she was again stunned at the light pouring in from every direction. There were long distant views down both ends of the lake and all the way across it. She knew this of course but every time she saw how dramatic it was it felt like a new discovery all over again. She could see everything from there. From the window that would soon provide the eastern view from her bed, she delighted in the scene she would wake up to every morning – a far cry from the scene from the small window opening in the room she was sleeping in now.

Quinn sat before the front windows with her coffee on the floor in front of her to take it all in. She crossed her legs in a yogic position and looked at everything around her. The electrical seemed to be finished and the plumbing was started. There wasn't much the guys could do inside while that was going

120

on so they had apparently been working on finishing the siding and trim on the exterior. From the outside, the building had looked just about complete as she'd come down the hill, and on the inside it was well on the way. The steady progress was really remarkable. It was almost ready for insulation.

Quinn heard the sound of someone coming up the staircase and wondered who it could possibly be. People had been stopping by boat to see what was going on, but so far no one had had the nerve to trespass on her property to satisfy their curiosity. The room went silent and Will looked over at her from the opening.

"I thought you might be here," he said.

"Oh, Will," she said. "What in the world are you doing here? Were you looking for me?"

"Nah," he said. "I just finished meeting with the folks next door to make some decisions about the new work over there. They're gonna' leave first thing in the morning so I didn't want to miss them."

"Did you get everything settled?" she asked.

"Yup. It's really no big deal. But it's better to get things clear before we start, so…"

Quinn smiled at him and looked out at the lake. He looked out too, from where he stood. You could see everything from anyplace in the room.

"The boys left early this morning, and I'm just missing them," she said pensively.

"Those two are some pretty neat guys," he told her. "You did a great job with them."

"I'm not taking credit for anything," she answered. "I've been really blessed with them – I could tell when they were little that they would be special people, and that's unfolding before my eyes…" She could feel the tears start but she didn't want Will to think she was just a sentimental old woman, so she blinked a few times to hold them back, looking away from him.

Will must have known it was a good time to change the subject.

"I put a screened door together for the bottom of the stairs. You feel like giving me a hand with it?"

"Of course I will," said Quinn. "I didn't know you were doing that."

He turned to go back down and Quinn quickly took the opportunity to get back on her feet. She stretched her legs to get the blood flowing again. Before she got down the stairs he had set the wooden door close to the opening and was dumping the contents of a little brown bag into his hand — it held the hinges and a slide bolt that would lock it from the inside.

"This is a really nice door, Will," said Quinn looking it over. "I had no idea you were making it. It's gonna really help draw the breezes up the stair when it's hot this summer...I honestly hadn't even considered how great that would be."

"That's the idea," he said, already getting things into place for the little project. "With no air conditioning you're gonna need plenty of ventilation up there."

He set the light pine door with its dark screens into place from the outside, separating the two of them as Quinn stood on the inside. Three bronze hinges were already screwed onto the side of the door, along with a bronze vertical pull that served as a handle on each side.

"Hold that steady while I mark where these hinges are gonna set," he said, lifting it up into place so that it was flush to the head of the jamb.

"Are ya there?" he asked.

"Yes, I've got it," she said, holding the door as firmly as she could so it wouldn't slip down while he was working.

She watched his rough hands as he started to screw the hinges into place on the jamb. There was a piece of gray duct tape hanging from his finger.

"Don't you carry any Band-Aids with you?" she asked him. "I don't know how sanitary duct tape is..."

"Oh yeah - but they always fall off so I have to take more serious measures," he said. His fingers were nicked and scratched. "Barely a day goes by that I don't bang myself up somehow."

Quinn listened to his breathing as he positioned the power drill into the screw heads and powered it to place the screws perfectly. His breath was even and calm. Then he checked them all again. She herself was less than calm.

"Okay?" she asked.

"Yup, that oughta do it," he said as he pulled the door towards him, opening it.

He stepped into the little hall so quickly he just about bumped into her but didn't, and gracefully turned to look back out through the new door. He was so close she could sense the scent of work on him – a slight sweaty smell that seemed to be mixed with pine and sawdust. When she breathed in she felt her entire body react with the subtlest shiver of energy. She stepped back a little with the surprise of it, but he didn't seem to notice.

"Where do you want this bolt?" he asked her, holding it up where he thought it might go.

"Right there is perfect," she said.

He had thought of everything, as usual. He screwed the brass slide bolt into place without her help, and slid it open and closed a few times to make sure it would work smoothly.

"There you go," he said with a grin, looking right at her.

"Wow. A beautiful brand new screened door – I love it!" she said grinning back at him, looking into his sparkling blue-gray eyes. His skin was rough from the outdoors but soft and wrinkled just a little at the corners of those mesmerizing eyes.

Quinn didn't want to move but somebody had to.

"I left my cup up there," she said as she ascended the stairs to get it.

Will gathered his tools and crushed the brown bag into his pocket.

"Well, gotta go..." he said. "See ya later."

By the time she got back to the top of the stairs he was already gone. Quinn lowered herself onto the top step and sat there staring down with the coffee cup in her hand. Below her at the landing was the pretty new door he had made - all his idea - and it was a good one too. It was Memorial Day, Quinn thought. Why was he out working when he could be home or out on the water relaxing like everyone else? The only answer she could come up with was that he just loved his work, like she did hers, and it wasn't something he needed to avoid. The craft he did was his creative outlet, and it had to make him feel good. She was just so happy to be the beneficiary of it... and amazingly, she just loved being around him.

That afternoon Quinn paddled out into some of the quiet warm coves to enjoy the solitude. The sun felt so good on her arms and back – she protected her face with the floppy hat, and it did seem to keep some of the flies at bay. To avoid thinking too much, she stayed close to the shoreline so she could see everything that was going on in the woods. At one point a huge fluttering startled her, and she realized she had inadvertently come too close to a heron who must have been standing almost right beside her. She ducked her head instinctively as he flew past, though he came nowhere near her. How could she have missed him? She hoped that he would come back to land on this side of the lake so she'd have the chance to see him up close.

Sure enough, after paddling very quietly for a while, she saw him enter the edge of the woods up ahead of her. She made note of the exact place by locating a rock that surfaced from the water there. Determined to be absolutely silent, becoming what she laughingly called her "inner Pocahontas," she glided so softly that only the water dripping from her paddle could be heard.

When she got close, she stopped paddling altogether and just let her boat float. Soon he came into view. She let her paddle drop noiselessly down into the water to stop the forward movement of the boat, and looked at him. Just like in the pictures, he was standing on one leg like an elegant statue. His pale blue-gray coloring and long black legs were a vision of beauty to Quinn. It was such a gift to be able to observe one of nature's most interesting creatures up close like this. She knew, too, that his presence was meant to bring great good fortune, and the knowledge that cosmic energies were protectively at one's side. He seemed to be perfectly comfortable standing silently as she watched him.

After a while Quinn backed the kayak away without a sound so that she wouldn't disturb him. When she felt she was far enough away she turned slowly and headed back towards home, content within as she hadn't been for a long, long time.

When she got back to camp it was just around five o'clock but she was beginning to get chilled, so she stowed her boat and paddle quickly and went up the hill to get out of her damp suit and shirt. First though, she laid and lit a fire in the big fireplace, then she went up to change.

She didn't feel like getting dressed again, so since it was Memorial Day, the start of the summer, she chose her ankle length white cotton gown, instead of the usual ticking striped flannel ones she had worn all spring. She threw the long bright salmon colored silk robe over it, grabbed her journal and went down to the kitchen for a glass of wine. Then she went to sit in the chair she had loved for years, close to the fire. It was already cheerfully popping and crackling brightly. She wanted to write about seeing the great heron that day.

Staring at the fire she pulled her legs up under her and began to write with her flowing black ink on the creamy pages about the boys' visit, the progress of the boathouse, and the appearance of the heron. She had seen the heron many times but her mother had told her he would always come when she needed him the most, and she'd believed it.

Indeed it seemed to be true too. She and her sisters had sometimes even prayed for the heron to come and help settle their seemingly insurmountable problems. They would huddle on one of their beds upstairs and whisper together what it might mean if they saw him, and what he might want them to do. In any case, they always felt better when the heron came, because he would look after them as no one else could do, and somehow show them the solutions they needed.

Quinn loved to write – to see the scrawling up and down on the page was so much more beautiful then typing everything on a phone or computer as they did now. Perhaps it was akin to her propensity for drawing – for putting something beautiful on the page, or the paper as with watercolor. She remembered how much she had loved what had happened with her first new attempts at watercolor, and became excited just anticipating the new directions she might be led to take this summer, painting with the group.

Her writing did not bring her to any conclusions, but it was just good to get it out – get it on the page so she could let all these feelings, hopes, and dreams go. Maybe the heron would be able to make something of them...

When all her inner ideas seemed to be on the pages she took the wineglass to the kitchen, making sure the screen was in front of the sinking fire, and her books were stacked neatly. She didn't feel like eating any dinner, and was ready to go up to find comfort in her nest of a bed and the great book she was reading. In the kitchen, she made sure everything was tidy and put away so as not to attract the mice, turned out the lights and started for the stairs.

Just as she took her first step, Will opened the back door and stepped half-way in.

"Were you going to bed already?" he asked.

Embarrassed at the early hour - it was only around 8:30, Quinn answered, "Well, yes… I was going up to read… What in the world are you doing here?"

"I had to come get a tool I left from down below," he said.

" Oh. Well, I was just going up", she said, taking another step.

"Can I come up and see what it looks like?" he asked. "I haven't been up there for over 20 years…"

Quinn thought for a second and then said, "Sure – come on up," as she continued on up the steps.

Will snapped the door shut and followed her.

When they got to the top of the winding staircase Quinn said, "I don't know what it was like the last time you came up here, but this bathroom was made from a bedroom that used to be here, when I was little," pointing to the bathroom on the right at the top of the stairs. "I remember we used to have to go out to the two-seater outhouse, or use the covered pot my mom kept for us in the hallway at night. We were always so self-conscious that everyone could hear us tinkling in the middle of the night, so we were sure glad when the bathroom happened." She turned on the light so he could see it.

"Anyway, Grandpa put this bathroom in the same time he fixed up the kitchen below with a sink with real running water, the new refrigerator and gas stove. He took the pump out of there that used to be the only water supply to the house. He was so proud to have modernized the place. And yeah, it was sure a lot more convenient afterwards. I know my mom was really happy about it. Oh, and believe it or not, he put in the washer and dryer then too. Before that they only had a washtub out in the porch, which is now the mudroom. They hung clothes on a line through the woods. What a chore - poor Grandma, and poor Mom…" she said.

Will looked in at the tidy bathroom and nodded.

"This is great," he said, "You got a ton of space in here…"

"Well, that's because it used to be a bedroom," Quinn reminded him.

She continued down the center hallway.

"My grandfather made all these rooms up here simply because there was so much space below on the first floor, and over the porch. They had eight children, so it was great for all of them. There were only three bedrooms in their house down at home to crowd everyone into - basically the boys got one room and the girls the other 'cause Grandpa and Grandma had their own room. It must have been great for them to get up here and be able to spread out for the summer."

Will looked into all of the rooms - Quinn turning on the lamps in them for a moment so he could see. They were all pretty much the same except for the ones that Kole and Jackson occupied. These two rooms were filled to the brim with the things of childhood adventures. Will couldn't help but to go in so he could take a look at the shelves of books, wooden toys and the myriad things the two boys had collected over the years. Their beds were rumbled and unmade – Quinn hadn't gotten around to changing them yet.

He didn't say a word though.

Quinn continued down the hall and brought him to the square window at its end.

"Here's the window we all would look out, to see what the weather was gonna be for the day, or to find the moon at bedtime…" she said. "The breeze coming in here kept the whole attic cool when the nights got really hot. We would climb up on this chest when we were little, and the boys did too when they were really young, to look out and get cooled off…"

Will looked down at the sturdy wooden chest with its brass corners and big latch, beneath the window. Then he looked back at Quinn, fighting the tears that threatened to fill her eyes - those days were so precious to her.

"And this is my little room," she said, taking a step into it. "I've slept here since I was a girl, and I love it." She bent down to light the small lamp at her night table.

Will peaked into the room approvingly, but went back to the open square window next to it at the end of the hall.

"I can see why you love it here…'" he said, looking out at the scene beyond, the moonshine illuminating the woods and reflecting on the lake below in a rippled pattern.

Quinn stood beside him and looked out the old square window too, which was flung open to the hallway, the big screen between them and the bugs. She felt a slight breeze brushing her hair slightly back from her face. Will turned towards her, took her chin in his hand and slowly brought his lips to hers, hesitantly as if to let her object and put a stop to it. She didn't.

His kiss was warm and soft. She found her body responding with a tremor that seemed to come all the way up from her toes.

Will looked out again at the clear illuminated night for a moment.

"It's beautiful from up here," he said.

She nodded, unable to say anything at all.

He touched her lips with his again, this time his tongue gently finding hers. She sensed a hint of whiskey, and it tasted good. She reached up to put her hands on his shoulders, and he pulled her closer, one hand moving through her hair and the other pressing against her back.

"Can I lie down here with you for a while?" he whispered to her.

"I guess you could," she said, in wonder at the very idea.

She very slowly backed into her room toward the bed, let her robe drop onto it, and slid in beneath the flannels and quilts. The moon was shining softly through the little window, so she turned off the light. She moved to the far wall, away from where Will sat down on the edge, taking off his boots. She lay breathlessly there against the pillows waiting to see what would be next. Will seemed to be completely relaxed and comfortable, but suddenly Quinn felt desperately cold, and she pulled the bedcovers up to her chin, looking at him.

Will took off his shirt and work pants and seemingly folded himself into the blankets on the bed next to her. She immediately felt the warmth of his body and breathed it in, but she was still shivering.

"It's okay," he said in a whisper, leaning back against the pillows. "Nothing has to happen… I just want to be here for a little while with you."

"I'm sorry," she said softly, "it's just been so long since I've had anyone this close to me…"

"Just rest right here in my arms," he said, wrapping one of them around her shoulders and pulling her closer with the other.

That felt so good that after a while Quinn's body calmed. Her breathing slowed and she looked up at his rugged face.

He kissed her on her forehead and her cheek, and kept his warm arms around her. He let her rest, as if he was almost falling asleep, but he wasn't.

After a while Quinn found that she was completely comfortable with her head cradled in the curl of Will's arm, and she turned her face to touch her lips to his chest. He moaned a soft sound. She lifted his tee shirt and took his nipple into her mouth and found him below at the same time. He drew his breath in sharply and tilted his head back at the blissful feeling, and that encouraged her. Then he turned to her and began to look for her with his mouth, finding and kissing her deeply.

Quinn felt her body melt with desire. The hardness of Will pressed against her. He opened the little buttons in the front of her gown and pushed it aside to look at her in the dim light. He cupped her breast in his hand and kissed the pinkness of her nipple with a soft sucking motion that made Quinn lose herself completely.

She was still afraid. What if she was not ready for him? What if the parts of her she had not used for so many years didn't work anymore? But the overwhelming passion of the moment overtook her sense of doubt and dominated her.

Will touched her in her most intimate place, and she almost cried out when he began to caress her back and forth there. Her breath was quickening, her eyes closed, and she felt in a way that she hadn't for literally years. Her body arched toward Will and she reached for him. He was there, and he pushed himself ever so gently into her.

He rocked with her very slowly and deeply until she called out, "oh..."

"Are you alright?" he whispered.

"It feels so good," she sighed.

"It does?"

"Oh yes it does," she whispered.

That must have been the response he was looking for. He began to push deeper into her and then she came, and she came for such a long time that it seemed to last forever, and he came too, with her, releasing a sound that she loved.

They kept their bodies entwined until their breathing slowed to a semblance of normal. Then Will kissed her and slid to Quinn's side, still holding her close to him with his face buried at her neck. Finally they both slept in the moonlight.

Quinn felt Will slip from the warm bed in the middle of the night, reaching for his clothes and dressing without a sound. He picked up his boots and padded down the hall and stairs — she heard the back door click shut, and his truck go slowly, almost silently up the driveway.

The bed had absorbed the scent of him, of them together, and she pulled the bedding around her to inhale its sweet fragrance, drifting back to sleep.

Chapter 16

For days, Quinn's heart felt so light that everything seemed to have changed. The whole world looked different, and even if she never saw Will again in her entire life, she had him to thank for it.

So many years had passed her by because of her fear of intimacy, but she had never realized it. There was a whole list of things that Quinn had used to keep herself protected, safe, and alone. Her failed marriage was at the top, and it went from there to include most dramatically her belief that she was unable to choose a man to share her life with because of the mistakes that she had made already, rendering her incapable. That idea had literally stopped her in her tracks and kept her in a stationary place almost permanently.

When Quinn woke up the morning after Will had spent the night with her, she knew that she was changed for good. It was not that Will had worked a miracle, but that he had penetrated the armor she'd had in place for so long that she didn't even know it was there. The barrier had been broken in exactly the right place and in the perfect way. She'd been blindsided, never even having the slightest clue that she had held such a defensive position, or how it could be blasted to smithereens in a mere moment in time.

The first thing she thought of that morning lying in bed was the heron. Had he actually worked his magical powers on her? She had just seen him, literally hours before Will had climbed the stairs up to the attic with her. Maybe he had come to shock her into a new reality — it certainly seemed that way. Surely he had gotten his reputation in native American lore for doing just that — suddenly appearing in a person's life, for the specific reason that something earth-shaking was needed — a change, a cure, a solution, an answer.

Whether it was the magic of the heron, or just a coincidental occurrence that Will had come to her so unexpectedly, she felt the transformation profoundly. Instead of feeling that her life was essentially on the downhill path toward old age, she suddenly now felt she was going in the opposite direction toward an inspirational life filled with possibilities. It amazed her to think that just one short evening could be responsible for such a reversal.

Will had stirred her being entirely. He had brought to life feelings and sensations that had been dormant for years, but he had also shaken the old patterns she'd been in. Like a snow globe – everything was floating in the space of her mind and was about to find a new place to land. Where, she didn't know and didn't even need to know. The adventure of being in unknown territory had brought her back to the freedom of a child who had everywhere to go and all the time in the world to do it.

She was determined not to change anything between herself and Will, because their relationship had already been an enigma to her. How could you change what was a mystery in the first place?

So she went about her days in much the same way, watching him as he came and went to manage the work that was rapidly proceeding on the boathouse. He still came into the kitchen to warm his coffee some mornings on his way down the hill. She did not try to detain him or engage him in mindless conversation – she knew he was a fiercely independent man with a lot on his mind, and she didn't want to interrupt him or make him focus on her. To her, he was perfect as is, and after that night, even more so.

She decided not to tell anyone what had happened. Not Lisbet, her boys – not anyone. It was just too astonishing to talk about, and it was hers. The gift of this experience, and the realizations it produced in her were just too intimate and precious to share, so she held them closely within her own heart.

But the effects were everywhere and in everything. Quinn felt so refreshed that every atom in her body seemed to have been renewed. She was bursting with energy, slept little, woke early and ate practically nothing. It was as if her body was living on air, or some kind of inner nourishment, and didn't need the weight of food anymore. So she remembered to keep herself hydrated, forced down water and blended drinks made of orange juice, yogurt, strawberries, bananas, apples and green stuff — usually spinach or kale, until her appetite decided to come back.

Long walks did not tire her out, so she took lots of them, and they gave her additional opportunities to be with all the myriad thoughts and ideas that kept springing up in her mind. It was impossible to make sense of them all, so she just let them come and go, smiling inwardly.

Meanwhile, the boathouse construction was moving at a rapid pace. There seemed to be lots of progress, and she loved going down in the late afternoons to look at what had happened during the day. The fireplace had been brought to the site, installed, and attached to the flue through the roof. The stone to finish it was stacked near the dock but she didn't know how it had gotten there. The plumber finished the water connections, installed the shower, water heater, supply tank and the radiant floor heating system in the new floor with its accompanying furnace set on the ground floor in a small closet. The wiring seemed to be complete when Will put in a new panel box, and had the power connected so all at once lights came on. The boathouse could now be lit softly at night, and it looked like a storybook picture from the water.

When the chaos of the Memorial day weekend became a memory, Lisbet's life settled down and she called to go paddling and for hikes, but they had to be mindful of the black flies that would torture them till the fourth of July. It was always something. Since school wasn't out yet, the summer people hadn't arrived so things were still relatively peaceful on the lake and in the villages. Quinn enjoyed seeing her friend and hearing all about what was going on between her and Ben, but it was pretty much always the same — they would go to group dinners together and he would accept invitations to Lisbet's house for dinner, but those occasions would typically end with a friendly hug and a peck on the cheek that left Lisbet in frustration, and an anxiety for things to change. She was willing, however, to stay on this awkward path that seemed to go nowhere in particular, rather than give up on Ben and direct her attentions elsewhere.

The idea of this made Quinn ever more grateful for the exquisite interlude she had shared with Will, that had come so out of the blue. She had done absolutely nothing to deserve or instigate it — it had been a heavenly blessing that she had needed on some interior level, and had arrived spontaneously. Because she had no idea how it had materialized made it all the more astounding.

So, she carried on as before but with a brand new perspective. There was a radiant joy within her that she almost had to take pains to hide. She wanted to smile all the time and let her newfound delirium show, but if she did there would be questions she had no intention of answering. There was no reasonable explanation she could give, but for her everything had changed.

The Plien Air painting group was meeting regularly despite the black flies, and Quinn tried to join them whenever she could. They were meeting at different locations every week, and she always looked for the way light was playing on the scenes so that she could create something unique with it. Sometimes her work turned out surprisingly well, but other times she was disgusted with it and thought it had been a waste of time. You could never tell what watercolor was going to do. All you could do was give it life on the paper, and see what would happen.

She had one or two pieces now that were pleasing, including the one she had done on her very first day with the group. The fact that it had turned out so well in a rather effortless way proved to her that no matter how hard you might work to make something happen, it might not make any difference. It would work or it wouldn't.

She thought about how meditation had given her the ability to see thoughts and ideas, and then let them go. She realized that in this moment of her life, she needed to practice that in a way she never had before — she needed to let go of everything. The more she did so, the more she was drawn back to meditation because it continued to provide her with the successful experience of letting go. Amazingly, a circle had been created for her where each of her new ideas seemed to be leading to new realizations, and these would reflect back to earlier teachings she had embraced that were now helping her in new ways. The teachings were there in her spiritual inventory, ready to be utilized as each unanticipated situation came forth, creating a deeper realm of understanding.

As June continued, Quinn heard from both of her sisters that they thought they would come up for the fourth of July weekend, so she began to do some heavier cleaning and preparations for them. Of course, it all might be for nothing because they often changed their minds, and never seemed to be able to coordinate their visits together. She wished that they could just relax and enjoy camp the way they all used to, so she was determined to make that a little more possible for them, since she had a lot more free time than they did. It was just about all they could do to pack up every last thing they were going to need into the car, technological devices included. They'd said they were looking forward to coming, but she was definitely unsure of that. Sometimes it sounded like just too much effort for them to get ready, and then face the long trip.

She meticulously went through camp dusting, washing, polishing and putting things back in a way that she never did for herself or the boys. She'd never been an immaculate housekeeper because she simply didn't really want to take the time away from everything else to clean house. When her sister Megan had claimed she was haphazard or even lazy about it, there was some truth in it. But for her sisters' visit, she wanted everything to be as neat as a pin. She wanted them to take even a modicum of the enjoyment she did in being there, but with no work to do.

Both sisters were disinterested in cooking, so Quinn planned some simple meals in advance that she thought they'd like. Her bread was always a huge success with everybody, so that would be her standby. She'd bring in plenty of hearty breakfast things and good coffee to wake them up with an irresistible aroma wafting up from the kitchen. Since they both loved to sleep in, there would be brunch, and then there would be just a nice dinner to plan. They liked to go out to eat too, and were always dragging her with them to the local places they wanted to go to once a year, but she always ended up really enjoying that herself, so she looked forward to it.

She was excited to show them the boathouse, but hesitant at the same time because they would be worried, as they always were, about her living up here alone. There were just too many things to be afraid of, like wild animals, loneliness, and the freezing cold long winters, all the snow, and the steep driveway – oh, the list could go on forever. Quinn didn't think there was any real way to really reassure them.

Chapter 17

On the Thursday evening before the holiday, Megan and her husband Colin pulled down the driveway in their big black SUV packed to the gills with supplies, fishing gear, a big cooler, and their basset hound, Gilly. As soon as they opened the door for her, she leapt out of the back seat and dashed to the edge of the woods to see what all the new scents were.

Quinn was getting an early start on dinner preparations when she heard them coming and hurried out the back door to greet them and help bring everything in – she was always amazed at how much stuff they needed. Gilly pulled as hard as she could against her leash, tail wagging furiously as she greeted Quinn energetically, then rushed to scour the edges of the driveway for traces of animals she might chase. They couldn't take the risk of letting her go free because the hunter in her could lure her to bound off after a deer or some other critter and it could be hours or days till they saw her again. So Colin handled her while Meg and Quinn carried things in, then Colin took his turn unloading while Megan held the beloved dog.

When everything seemed to be stowed in the kitchen or upstairs, they brought Gilly in and hooked both screen doors shut so she couldn't push them open. She immediately ran around the camp sniffing at every nook and cranny, probably expecting to find a hapless mouse. Quinn pictured them all huddling quickly into their hiding places, tucked in early for the night...

Megan gave Gilly some water in her usual spot beside the wood stove, while Quinn stacked the food and drinks they'd brought in the refrigerator. Colin reached for the small bottle of whiskey he'd remembered and poured some over ice in a tumbler that Quinn had already prepared for him.

"Here's to camp!" he said lifting up the glass as Quinn poured some wine into glasses for herself and Meg.

They lifted their glasses too, touched them together and headed out for the porch, grabbing Gilly's leash from where it was dragging on the floor.

"Man, it looks great out there," said Colin standing at the top of the porch steps leading down to the path to the water. "I can't wait to take my pole down there and see if anything's biting..."

"Don't let us stop you," said Meg. "He made us pull over to pick up a license and some bait on the way."

"I just didn't want to waste time going back to town after we got here," he answered defensively, already on his way around the side of the house to fetch his pole and elaborate tackle box from the car.

"Well, he's happy now!" said Megan to her sister, taking a little sip of her wine. "We can do whatever we want and he'll barely notice as long as he can be fishing."

"I'm so glad you guys decided to come," said Quinn. "You both need some breathing room and relaxation in the worst way."

"I know," Meg sighed. "We're both so consumed with work we can hardly even find the time to plan a trip, much less take it. I'm not sure I even know how to relax anymore."

Megan worked as an accountant in a big firm, and Colin was a high-powered lawyer in Washington, DC. They both had to commute every day, and were expected to put in horrendous hours, even over the weekends.

"Well I want you to really take it easy while you're here," Quinn offered. "Everything's all set for you, and I don't want you to do a thing...that reminds me, I need to go in and turn the oven on – I've got a nice stuffed chicken ready to be roasted."

Her words faded away as she went through the screen door, letting it slam behind her. Megan tied Gilly's long lead to a rope that was strung around a porch post so she couldn't follow Colin down the hill, though she was sure determined to do so if she could. She paced back and forth at the top of the steps with her eyes peeled for Colin.

Quinn came back out with some raw vegetables, cheeses, olives, and crackers, setting the big wooden board down on the long bench in front of them. The sisters sat back in their rocking chairs and looked out over the water. They could see Colin below on the dock casting his rod, his whiskey glass perched on the dock at his feet.

"Have you heard anything from Lily?" Megan asked.

"Not yet, but a few days ago she emailed and said she was gonna try to get up here tomorrow. It would be so great if she makes it," said Quinn, "but there's no way to know till we see her."

"She's got a busy life right now, but she needs to get away once in while too," answered Megan. "I've been so looking forward to being here with the two of you like we used to."

"Me too," said Quinn, and they looked over at each other warmly, nibbling cheese.

When the chicken was ready, Colin could smell it all the way down at the dock, so he set his pole just inside the boathouse next to Kole's and came up the hill without needing to be summoned. Quinn pulled out a big tossed salad in an aged wooden bowl that she had actually burned a design into as a child, and tossed it with lemon and olive oil. They served themselves from the kitchen and brought their plates out to the porch again to balance on their laps. A basket of hot bread wrapped in linen sat in front of them, with a cut glass dish of butter and a pot of raw honey.

Colin lit the fire inside after dinner, and Quinn brought hot coffee and shortbread cookies out to encourage the couple to relax in the front room. While they settled into old familiar chairs, she washed the bit of dishes they'd used, and put the leftovers away, refusing help. Gilly stood at her feet to keep her company in the hope that some tidbit would fall to the floor just for her.

After the dishes were done Quinn slipped upstairs to light lamps and turn down the bed that she'd made ready for them, checking to make sure she'd piled enough fresh white towels on their dresser. There were fragrant pine stems in a vase with a handful of wildflowers beside the bed, and a bar of local handmade soap that made the whole room smell vaguely of lavender — the scent that was supposed to be restful for a good sleep. She put two foil-covered chocolates on their pillows, just for fun.

When she got back down and went in to sit by the fire herself, Colin had his feet up on a caned footstool with his head in a book and Megan was checking something on her computer.

"Hey you!" said Quinn. "No working!"

"I just thought I'd make sure..."

"Meg, they can manage without you for a day or two... now close that thing down and pick up that book you've been wanting to start, hear me?"

"That's what I keep telling her," mumbled Colin into his book, "but she never listens..."

Megan saw that she was overruled, so after a few minutes she closed the laptop and reached for a book from the little stack beside the lamp on an old twig table by her chair. She sunk back deeper into the cushions and leaned her head back, opening the hardcover.

"Now that's more like it," Quinn told her, approvingly, while lighting candles on the mantle. "I don't want to see you on that machine again for the rest of the weekend."

Megan rolled her eyes at her sister, and Colin smiled quietly without looking up.

It had been such a long drive with many preparations done for the trip, so Meg and Colin climbed the stairs fairly early to get comfortable in their room. Quinn knew that they kept late hours at home, but it was so quiet for them here without the distraction of TV which they halfway watched every night, that she was glad they gave in to the peacefulness of the setting.

She was already in her gown and robe by the time she heard them come up one after the other, with Gilly's nails clicking on the steps along side them. You could hear everything up there with the walls of the bedrooms not even reaching the rafters and the open space above, so Quinn was careful to be very quiet so that at least the illusion of privacy could be maintained. She draped her robe over the bottom of the bed, tucked into the softness, leaned against all her pile of pillows and picked up her own book. Never once did she do this now, without thinking of the night she had curled into Will's protective arms, and wonder if it would ever happen again.

Megan and Colin had been married for many years, and though they each had terribly demanding jobs that took so much out of them, the little spare time they had, they always spent together. They had raised a wonderful son who was now happily married and had a career he loved as a talented photographer, living just a few hours from them. They seemed to have an unspoken agreement about household chores because they kept a spotless home and apparently never had to argue with each other about getting things done. Colin even ironed his own shirts because he wanted them to be done perfectly and ready to be laid out the night before work. The housework was shared, amazingly without resentment, Megan doing the laundry and Colin taking the yard work. They didn't cook at home, and merely had to agree each night on what they would eat for dinner, and when each of them would manage to get home, which was always late.

Quinn admired their relationship, even envied it. She had never experienced a partner who cared for her unselfishly like a dear friend, and she wondered what it would be like to crawl into bed beside a warm loving body night after night.

With those thoughts running through her head it was hard to concentrate on reading. Before long, the soft murmuring sounds and comings and goings across the hall dimmed to silence. The loons called in the far distance, one to another, almost as if on cue. Quinn's own eyes began to flutter and her head to nod in the lamplight so she turned out her light and let herself slip into sleep.

It was still dim in the attic when Quinn heard Colin pad down the hall to take Gilly out the next morning. The back door opened softly below, and she heard Gilly's leash clink and rattle as she walked the perimeter of the woods. No doubt there were lots of new smells for her from the myriad animals that prowled silently out there every night.

Colin brought her in, clicked the leash off, plugged in the coffee that Quinn had left ready for him, and started Gilly's breakfast. Quinn knew that he had taken on that chore at home so Megan could sleep as long as possible. He'd always been an earlier riser, so it worked out fortunately for Meg.

The aroma of the coffee pulled Quinn right up out of the bed. She slipped her robe on, headed to the bathroom and on down the stairs. By the time she entered the kitchen Colin was already on his way down the hill with coffee to see if the fish were interested in his bait that early. Gilly was tied to the porch making a bit of a fuss but she settled right down when she saw Quinn standing at the door with a mug of creamy coffee. She wagged her tail wildly in a greeting, pushing her head into Quinn's hand when she came out onto the porch.

Quinn petted Gilly's head and long silky ears, crooning good morning to her while her coffee cooled a bit, then sat back and breathed in the fresh morning air. She figured the men would be working on the boathouse that day, so the momentary quiet was all the more precious. It looked like it was turning into a perfect day, so she was so grateful for that, and glad that Colin was able to take advantage of it to do one of the things he loved the most. She wished that his son was down there beside him, making jokes and the two of them laughing softly like they always did when they were together.

When she went back to the kitchen for a second cup, Will opened the back door with his own cup in his hand.

"Mornin'," he said cheerfully.

"Oh, good morning to you," she answered, unable to hide a smile.

Will moved to the microwave and put his cup in, pressed it on and turned to her. "Company for the weekend?" he asked.

"My sister and her husband got here last night, and we hope my other sister will arrive this evening too," she answered. "You too?"

"Oh yeah, I usually have a houseful for the fourth," he told her. "Gotta try to make it an early day today so I can do a little cleaning."

"You? Oh, I can't imagine you live in a messy house, as neat as you keep the jobsite," she said incredulously.

"Yeah, well, you'd be surprised then," he said as the bell rang to signal that his coffee was warmed.

He turned to open the microwave door, carefully grabbed the hot cup and closed it again, moving toward her just a step. He raised his other hand slowly to brush a stray strand of her hair back, ever so delicately, a serious look on his face.

Quinn felt a warmth coming up her back, spreading over her shoulders, up her neck and coloring her cheeks pink.

"Would you have the time to come down and go over the kitchen with me this morning?" he asked her.

"I'd love to do that… when do you want me, now or later?"

Suddenly she realized the accidental double entendre of her question.

"Can you come now?" he smiled, getting it too.

"Sure, just let me change then," she said, trying to keep from becoming embarrassed. "Megan is still asleep and Colin is already down there fishing."

"Okay, great - I'll see ya down there," he said, still grinning. Then he turned and went out the door, closing it soundlessly.

Quinn went to fill her cup, watching him go around the camp and head down the hill, through the window over the counter. Gilly gave a low growl and a bark as he passed the porch, but Will wasn't even startled. He probably sensed her even before she sensed him.

Quinn sighed as he went out of sight, grabbed her cup and headed up the stairs with it, walking quickly but silently to her little room. Her body was humming as she pulled off her night things and hung them on a hook behind the door, then slipped into her sports bra, a gauzy white shirt and some black yoga pants. Knowing that Will would want her to have shoes on, she took some white anklets from a drawer and went back down the hall. She made a pit stop to rinse her face, apply some concealer, powder and blush with a touch of pink glaze for her lips, brushed her already clean hair over her head and then fluffed it around her face.

It was only minutes before she was on her way out the back door through the mudroom, sliding her feet into socks and sneakers and descending the hill. Gilly looked at her with bewilderment from the front porch as she passed by.

Quinn had to slow down to compose herself and keep from sliding onto her bottom in the slippery pine needles that covered the hill in a thick carpet. When she had shoes on it was so much harder to keep the delicate balance between being careful enough not to fall, and looking like an old lady shuffling in her slippers. It was a relief when she got to the dock. Colin turned to greet her with his pole in one hand.

"Any luck yet?" she asked him.

"No. I'm gonna have to get Meg to come out in the canoe with me so I can go to some of the ole places that used to be good," he said.

"Will needs me to have a look at some stuff about the kitchen up there," said Quinn. "I'll get breakfast as soon as he's done with me."

"Take your time," said Colin. "You know how your sister loves a lie-in."

"Yep, I was counting on that. There's plenty more coffee, so help yourself to that. She'll wake up when I get the bacon started."

With that she pulled the new screen door open and went up the steps to where Will was waiting at the west facing window with his tape measure in his hand.

"Okay, what have you got planned for here?" he asked. "I want to build the base cabinets in my shop and bring them over, but I also want to have the appliances here first so I can fit everything together on site."

"There'll just be the small 24" range and an under counter refrigerator," she said coming towards him. "That's it for appliances. I can get them here and we can store them downstairs till you're ready for them."

Will nodded his head, and moved to the window. "Good. Okay, I know you're gonna want the sink centered under the window, so I'll need that too. How wide is it?"

"We need to allow for a 36" base. It's just narrower than that but not by much."

"Okay," said Will, making a mark at the center of the window and measuring the 18" to each side. After he marked those dimensions, and he checked the space remaining from there to the two end walls on each side.

"I want the range to be about 9" from the right wall leaving a narrow tray cabinet there, and the fridge right up against the left wall. Everything else should be drawers."

"Don't you want any doors with shelves?" he asked.

"Nope," she said. "Drawers make it easier to see exactly what you've got without having to get practically on the floor to see what's in the back - just a regular top drawer with two deep ones below it. Remember I've got the pantry for food and additional storage."

"I thought that was for clothes," Will said.

"Yeah, but it's for other storage too," said Quinn. "It'll be a multi-tasking closet."

"Okay, we'll get to that in a minute. I think I remember you wanted all open shelves above with no wall cabinets, right?"

"Yep, exactly," she answered. "The shelves should be 12" apart in height and all the way to the ceiling. I'm gonna need every inch of storage space I can get. Can you give me a little bit narrower shelf – say about 8" deep – about 6" off the countertop? That'll be for condiments and spices."

"I can do anything you need," he said. "Are you gonna give me a drawing of this plan so I can make sure I've got everything?"

"Sure, I can do that. Is a hand sketch alright?"

"As long as everything's on it that'll be fine," said Will.

He made some quick notes on a scrap of board with his pencil.

"Okay, let's talk about materials," he said. "I've got some hickory from an old barn that I think would be enough for the fronts of everything, even in the bathroom if you wanted to match it there. We could use cherry or oak for the tops unless you want a hard surface."

Quinn's face lit up. "The hickory sounds fantastic, and I love the warmth of cherry. That'll be perfect. The sink is gonna be an under mounted farm sink, so make sure you coat the top with plenty of poly. I'll be draining dishes with a rack in one of the bowls, so there doesn't have to be a wet space on the counter, but it's still gonna get wet – even though I'm careful," she said.

"What about the shelves then?" Will asked, tilting his head to the side.

"What do you think?" she asked him.

"Well it's your design, you know, I just work here..."

"Your input really means a lot to me. You're the craftsman... I wanted a handmade interior and you're the only one I could trust to do it right."

The cheek of Will's face quivered slightly, a movement that Quinn loved, but had only seen men do, when they were under some sort of perceived pressure.

"How about cherry veneer with a hickory edging?" he asked.

"That sounds perfect," she said. "Can you make brackets with solid hickory branches?"

"Sure, if that's what you want."

"Yes – and make them as wild as you can. Don't bother making them alike. I'd like them to look like we took them right out of the woods and put them on the walls," she said with an excited grin.

Will rolled his eyes, but he smiled. "Okay – whatever you say… just give me a sketch so I can make sure we're both on the same page."

He walked over to the closet that was already framed in.

"So you want almost all shelves in here?" he asked, beginning to take measurements inside the doorframe.

"Yes, but they can be pine in here. Let's put a 24" wide hanging space behind the door, and the rest of that sidewall double hung. Let's do the rest in shelves, with some shoe shelves all the way around, about 6" from the floor. I need plenty of space for my flip-flops."

He looked at her wryly. "And some work boots," he said. He looked at her feet but did not comment on the sneakers.

"Of course. I was just going to say that," said Quinn.

Will scratched some more notes onto the board in his hand. "Okay, what about the vanity?" he asked, moving into the framed in bathroom.

"Match it to the kitchen base, with as many drawers as you can, but in here I want a white cultured marble top with integral bowl," she said. "I'll get that ordered when I order the rest of the plumbing fixtures and fittings. I don't want it to be in your way."

"Actually you can order it now, and then we can have them hold it till the last minute in the shop," he said. "I'd like to have that come just about on the day we are ready to install it."

"Will do," she said.

They looked at each other with obvious pleasure.

"Well, that about does it," said Will. "I've got all the rigid insulation for beneath the radiant floor on my truck, and the guys are gonna bring it down and put it up today. Then they'll do the batt underneath it. We'll squeeze in as much as we can to keep you warm in here. In fact I think I hear them down there with it now."

"That's great," said Quinn sincerely. "I'm so happy with everything."

"Yeah, it's lookin' pretty good," he said, looking over at her. He took the board he'd been writing on and moved toward the stair. "Well, I'll leave you to your family then."

"Thanks for everything, Will," she said quietly.

"My pleasure," he told her, and started his way down.

Quinn closed her eyes and leaned against the wall, taking a deep breath to center herself. She stood there for a moment, listening to Will give the guys downstairs their directions for the day. She did love the sound of his voice, for some reason.

She knew she could not waste any more time in a reverie, she needed to get up the hill and start a fine breakfast for Meg and Colin, so she imagined a force pushing her toward the stairs down and out the back door. Then she toed off her sneakers and stooped down to pull off her socks. She wanted to feel the morning warmth of the pine needles beneath her feet as she climbed up the hill to camp.

Chapter 18

*A*fter a leisurely brunch of pancakes, sausage, eggs and toasted fresh bread, the women cleaned up the kitchen while Colin went down to get the canoe and Quinn's pond boat out for a paddle. Gilly had run down with him with excitement and now paced the dock anxiously, knowing they were up to something and worried that she might not be included.

The two sisters slipped on their suits under loose cotton shirts, collected a couple of big towels, hats, and some water bottles and headed down to join Colin. He had tied Gilly to a peg just inside the boathouse so she could wander in and out, or lie down in the shade or on the sunny dock without being able to jump into the water. His fishing gear was tucked into the bow of the canoe so he could fish from there and Megan could navigate from the stern, as they'd done many times before.

Colin got into the canoe first so Megan could push it out and get into the back seat. Quinn stood in the water to hold the boat steady for them while Megan eased into her caned seat and pulled her leg in, the boat rocking somewhat until both of them got their balance with the paddles in the water. They pushed off from shore into the flat, clear water under a bright sunny sky. Quinn let the canoe take the lead so that Colin could direct them to all of his favorite fishing spots and take his time in each of them. The girls didn't care where they were going – they just wanted to be out in the beautiful day on the water, so Meg paddled as her husband gave directions and Quinn zigzagged in her boat behind them to keep them company.

People were coming in to camps all around the lake, so boat traffic was beginning to pick up along with the noise of outboards, inboards, jet skis and seaplanes. Flags were appearing to signal the presence of folks "in camp", and it was a mixed blessing to know that while it was great to see everyone finally returning for the summer, it would change the atmosphere from one of quiet reserve to the somewhat chaotic noise of people out enjoying themselves on the water at almost any time of day or night. Sometimes a rude interruption would break right into a tranquil peace. Motor boaters were of a different mentality than paddlers – everyone knew that.

They glided along the edge of the shore into the warm coves and back out to the cooler waters, Colin dropping his line in whenever he felt the energy of fish. The women just gazed at all there was to see. Quinn kept her eye out for the heron, but she was pretty sure he would have better things to do than stand around statuesquely today when there was so much going on at the lake. They went down into the wild end to take a look at the loon's nest, but the birds were long gone from there, swimming and fishing contentedly where the waters were quiet and somewhat protected from the onset of busy boat traffic.

By the time they got back in, Gilly was anxious to be released from her guard post, the men were gone from the jobsite, and it was time to start thinking about supper. Since Lily might be arriving, they had decided to stay in camp again to be sure to be there if she indeed was coming. With deliberate care, they each slowly emerged from the boats with no small amount of groaning, lifted the boats up into the boathouse and made their way up the hill trying to keep their breath.

"Where've you been?" called a voice from above them on the path. Lily was on her way down to meet them.

"You're here!" exclaimed Quinn, grabbing her sister for a big hug.

"Yeah, I decided to insist on taking today off, and left early this morning. I even had the car packed last night so I was ready to go when the sun came up." She shook her head. "That drive is a real pain with all those trucks on 81."

"You got that right," said Colin. "But it's the only way unless you just want to waste time on back roads."

Megan gave Lily a hug too when they met on the path. Even though they didn't live too far from each other they didn't get together much because they were always too busy with work.

"Did you unload yet?" asked Meg.

"No, I just brought a few things in for the refrigerator when I passed through the kitchen and came straight down here. I've got my suit on under this and I'm gonna take a swim right now."

"Oh, that sounds good," said Quinn. "I'll come with you."

So Quinn took two towels from Megan and followed Lily down to the water while Meg and Colin continued up the hill with Gilly.

They dropped their shirts onto a couple of Adirondack chairs, slipped off their flip-flops and Quinn stood watching as Lily walked trancelike to the end of the dock and leaned right into the water. She herself was unwilling to do the plunge, so she stepped down the wooden ladder till she was waist deep, and then slid onto her back with a sigh, moving outward with the momentum and beginning to paddle her feet to stay afloat. She dipped her head back to soak her hair and look up at the cobalt sky. It looked and felt like heaven.

Lily came up for air and brushed the water back from her face and eyes, treading water. "It's as good as it gets, isn't it?"

"Yes it is," Quinn answered, grinning. "Some things never change..."

They swam around, looking down through the clear water to the rounded rocks below. The lake bottom dropped off sharply from the shore, so they were in deep water, but they could still see everything. It was so good to realize that the waters had not become polluted as they had in almost every other place in the country.

After a while Quinn started to feel like she needed to go figure out dinner. "I'm ready to go up," she said, climbing the ladder to the dock.

"I'll see ya there," said Lil. "I wanna stay in for a little longer."

Quinn grabbed a towel, dried her face and arms and wrapped it around herself, slipping into her flops as she made towards the hill with her shirt in her hand.

"I brought some steaks and potatoes with me," Lily called to her. "They're in the fridge."

"Oh, that's wonderful!" Quinn said, turning back to see her sister deep in the water with just her head showing. "That certainly solves dinner. I'll see if Colin's willing to grill them for us."

Lily nodded her head before dipping it into the water for another dive. It was so good to see her relax and enjoy the water she had always loved so much since she was a tiny girl, the baby sister.

When Quinn made it to the porch, Megan and Colin had already brought some drinks and snacks out for a happy hour. A glass of red wine sat there waiting for her, so she picked it up and took a sip. "Thanks for putting all this together, you two. What a treat."

"We were ready, so we went ahead," said Colin. "We saw some steaks that Lily must've brought with her. I can grill those if you want."

"That sounds perfect," said Quinn. "She said she brought some potatoes too, so I could put those in to bake while we relax." She put her glass down on the bench. "I'm gonna run up and get out of my wet suit – be right back."

In the kitchen she pulled the potatoes out and gave them a good washing at the sink, turned on the oven, then went up to change. She didn't feel like putting her clothes back on so she picked out a loose, long sleeved rayon dress in a delicate red print, and slipped it over her head. She dried her hair a little, but let it finish itself knowing that it would mean more curl than usual. It was summer now, after all.

She checked in on Lily's room to see about towels and light the bedside lamp for her. A light on in your cozy room seemed to make you feel more welcomed, she thought. When she was satisfied with the room she hurried down the hall, only to run into her little sister on her way up with an armload and a cloth overnight bag over her shoulder.

"Is there more out there I can bring in for you?" she asked.

"No. I traveled lightly this trip." She passed Quinn and continued up the rest of the steps. "I'll just change and be right down."

"Okay – see ya in a minute then." Quinn detoured into the kitchen to put the potatoes in, pulling out the makings for a salad while she was at it. The wooden bowl was still on the counter so she filled it with washed lettuce, spinach and kale, then chopped cucumber, celery and onion. She threw those in on top, with some craisins, walnuts and feta cheese.

Lily poked her head in and said, "You're not gonna stay in here cooking, are you? Come on out to the porch with us."

"Oh, I'm coming right now," said Quinn. "I was just waiting for you." She put everything down and followed her sister out to the porch, where Colin and Megan seemed to be well into the process of relaxing and enjoying the evening. Gilly was circling the bench where the food was, looking at it with great interest but knowing better than to grab anything with her two people watching her so closely.

"Let me know when you want me to light the grill, ladies," said Colin. "Looks like everything we need is here, even charcoal."

"Let's let the potatoes bake a bit," said Quinn.

"Sounds good to me."

Everybody apparently agreed with that, and the four of them rocked back in their seats with appreciation that they had plenty of time to enjoy the first evening of summer, and the whole weekend too.

In the morning Quinn followed Colin downstairs after Gilly wakened him. She started the coffee while he tended to the dog, so it was ready while Gilly was still eating her breakfast. The two friends waited for her to finish so she could go with them, then took their cups out to the porch to watch the sun come up through the trees.

Within moments Lily came through to the porch with a steaming cup, already in a dry suit with a shirt over it.

"I'm going for an early paddle," she said. "Don't hold breakfast for me but I'll probably be back before you're ready to eat anyway." She went down the steps and onto the downhill path, with Gilly straining at her leash to follow.

"I'm so glad she's getting out there," said Quinn. "There's nothing like an early morning paddle to soothe the soul."

"Well, I guess so," said Colin, "but I'd rather be fishin'."

Quinn knew that he would be down there with his pole as soon as Lily got herself launched, and sure enough when they saw her slide out into the water in one of the old kayaks, he was on his way. She and Gilly watched him quietly.

Quinn made Megan's favorite, french toast, for brunch that morning. As expected, the sizzle of bacon in the pan brought her sleepy sister down to the kitchen. Quinn insisted that she needed absolutely no help – the table was set with a big bowl of delicious looking fruit in the middle, and everything else was ready as soon as they were. But she didn't want to rush anything, insisting that Megan enjoy a leisurely cup of coffee while Lil was still out on the water.

Megan acquiesced and joined her husband on the dock with a refill for him, sliding into one of the Adirondack chairs to watch the early activity on the lake. There were several fishermen across the lake, slowly trawling in fishing boats. A couple of skiers took advantage of perfectly flat conditions, sliding back and forth on slaloms, and a few kayaks and canoes came by with coffee mugs balanced artfully on the edge or in the hands of the paddlers. It was a pleasant scene.

When they saw Lily appear coming around the edge of the cove, the couple brought Gilly with them up the hill for the now eagerly awaited breakfast. Everything was ready in the oven warming so they sat down to eat – Lily not far behind.

While they ate companionably, Quinn convinced everybody that they all needed the exercise of an easy hike, preferably to up to Rocky Mount. So after the dishes were done and the kitchen tidied, they all found footwear that would work for the stony trail and gathered their gear together into Megan and Colin's car, which would hold all of them comfortably with plenty of room for Gilly.

They drove just a couple of miles to where the trailhead awaited them. There were lots of cars and trucks already parked there, with families loading up with backpacks and picnic baskets for the hike. Colin wove the car at a snails pace through the parking area looking for a space, mindful of all the little ones playing and balls that could roll out into the road at any minute. It was a lively place. He parked at the far end so they'd have some room away from the cars to get Gilly out comfortably and adjusted to the atmosphere.

Then the four of them got out and strolled across the wooden footbridge that led to the bottom of the trail. The whole hike was going to be uphill, so they were in no hurry, but Gilly was beside herself with anticipation.

The trail wasn't too demanding, and though there were people on it, it wasn't too crowded. They'd brought plenty of water, and Quinn had tucked a bag of ginger snaps and various other packaged snacks for them in her pack.

Gilly happily led the way, unless she met another dog coming in her direction, at which point she had to bark, sniff and tug energetically at the leash until her people dragged her off up the hill. Then she would immediately take the lead again as if the others probably had no clue where they were going without her leadership. The temperature was perfect, the company amiable in conversation; so they took their time, stopping to take pictures and look at everything.

When they arrived at the highest point, there were people milling about looking at all the stunning panoramic views over the huge rocks and down into the valley. The winding path of route 28 was visible below, with cars crawling along it like miniature toys. You could see for miles. Gilly took a long drink from the portable bowl they'd brought for her, and then busied herself sniffing at all the fantastically interesting things at the top of the mountain.

Quinn knew that no one would have thought they'd be hungry again after the generous brunch, but when she passed around the bag of snacks everybody took something to enjoy as they sat or laid on the boulders, felt the breeze in their hair and looked at the beautiful views surrounding them.

Quinn had even remembered some chocolate, and she passed a small piece to everyone. They sat staring at the views in every direction, pointing out landmarks they recognized, in no hurry to get back on the trail. Colin laid back on the ground with his head on his sweatshirt and even dozed off for a few minutes with Gilly's head lovingly settled on his lap. The girls talked about fond memories of climbing to this very place with their mother and the childhood summer friends. She always brought a picnic lunch for all of them. The place was beautifully unchanged, a pristine spot that they always loved visiting despite the long upward haul it required.

When everybody was rested they meandered slowly back down the trail, taking their time again and taking more photographs. When they got near the car they decided it would be a good night to eat out, after happy hour on the porch, of course.

For the next two days the weather held, and they kept to pretty much the same schedule, letting Megan sleep in mornings if she wanted to, getting out on the water, swimming, and Colin getting lots of fishing in. They didn't have to be concerned whether he caught anything because he threw everything back anyway. The girls went in to town to look around and visit all the old places they used to walk to when they were growing up. Some places had changed completely but others were just as they had remembered them. On Sunday night they went to the ice cream place and each got a huge cone to eat while they watched all the people enjoy their last night of the weekend.

Megan and Lily began to sigh deeply, thinking about the long trip home and return to work again. A couple of days wasn't enough rest for them — they were just beginning to really relax when it was time to get everything packed up and leave. Colin must have felt the same way but he was quiet about it. Years of having to tow the line in a big law firm had brought him the status of partner, and the long hours and commitment were something he had expected when he got out of law school, so he took it in stride. Not that he liked it. Now that he had a slew of associates and interns working under his direction, he could sometimes leave the office at a decent hour, but he usually brought work home with him and spent most evenings at the desk in his home office.

Quinn was somewhat surprised and certainly relieved that the girls had not brought up any complaints about the rebuilding of the boathouse. In fact they both liked the way it was turning out and were impressed with the new living space, complimenting it. They did ask her how she thought she was going to be able to manage the long cold winters there all by herself, but when she told them she'd be fine they seemed to accept her answer and did not press her further or talk her out of it.

She knew that they must be conflicted about the fact that she, their eldest sister, would be able to stay here and live, with a work schedule that was so relaxed it was almost non existent, while they had to live in a hectic metropolis and keep on working at jobs they had long ago become disillusioned with. The whole situation was regrettable for them and Quinn wished that there was some way she could help them change it. They both had plenty of savings put away but they were still afraid to give up the security of working. It was a scary idea to think one would cease adding to the pot, and begin drawing from it.

But there was nothing she could do. She encouraged them both to start planning to begin the part of their lives where they could love living every single day, instead of drudging through it until some distant point in the future when their real life would begin — and then they could be happy. She wanted them to be happy right now, as she was.

On Monday morning the two cars were packed up early, and all Quinn could talk them into were thermoses of coffee for the road. She didn't blame them because a nice breakfast was always good to look forward to after the first few hours on the road. Gilly would have to stop anyway. They would go together at first, then split up later as each vehicle headed towards their individual homes.

She waved to them as they slowly ascended the driveway, kicking up a bit of gravel as they went. Colin beeped the horn in a cheerful goodbye when they reached the top and the two cars pulled out onto the main road.

Quinn felt torn. The weekend had really been fun, and a wonderful success as far as she could determine, but she felt a certain sadness. She would have yet another day of the holiday weekend today, and many more to follow that, where she didn't have to answer to anyone, or go to a job she was sick of. She had everything she wanted right where she was, almost.

Chapter 19

Whenever the camp emptied itself of loved ones, a transitional feeling of aloneness always overtook Quinn. It was so unavoidable and familiar that she was prepared to have to work with it. There was always the laundry and clean up to be done to distract her, but it was still Monday of the holiday weekend so she didn't feel like doing household chores just yet.

She had missed meditation the last few days, so when the two departing cars disappeared onto the highway she went upstairs to her little room, lit a scented candle, and climbed onto her bed so she could sit up straight, legs crossed in the half lotus position with pillows at her back to support her. She placed her hands palms up on her thighs and closed her eyes. There, with several deep-cleansing breaths, she allowed her breathing and heart rate to slow. Thoughts swirled around her brain, but that was to be expected so she reminded herself to be patient with them.

Noise from the lake echoed from below, with everyone trying to get in their last boat rides and skis, or anything else they could think of before actually getting into their cars packed to the hilt with kids and stuff to head home. The summer people could relax and watch the show, and now Quinn could do that too. She lived here – a new concept that she was actually still adjusting to. The sounds did not disturb her.

She silently repeated a mantra that had been given to her 30 years previously, that she had never shared with anyone, and it helped to quiet the thinking and empty her cluttered mind. Many thoughts came, but she just looked at them and let them pass. Soon she was breathing slowly, softly, and the only thing she noticed were the magnificent colors that occasionally appeared in shades of indigo, blue, violet and sometimes bright white, behind her eyelids.

She didn't know how long she'd been there, but it didn't matter in the least, in fact the longer the better. When she finally opened her eyes, the room seemed very bright, but pretty too – an atmospheric restful place in which she felt calm and safe.

Her legs were aching when she untangled and stretched them out in front of her, leaning over to grab her toes for a few seconds. Then she slid them over the side of the bed and rose to have a look out the little square open window. The trees had leaved out to such an extent that she really couldn't see the water from there anymore, though she could certainly hear it. The smell of summer permeated her completely and she breathed it in deeply to let it fill her.

A long hot shower sounded so good that she wasted little time getting to the bathroom to turn on the faucet. Hanging her gown and robe on the hook behind the door she stepped into the old tub, pulled the curtain around it and stood under the streaming water. With her head tilted back, she let it pour over her, once again thinking how very lucky she was to be here doing this instead of driving all day in a car. She used her fragrant shampoo to make lots of suds in her hair and soap scented of lilies of the valley for her body.

When she was done she dressed in her favorite loose clothes, dried her hair and went downstairs to see if there was any fruit left to eat. There was.

Taking it out to the porch, she began thinking of a painting exercise she had been planning in her mind, so when she went to take her bowl back to the kitchen she brought a jar of water, her tablet of watercolor paper and her tin box back out with her. She wanted to do a little study of the boathouse.

Her tablet in her lap, she pulled out a soft leaded pencil from the box and began sketching the boathouse as it would appear from the middle of the lake – she knew by heart exactly what this looked like. She kept the lines as light as she could, so that minimal paint would be lifted from the paper when she had to erase them later. It took a while, but when she was satisfied with the image, she set it aside and opened her palette, setting it on the bench before her next to the water jar.

With a paper towel that had been tucked into the box, she used a bit of water to dampen the surface of the palette, and cleaned some of the old paint colors away. To get the soft transparent tints she'd been thinking of, it would be necessary to use clean water with just a touch of pigment, and she didn't want any old dark muddy colors spoiling the new ones.

Experimenting with different shades and tones, she tried some test mixtures on a separate sheet of paper knowing it would be important to have the tints she wanted at hand when she eventually wet the paper for the wash. It would be good to have as much control over the drying of the paper as possible once she started rather than having to hurry up and get the paint mixed and onto the paper while it was already drying.

In her mind, she could imagine the atmosphere she wanted to create, a misty ethereal one with almost no background detail. She wanted to demonstrate how the sky, fog and water could sometimes blend together as one. She had seen that magical combination many times, but didn't know if she would be able to portray it on paper.

It was probably going to be difficult to get this to work, so Quinn was pretty sure she would have to try it several times, maybe in several sittings, to get it right. Especially since she wasn't even sure how to do it – she just knew the feeling she wanted to capture. She wanted to let the detail of the boathouse float in the foreground, and that would be a challenge with everything in the background wet on the paper.

So she plunged in, ever so tentatively, wetting the entire sheet except for the boathouse. Then leaving white at the top of the paper, she added a very light tint that she had already mixed, beneath it, letting that bleed down toward the practically unseen shoreline, where she again returned to almost white again. Then she added a slightly altered tint again for the water, leaning back to let the whole thing do what it was going to do as it started to dry. She didn't know what it would do, and that was the beauty of it. She left it alone to see what would happen.

As she waited and watched the color move into the paper, Quinn again thought how like life itself it was. The color worked into the texture and fabric of the paper, just as the moments of one's own life wove their own pattern in a way that there was really never any control over. All you could do was to be there, let it happen, and wait.

It was hard to do, but it was getting easier for her. One of the benefits of being her age was having the sanguinity to be able to wait to see what would happen next instead of planning with everything you had for a certain outcome. Many times in her life she had seen that when she got exactly what she'd wanted, it was not what she expected or needed. In fact, sometimes it was terrible. Learning how to let the energy of the cosmos bring to her what she needed was easier in a way, except for the problem of uncertainty. You never knew what was going to happen. You had to relax in not knowing, and that was an even bigger challenge.

When the paper dried, Quinn was pleased but decided to try the exercise again to see how some other colors with a little less or more tint would turn out. This time she sketched in the boathouse even more loosely, with no detail at all. She could always add that later after deciding which result she liked best. Wouldn't it be nice if you could get a do-over in life too?

She felt like a kindergarten kid playing with paints. It didn't matter if the results were good or not, no one was going to see or judge it — she could just throw all her work away later if she wanted to and no one would know the difference. So she spent the rest of the afternoon having fun, while the world went on around her.

Time must have flown past, because when Quinn finally had to go in to use the bathroom she noticed it was already late afternoon. How had all that time slipped away? She had no idea she'd been out there that long. She stood at the sink drinking a big glass of water.

When she went back out, she gathered her pencils and wet brushes, closed the tin box, and picked up all the paintings she had worked on. A few of them looked pretty good, but some were going right into the pile of papers by the fireplace. She threw the water from the jar over the porch railing and brought the water jar and all the other things into the kitchen. The brushes needed washing with clear water so she cleaned them in the sink, shook them a little to remove the water, and set them on the dish drainer, then washed out the water jar and set it in there too. She spread the watercolor sketches out on the kitchen table so she could look at them later to see if any were really worth keeping, knowing a little distance from the work would make her evaluation more accurate.

There were lots of leftovers in the fridge from the weekend meals, so she wouldn't have to cook anything for dinner, but she didn't feel like eating – she wanted to write.

Even though it was still warm outside, the sun was beginning to sink in the western sky, so she laid a fire in the big fireplace to take the indoor chill off the place. Her journal and pens were sitting on one of the many bookshelves, so she found them and set them on the table next to her favorite chair. Then she went to the sideboard to pour a glass of wine from one of the bottles that had been opened over the weekend, and put it beside her book while she lit the fire. It crackled to life right away so she stepped back and set the big screen before it. Now she was ready to sit.

Quinn opened her journal to the last entry, marked by a ribbon, and read over what she had written. It was always good to be able to see how she'd been feeling the last time she'd written anything, and how things had evolved since then. Sometimes the concerns she'd had were whisked away by the passage of time, and replaced by the encroachment of new ones. But then there were times when things were just moving along rather seamlessly, like now.

Staring into the fire was a good way to let her thoughts wander, because she wasn't sure where to start. She didn't want to write about Will, because someone might pick up the book and read it some day, and she wanted those thoughts to be her own private ones. Soon she began writing about the progress on the project, and the feelings she had about the weekend with her sisters and Colin. It was all good.

After a while she went into the kitchen to find some of the cheeses left over from the weekend happy hours, opening a package of club crackers to go with them. There was a small bowl of olives there too, so she grabbed those and put it all on a board to snack from. The cheeses were better varieties than the ones she occasionally bought for herself – she had wanted to make things special for her sisters. Now she got to enjoy the delicious cheese herself.

As soon as she sat back into her chair, she heard the back door open, and Will's voice from the kitchen.

"Ya here?" he called.

"Yes, I'm right in here, Will. Grab a beer and join me," she said.

She heard the fridge open and close again, and the top pop off a bottle. Then Will came around the corner of the stone fireplace towards her, stopping to look at the fire, which was now burning gently. He took a drink from the green bottle, and looked over at her. He wore a clean black tee shirt, loose brown painters pants, and the ever-present scruffy work boots. His face was deeply tanned from working outside almost every day, as were his arms and hands. His expressive blue eyes looked almost indigo in the evening light.

"How did the weekend go?' he asked settling himself down in a cushioned chair opposite her. He leaned back and crossed one leg over the other at the ankle.

"It went surprisingly well – better than I had even hoped," she said. "Nobody started any arguments, and they basically seemed to be able to relax and have a good time. I feel pretty relieved."

"It's always a challenge when the family piles in," he said. "My son was here with his girlfriend, with some friends of theirs, and that seemed to go well enough too. I think they're getting serious."

"Do you like the girl?" Quinn asked.

"Doesn't make much difference how I feel. He's gonna have to live with her."

"Well, yeah – but you want him to be happy, right?

"Of course I do. I just hope they treat each other right."

There was so much more to it than that, but Quinn didn't want to get into a heavy sort of conversation about Will's family matters. She knew he wasn't one to philosophize, and was extremely private about his personal life. He probably didn't need or want interference from the outside either, so she let it go.

"Well, I'm glad you got to see them," she said, looking at the fire popping softly.

"I had to come over and meet with your neighbors again – they're getting impatient to get their deck work done, but I just haven't had the time to get it started."

"Oh, I heard they were gonna have a lot of family coming up in August… they probably want it done before then," said Quinn.

"Yep, you got that right, but it's not gonna happen," said Will. "They should have given me more notice if they had a timetable. Their deck is stable enough for another summer anyway. That's the kind of job I can easily fit in in the fall, when the cold weather starts."

"Well I hope they'll understand."

"They're gonna have to," Will said with a deep sigh. He took a long pull on the beer. "I'm sorta glad the weekend's over."

They talked some more about the kids and family, then moved on to the boathouse, and what was going to happen next. They were both pleased with the progress so far – things had really moved along rapidly since the project had started, and it looked as though it might all wrap up by the time the leaves started turning. Neither of them wanted to think of the summer going by that quickly though.

Quinn got up to take the cheese board back to the kitchen. "Have you eaten yet?" she asked him.

"Oh yeah, hours ago. We grilled out late this afternoon before they left," he said.

Quinn wrapped up the cheese again to put it in the refrigerator, and closed up the crackers in their box. She wasn't sure what to do next, but some pretty intriguing thoughts were running through her head.

Will came in behind her and moved in close to her back as he set his empty bottle on the counter. He threaded his fingers under her hair at the back of her neck, slowly turning her towards him by the shoulder, and bringing his mouth close to hers. Before she could say a word he nibbled her bottom lip until she opened her mouth to him, and then he kissed her penetratingly.

Quinn's entire body responded, tingling all over and melting with the intrinsic memory and feel of his body. Her heartbeat quickened and her hands involuntarily rose to his chest.

"Are you ready to go up now?" he asked.

"Do you want to come?" she asked.

"Yes," he said.

Quinn reluctantly pulled herself from him and went to the front room to turn out the lights and close the door to the porch. The fire was almost out with the screen in front of it. She took a last look around and then headed for the stairs. At the top, she turned into the bathroom. Her gown was there at the back of the door, so she took off her clothes and slipped into it.

Will took off his boots by the kitchen door, and went to use the bathroom out in the mudroom. He turned out the remaining lights, snapped the back door closed and followed her up.

When she went down the long hall towards her room, he was standing at the end by the square window waiting for her. A refreshing cool breeze came in from the water, and they both felt it, but said nothing. Quinn went into the little bedroom and crawled over to the far side of the bed under the covers.

"Where are you going?" he asked her.

She just smiled, and laid her head on the pillows.

He dropped his shirt over the chair, and sat on the bed, pulling off his cotton pants. Quinn's heart was beating like crazy and her body began to tremble. She closed her eyes to try to calm herself.

This time Will wasted no time talking and comforting her. He leaned in to kiss her some more, with his arms on either side of her and his hands on her head. She let herself go completely into it, forgetting about anything else in the world. The kisses were so powerful she was transported to a magical place where thinking didn't exist.

While he kissed her Will's hands were everywhere on her body, making her feel crazy with desire for more of him. He felt it too, but he took her to the edge by caressing her, and then finally pushed himself firmly into her and held himself still there for a moment. Her body quivered with the need to move, and when he let her go by lifting and pushing again they didn't stop moving until she cried out in a joyful ecstasy. He was right there with her.

They were both out of breath, and he nestled his head beside hers while their bodies came to the blissful realization of what had just happened. Quinn was surprised at the level of passion that had overtaken the two of them. Her whole body felt the impact of it. Once he touched her it was as if a fuse was lit and nothing was going to stop it until the fire happened. It was amazing.

They looked at each other in the moonlight.

"Was that okay for you?" he asked her, chuckling.

She laughed quietly too. "Oh my god… how 'bout you?"

"Not too bad," he smiled, holding her even tighter for a moment, then sliding to her side. He pulled the quilts up over them and looked up at the mellow light reflecting around the room.

Silence seemed to be the perfect answer to everything right then. Quinn kept her hands on Will as he let his body relax and finally rest. He turned slightly towards the window, the breeze drifting down on his face, and she turned herself toward him, kissing the back of his neck as her body folded in behind the bends and turns of him, and they both slept.

Chapter 20

*B*efore dawn broke, Will slipped from the bed and dressed silently. Quinn wondered if he actually believed that she could sleep through his leaving, but she kept completely quiet, to let him go. She knew that he needed to retain his distance from the crew, never letting them know too much about what he was up to, so he had to leave.

She listened from the bed as he went downstairs and left through the kitchen door. His truck started from the far side of the camp, so she knew that he had taken care not to leave it out in the open for the neighbors to see before they left that morning.

The bed smelled wondrously of their lovemaking. The fragrance was of life itself, she thought, pulling the bedding up to her nose to be closer to it. She had been afraid that she would never again have the opportunity to experience the subtle scent of a man's sweat and sexual body fluids, not to mention having them mixed with her own.

She was amazed too, that everything worked. Supposedly, as a woman aged, she dried up and might have a hard time responding to male sexual overtures. For years she had feared that this might be the case – she and Lisbet joking that they needed to keep a tube of feminine lubrication in the medicine cabinet, just in case... but she'd never believed she'd have the chance to use it, much less contemplate whether she'd need it.

It turned out that the opposite was the case. Her body melted and liquefied when she even thought of Will's touch. It tingled in all the right places, almost rising and readying itself for the gratification it longed for and needed. Now she knew that she was indeed still vitally alive – it wasn't just the quirk of a one-time thing. Her body had not abandoned her at all, it was there anxious and ready for the stimulation it had been missing for so long.

Quinn went to the bathroom, pulling her robe around her in the chill of the pre-dawn air. It was still dark as she padded back down the hall towards the window, but she wanted to take in the early morning scents too, so she left it open.

She lit her candle, and set herself up in the bed to meditate. First though, after she'd quieted, she said a heartfelt prayer of gratitude for everything. She felt surprised, and didn't understand whatever she could have done to deserve such a blessing. Not that she needed to deserve anything – she was just being herself and maybe that was enough. She knew that love in any of its forms was a gift from the cosmos. And she was grateful, beyond any measure, for that precious gift.

In the July days that followed the air became warmer and cool breezes had less effect. Quinn opened up the many camp windows and made sure screens were in place. She kept the front and back screen doors free to bring the cross ventilation coming through the rooms.

In her room, she replaced the flannel sheets with white cotton percale, adding a yellow woven thermal blanket on top and a quilt at the foot of the bed in case a cool front came through overnight. It took a while for her to get all the towels and bedding in the attic washed and put away from the holiday, but she didn't mind the chore – she liked working with fabrics and textiles and enjoyed arranging the beds again with summery linens in case anyone decided to come up and visit.

The crew worked diligently on the boathouse, and Quinn went down to observe their progress almost every afternoon after they left, sometimes taking a glass of wine with her to linger close to the water as the day ended. They finished the radiant floor insulation and closed it in from below with plywood so that the boards could be unscrewed if they ever needed to get to the system for repairs. Blown in foam insulation was installed everywhere else, and after that was completed they finished the ceiling of the main room upstairs with wide planks of knotty pine, continuing it down the walls to the floor. Then they brought the old logs from the original roof up from where they had been stacked, and installed them beneath the pine in approximately the same locations they'd been in for almost a century.

The beautifully trimmed ceiling really made the space come alive with distinction. The men were careful to conceal nailing so that the logs looked as if they had been there forever, except now they were clean and golden colored – not dark with the ravages of time and the pestilence of insects. Quinn loved watching what the men were doing because it was really a work of art. They had to painstakingly fit each piece in, trimming it over and over without taking too much off, so that there would be no telltale gaps, and the logs appeared to be supporting the roof as they actually had for so many years. Before climbing down, the men wiped the logs one last time of the remains of any sawdust so that dust from the air wouldn't tend to collect on them later.

When the ceiling was complete, it looked magnificent. Quinn was so delighted with it, and she credited Will with the precision with which the guys had done the work because she knew he insisted on it and had kept a close eye on the process to make sure it was done the way he instructed. On some days he had stayed with them to help, especially in the beginning when they were getting started, or when they had a particularly big log to raise into place.

Next, the men addressed the window trim, and the installation of the solid fir doors and pine trim, though there were only three of them. The little living space was really coming together.

Meanwhile Quinn finished the watercolor painting of the boathouse in the mist by selecting the background she liked the best, and adding the slightly more detailed boathouse to the foreground. She was happy enough with it. The outdoor painting group met once a week if weather permitted, and Quinn made an attempt to go with them whenever possible because it encouraged her to continue painting. There was no pressure with the group – it was all for fun with them, and she loved that.

She bought a cream colored mat that she could use to throw over her paintings to better evaluate them. One of her early teachers had taught her to place the matted work on the floor to look it over, because the distance was just about perfect for viewing, rather than up as close as it would be from a table. When she did this, some of the paintings seemed rather good. They were still not quite as loose and easy as she wanted them to be, but she was still working on that. It meant that she still needed to let go a little more, which seemed to be the metaphor for her entire life. Maybe, she thought, when the watercolors were working perfectly, her life would be too.

The boys got in touch with her from time to time and filled her in on their lives. Kole had a new girlfriend now, but he never had any trouble finding one because of his stunning good looks. It was what to do with them afterwards that was the challenge for him.

Kole found that every girl who liked him a lot began nesting for life almost immediately after spending any time with him. He always needed lots of time to get to know them, but they would seemingly make up their minds right away that he was perfect. His mother had preached all his life that he needed to make great friends with a woman before bedding her, but he found that most were so willing, even from the first night, and it was hard for him to be the one hesitating. But he was getting plenty of practice with relationships, and at the same time tiring of having to have the inevitably hurtful conversation when he came to the painful conclusion that this one wasn't going to be the right one either.

He knew that he needed to make it clear from the get-go that he just wanted to be friends, so his story developed along the lines of having just broken up with someone he was very close to, and not wanting to experience that again any time soon. Of course that often had the opposite intended result of attracting women even more, because they wanted to comfort him. What was a man to do?

Quinn always listened to her son attentively, because she loved him so much and sincerely wanted to be of help even though she knew in many ways he would have to figure this out himself. She was so relieved that he understood how painful it was to be hurt by a relationship – sometimes taking literally years to recover as it had for Jackson after his breakup from the woman he met in college and planned to marry. She was glad that he didn't have the callus attitude that a woman getting too involved was her problem, leaving a string of broken hearts behind him. He didn't want to be the cause of that kind of pain.

So now Kole was trying something new, demanding on the friendship first, and if it didn't work, he moved on. It was sexually frustrating for him, but he felt he was making progress in learning how to discriminate which women really had potential as partners rather than just a quick roll in the hay. Quinn was delighted with the reformation.

Meanwhile, Jackson and his friend Eilish from med school were becoming very close, but both of them were still afraid to commit to each other until they knew what each of them needed to do for their residencies. They could end up at opposite ends of the country, and then the test of time in a long distance relationship would kick in. Quinn knew that their hearts were exactly in the right place. They each wanted the other to be completely fulfilled in their hard-earned career, and that wish overruled their other desires for the time being. Neither wanted the other to have to sacrifice for the other.

When Quinn considered her feelings for Will, she remembered all the ideas that she had already learned and taught her sons. It was easy for her to imagine that the independent nature he had might be a defense he had adopted after being hurt in his divorce — or it could be the way he had always been. Either way, she loved that strength in him, his confidence in knowing what he was doing and what he wanted. She would never want that to change.

She also knew that an independent streak was a part of her own nature too, surprisingly. She had certainly been a doormat in her early life, but she had struggled to make her own way to such an extent that now she felt completely comfortable making her own decisions, never asking anyone for advice or any particular support. She took a great deal of time looking at all the angles of a decision she might need to make, but basically she trusted her own heart to show her with intuition what to do. It was never black and white like in a guide-book, and never without risk. You had to risk something to attain something great, she believed.

Lisbet was having a good summer too. She and Ben were spending more and more time on the phone almost every day, and he seemed to be relying on her opinions and feelings, sharing just about everything with her. But he didn't offer get-togethers unless it was something previously planned by his friends and he invited Lisbet to accompany him. Lisbet, however, continued to invite him over to make and share dinner with her every week, and he usually came but not always. She just didn't know where it was really going to go, and was afraid to ask him for fear of frightening him off with some sort of perceived pressure.

It was the opposite of the way with Will. He seldom called Quinn, but often suddenly appeared before her out of thin air, and that was fine with her because she loved being surprised by him. She was immensely grateful to him. He had for some reason felt comfortable with her and courageous enough to take a risk of his own by penetrating the invisibly protective wall she had around her, when she had been vulnerable. She didn't think that he had even planned it. The two had come together magnetically at a magical point in time when they needed each other.

So Quinn left Will completely to his own life, because she only wanted to be there for the part of it he wanted to share with her, and she knew he was in the process of gradually finding out what that would be. It would never serve her to interfere with that evolution because it was not only his but hers too. She could feel a transformational power taking place in her life, and she was determined to humble herself to it, letting it do its work on her.

One cloudy Saturday morning while Quinn was waiting for the kettle to whistle, the phone rang.

"Hey," she heard Will say.

"Good morning," she answered, happy to hear his voice. "What's up?"

"I'm about to bring the kitchen cabinets over there and I wondered if you'd wanna come help me, or just keep me company," he said.

"Yes!" she said excitedly. He was about to install her new kitchen!

"I don't need any help getting the boxes down the hill – I've got the hand truck. So just come down whenever you want to and I'll be down there working."

"Okay, I'll be there in a while then," she said.

"See ya then."

"Okay," she said and hung up the phone. She poured the hot water for her tea and added some cream, hurrying upstairs to get into the shower. Her adrenaline was pumping as it always did when there was something new about to happen.

She finished her shower, dried her hair and put on a pair of tattered, worn-thin jeans and a white cotton shirt, just in case she had to actually do any work.

She applied her makeup lightly and left her hair as naturally as she could, while sipping her tea. She heard Will's truck come into the driveway and she watched from the bathroom window as he loaded the first wooden cabinet box onto the hand truck and wheeled it out of sight down the hill. He had a few more to bring down there.

She found some socks because she knew she'd have to wear shoes today if she was going to be around Will while he was working, and went down the stairs to the kitchen.

Thank goodness there was some homemade bread, so she sliced it thinly and spread a few pieces with butter, peanut butter and strawberry jam. She folded some waxed paper around the sandwiches, and put them into a woven basket with a bag of unopened chips and some bottles of water. There were some shortbread cookies in the cookie tin so she bagged up a few of those and threw them in too. She rinsed a few strawberries in the sink and stood there eating them, though she really wasn't hungry.

When she got to the top of the steps of the boathouse, the two appliances - a range and small under counter refrigerator, were already in place and Will had moved the cabinet boxes either into place or close to where they would go. She set the basket down on the floor and joined him there.

"Can I do anything to help?" she asked him.

"Did you bring any coffee?" he asked her.

She hadn't thought of that. "No, but let me go up and get some. I'll be right back."

She went back up the hill to the kitchen and brewed a percolator full of strong aromatic coffee, pacing the floor a bit while she waited for it. It looked like the sky was darkening outside and could bring in some rain any moment. When it was ready, she poured the steaming coffee into a large thermos with some cream, and screwed the cap on tightly. Then she unplugged the pot, grabbed two mugs and headed back down the hill quickly before the storm started.

Just as she got to the top of the stairs they heard a few loud pops of rain hit the metal roof.

"I think you made it just in time," said Will, tapping one of the cabinets into place while checking it for level.

Quinn set the two mugs on a sawhorse and poured the fragrant hot brew into them.

"Wow, that smells good," Will said as he reached for one of the cups. He sipped it carefully because it was still really hot. "Mmm, that's perfect."

Just then the rain started to come down harder, beginning to pound on the new roof. They could see white caps on the lake kicking up, and the dark sky lowering and moving in. With windows all around, it seemed like the storm was right in the room with them. Quinn went to close everything up to keep the windy rain from getting the whole place wet, while Will went back to his work and the storm thrashed around them.

"You can open up that box and pull the sink out," he told her, nodding toward a box on the floor.

He had already unsealed the carton and checked the new sink for a perfect fit into the cabinet that he'd made for it, but had put it back in the box to keep it safe from chipping or breakage until he was ready for it.

Quinn got down on her knees, popped the tape open and slid the white porcelain sink out onto the floor. "It's beautiful, isn't it?" she said, running her hands along its sleek surface.

"It'll do," he said.

When all the base cabinets were set and leveled, he bent down to lift the heavy sink into the center one beneath the tall windows facing the now turbulent lake. After he adjusted it in place for level and square, he went to where the countertop was resting against a wall.

"Can you get the other end of this for me?"

Quinn went to the opposite end and lifted it gently, and they both moved the heavy piece over and set it carefully into place, fitting it around and behind the sink and over the base cabinets on either side.

"I'm not going to anchor this yet," said Will. "We'll wait until the plumbing is done, and then we'll tack it in there permanently. At least this'll be all set for them when they come though."

It also gave Quinn a chance to see how very lovely her kitchen was going to be. "It looks wonderful, Will," she said.

"Yeah, it came out all right."

Will stepped back to get the full effect while Quinn ran her hands across the smoothly finished cherry surface of the countertop. She tested some of the drawers, and their action was like sliding a knife through butter. The insides were precisely joined together like those of a finely made Japanese box.

"Just beautiful," she sighed.

Will was already bringing the shelves over, leaning them carefully against the wall. He put some paper from the empty sink box on the counter, and set the many brackets he'd made there on the new countertop so they'd be within easy reach. Consulting a little notebook he'd taken from his pocket he started measuring and marking places on the wall above the countertop where the wooden shelf brackets would go, aligned vertically.

Quinn fingered the brackets that looked like they had just been picked up off the floor of the woods, or cut from a tree. They each had to have a sturdy horizontal piece that would extend out from the wall to hold a shelf, and a vertical piece that would provide support against the wall, but beyond that every one was different. A couple of them had wild looking branches extending out to the sides.

She followed Will's commands, holding things in place while he checked level or alignment, and together they anchored all the brackets into position. They were in no hurry, because the rain was pouring down noisily on the roof and over the eaves leaving them really no choice but to stay where they were until it let up. Will moved the ladder over and set the top shelf up first, over the window trim. It was so high that Quinn would need the ladder again to put anything up there later, but that was fine because only her special pieces would go there, where she would seldom need to get to them.

Each shelf was already trimmed on three sides with bark to match the brackets, and everything had several coats of poly applied to keep it from splintering, and make it easy to wipe off. Will slid each heavy shelf into place, making sure that the spaces at each end were perfectly even.

While he worked, Quinn stood back looking at the big picture whenever he didn't need her help. As the wall came together, she was amazed at how exactly everything fit into place, and how exquisite it all looked. All the parts, when combined, made for a perfect whole.

She watched Will too. He had a plan in his mind, along with a few notes, of how he'd put this puzzle together when he built it and now he fitted all the pieces into place effortlessly, or so it seemed. She loved observing the grace of his body as he stepped forward to adjust the work, or back to get a better look, tilting his head to the side to consider each thing. His eyes were quick to recognize even minute details that didn't meet his approval, and he kept adjusting all the elements. His craft was every bit as creative as hers when she was drawing a house or doing a painting.

When he seemed to be fairly happy with everything, he pointed to the basket on the floor and said, "Any food in that thing? I'm gettin' hungry."

"Of course," Quinn said, bending towards it. She decided to slide down onto the floor next to the wall so she could lean her back against it. Will came over and sat cross-legged across from her, the basket between them. She lifted out the packet of sandwiches and set them on the floor in front of Will, opening the folded waxed paper. When she pulled the bag of chips open and shook a few onto the paper, he put one of those in his mouth with a bite of sandwich.

"Wow. This is great," he said, as if it were a feast in a fine restaurant.

Quinn smiled and took a half for herself. She bit into it and had to agree how good a pbj was right now. "And there's cookies too," she said.

The storm seemed to have blown through its rage, and was letting up now, but rain still pattered heavily on the roof above them. They ate listening to the mesmerizing sound as if it were music.

Will finished his sandwich and looked at the half that was left from hers. "You gonna want that?" he asked her.

"I can't deny you food, Will," she said with a grin. "Go ahead."

She didn't have to offer it twice. When he finished that he went for the baggie of cookies, and turned toward the front windows to watch the rain continue to drip, though it was falling slowly now and looking just about ready to quit.

"I've gotta go back to the shop," he told her, not looking back but taking a long drink from one of the water bottles.

"You just go when you need to, I'll clean all this up and sweep up here. I have nothing on my agenda for this afternoon anyway," said Quinn.

"You sure?" he asked.

"Go," she answered, tilting her head toward the door at the top of the stairs.

Will got to his feet and began collecting his tools together. When he had them all he grabbed the hand truck in one hand and stepped towards the stairs. He looked at her for a second and said, "See ya later," and disappeared down the steps.

Quinn gathered the paper up and closed the bag of chips before putting them back into the basket. She noticed that there was one cookie left, so she took a bite of it and got to her feet, tossing the empty baggie in too. She set the basket up on the sawhorse and put the cups and thermos in it.

Her broom was standing in the corner. She started sweeping right from there and made her way across the room, gathering a few nails and sawdust as she went. The rain was barely dripping now, so she knew she wouldn't get too wet getting up to the house.

When the room was clear she swept everything up with the dust pan that was hanging from a nail, and dumped it into the trash bag the guys had lined a pail with. She took one last look at the sweet little kitchen where she was going to be making all her meals in the very near future, pulled the basket to her side and started for the camp up the hill.

The rain came and went for the rest of the afternoon, so Quinn started a fire and curled into her chair to do some unabashed reading. The popping fire soothed her, the old camp was comfortable and cozy, and she fell asleep for a bit.

When she woke up she realized she had plenty of time to do some writing, so she replaced her book with her journal, a glass of red wine, and Cold Play on her Ipod dock.

Her thoughts were random but pleasant. Sometimes when everything was going so well she became afraid that it was just too good to be true, and something might happen to spoil it all. There would always be ups and downs though — no way to escape that. It was not productive to be too excited when things were easy, only to dip into sadness when they again became more difficult, as they inevitably did. The only path that made any sense was to be fully present for whatever was right there for her now. She said a silent prayer that her mind might be eased, allowing her to trust in the process of the unique unfolding of her destiny.

Chapter 21

August was suddenly upon them. The summer was flying past, and no one knew where it had gone already. The third month was the time all the family members would descend to take their long awaited vacations. It was something they looked forward to just before they would have to buckle down for the long descent of fall and finally another winter.

Lisbet was in her overwhelmed mode, working too hard to get everything just right for her siblings who would come for a couple of weeks to stay in the family camp just down the lake from Quinn's. She insisted on having not only the inside but the outside in pristine condition before anybody got there, even though the people coming were full grown adults perfectly capable of doing a little yard work or cleaning. After all, the camp was theirs too, and not all Lisbet's responsibility. But she couldn't have them arrive without everything the way she thought it should be, so she kept working.

On the bright side, when Lisbet came down to work in the family camp, it gave Quinn the chance to take advantage of her inability to resist a paddling trip, so she never passed up an opportunity to suggest one. The two woman went out on the water for short trips, and even a couple of all day trips to nearby lakes when they loaded their boats onto Lisbet's big truck, packed a lunch, cameras, towels and hats, and took off. It was a great escape for them, and a chance to go swimming unobserved, for they knew of many secluded locations where they just about had the whole lake to themselves.

One morning Lisbet called and asked Quinn to meet her out on the water in an hour. Quinn was more than delighted. She fixed a couple of sandwiches in case the trip got long, got her suit on, gear together, and headed down the hill to the water.

A couple of stone masons were working on the fireplace up in the boathouse, so Will had assigned his crew to another project. In fact, they might not even be back there much more for the rest of the summer because the carpentry was pretty much finished. Anyway, no one really wanted to be there when the masons were there because there was such a mess being created with the big boxes of cultured stone, grout in trays, and a coating of stone dust everywhere. Thank goodness they were kind enough to do their stone cutting outside, at the edge of the woods.

On her way down to get her boat Quinn went upstairs to take a look at the work, trying to stay out of their way. When she came into the room, two of them were up on scaffolding working on the stone, and the other was going up and down the stairs cutting pieces for them. They had rock music going on the radio and were yelling loudly over it. What a difference from the calm peaceful setting Will always insisted on. No wonder he didn't want to be there when they were.

Despite the chaos, the work looked great. They were mixing in the natural colors of two types of stone, using mostly flat ledge shaped pieces, but larger more square ones on some corners and interspersed through the body of the fireplace. Quinn could see where Will had marked out a 3" high slot all the way around, about 5 ½' from the floor for the mantle he would be making. She had asked him to fit it into the stone, and make it look as wild as the brackets in the kitchen did.

As soon as Quinn stepped into the room the roving stonecutter went over to the radio and turned it down. That was a relief.

"It looks wonderful," Quinn said brightly.

"You like it?" one of them asked.

"It looks even better than I had hoped."

The guys nodded approvingly, as if she should have expected that.

"Just let me know when you think you'll be ready to wrap it up so I can have a check ready for you," she said.

"Will do," said the same guy.

She thought he was the one she had talked to on the phone about the project, but had never met any of them before they arrived for the work.

"Does it look like you'll have enough stone?" she asked.

"I think it's gonna turn out just right," he said, nodding again. "We found some large kinda flat pieces from the lake we thought you might like for the hearth."

Quinn looked over at the big stones he was referring to.

"Oh, those look wonderful," she said. "I've been looking for some that would work, but could never find the right ones."

"We know where to look," he said, continuing to scrape grout around a piece he had just put into position.

"Okay, I'll leave you to it," she said, and headed down the steps for her kayak in the boathouse below.

Lisbet was waiting for her in her kayak when she got to the dock, holding her boat close to the dock with her hand. Quinn dropped the bag of sandwiches into her boat and said, "I'll be right there."

Lisbet let go of the dock and let her boat float out a little. She had her paddle in her lap and looked to be in no hurry for anything. Within a few minutes Quinn was gliding beside her and they picked up their paddles to move away from the shore a little.

"Is everything okay?" Quinn asked.

"More than…" her friend answered with a sly grin, lowering her head.

"Uh oh. Something's happened."

"Something sure has."

Alright…spill it," said Quinn.

Lisbet began telling her story, a tale she had been dying to be able to tell for a long, long time.

She had asked Ben to come out to her retreat camp with her to get it ready for an extended stay while all the relatives and grown kids came and took over the family camp and her own house for their August vacations.

He was willing, if not glad to do it. He asked if he could bring his fishing pole and of course that delighted Lisbet because it meant that he was planning to take some personal time out there as well as help her with whatever chores she had for him. She was planning to give him lunch, but quickly put some groceries together for a possible dinner and who knows what else. Lisbet wanted to tell him to bring his toothbrush!

But she held her tongue and the two met in town to follow each other for the drive out to the cabin in their own cars, because Lisbet was going to stay for a few days at least. When they got there Lisbet opened up the place and started airing it out, dusting a bit and sweeping the rooms. Ben refilled the stack of firewood inside, brought kindling in for the cook stove and moved some of the outdoor furniture for her so she could sweep the big covered porch overlooking the lake and the pretty rug she had there creating an inviting seating arrangement.

She put some bread dough together and set it to proof, then they made some sandwiches and took them out to the porch with some chips and drinks so they could eat looking over the water. There was a panoramic view of Lisbet's private lake from there, all the way around the log cabin, which was positioned on a wooded peninsula covered with tall white pines.

After lunch Ben took his gear with him to fish at a nearby falls of water that he especially favored, and Lisbet let him go alone while she did some fly fishing right at her own dock. The day was beautiful, and when she tired, she rested on one of the Adirondack chairs out there and lifted her face up to the sun. It was like heaven.

In the late afternoon, Lisbet formed a round rustic loaf with the bread dough and put it in to bake along with some sweet potatoes, then peeled and chopped onions to sauté with sliced mushrooms. She set the table inside with the beautiful silver and china that she had collected from auctions held at the historic camps when they were sold into private hands. She had always made an effort to preserve the antiques of the Adirondacks, because she appreciated them so much, and vowed to keep using them instead of hiding them away in some attic never to be seen again.

There were already flowers in pots around the porch, but Lisbet wandered the nearby woods to collect some fresh wildflowers and pine boughs. She put them in silver vases and set them out on the table and on the mantle over the huge hand built stone fireplace. There were candles ready to light.

This attention to detail was part of the way she lived – the way she did things all the time, as if every day was a special occasion. In each of the many

179

places Lisbet laid her hat, she created an atmosphere that was not only beautiful, but authentically old Adirondack. That was where she came from.

When Ben came back from fishing, he told her he'd caught a few but had thrown them back to their watery homes. That was fine, because she'd brought a couple of specially cut steaks that they could grill if they wanted to.

He definitely wanted to – it sounded so good and the smell of the softly caramelized onions and just baked bread was irresistible.

He went in to wash up, while Lisbet poured him a glass of red wine, and made herself an Arnold Palmer. They took these out to the front porch to look at the sun begin to sink lower onto the lake. She didn't bring any appetizers because there was so much food to eat for their dinner.

After he relaxed a little with his wine, and they talked about his fishing expedition, Ben went to light the gas grill on the side of the porch near the kitchen. After a bit he went in to pick up the platter Lisbet had prepared with the steaks and utensils he might need. She joined him at the grill, slipping in and out of the kitchen to check on the rest of the food and light the candles at the table.

The dinner was fantastic – the steaks were done to perfection and everything else Lisbet had made brought the flavors together perfectly too. They sat and ate the dinner slowly and enjoyed every morsel by the light of the candles and the crackle of the fire she had lit in the big fireplace.

After dinner they both took everything to the kitchen together, and Ben did the dishes while Lisbet put the leftovers away. In lieu of dessert, Lisbet encouraged Ben to enjoy some more wine and a cigar out on the porch. It wasn't a hard sell, of course, and before long they were both out there leaning back in the antique cane and hickory chairs made just for that purpose, their feet up.

This was the point in any evening Lisbet spent with Ben that she began to imagine what it would be like if he would just come into the bedroom and lie with her. God knows she had let him know how much she cared about him, but she could not take the next step herself. She wanted him to do that. So she kept up the conversation and her thoughts to herself.

When it got dark she told him she wanted to go in by the fire and away from the bugs and the chill. He followed her in and stoked the fire until it was burning brightly again. Then he came over to the sofa where she was sitting and sat beside her, as he always did. Even his kiss did not surprise her, as he'd done that many times before too. But there was something different this time.

His kiss was very soft and almost hesitant. She looked into his eyes and they were on hers. Then he turned a little more towards her and held her chin as he kissed her some more, very delicately. She felt her entire body loosen and melt into his arms.

He asked her if it would be all right if he spent the night there, because it was late and he'd had several glasses of wine. Naturally she agreed that would be fine, while in fact she was happy beyond her wildest dreams that he had finally suggested it. Now, would he go to the guest bedroom, or to hers? She was afraid to think of what the answer might be.

She told Ben she was going to get ready for bed, and where everything was that he might need in the bathroom. She said nothing of the sleeping arrangements, and went to her room to undress and put on her silky white nightshirt that fell to mid-thigh and showed off her magnificent legs – her greatest asset. She left it casually unbuttoned at the top. Her body was shaking with nervousness and the fear that he might reject her and go make himself comfortable in the guestroom. She didn't know what to do next.

She needed to use the bathroom right next to her room, so she slipped in there and closed the door. She was afraid to even look in the mirror, for fear that the reflection there would be just too discouraging. The night was comfortably warm, but she began to shiver, and hurried back to her room so she could get under the covers.

She closed her eyes and gave in to a forlorn feeling of how the evening would probably end, like all the others when he went home at a reasonable hour after kissing her goodnight at the door. She looked out the windows at the side of her bed at the moon that was beginning to rise with a heavenly glow over the lake, and her body calmed a little.

After a while there was no more noise in the bathroom or the living room, so Lisbet began to wonder if Ben had found everything he needed and would be comfortable. Maybe he had gone to bed already in the guest room.

She had just closed her eyes and tried to empty her mind when she noticed his scent near her, and heard him ask in a whisper if he could come into bed with her.

She turned to him in the semidarkness and lifted the duvet to welcome him, and he slid gently beside her into the big soft bed. He put his sturdy arms around her and held her closely, resting back on the pillows. Lisbet put her head on his chest, her arms around him too. She was too overwhelmed to do anything but fold into him and try to breath.

They lay there for a long time just holding each other, but finally he said to her, "You are my best friend."

She smiled into his beautifully blue eyes, twinkling in the moonlight, and said, "and you are mine."

Then Ben kissed her deeply and kept doing so as he touched every part of her slowly, from her shoulders to beneath her nightshirt over her breasts to her waist and hips and finally to her bottom as they pressed into each other still holding on. They kissed and made love tenderly into the long quiet wilderness night.

By the time Lisbet finished her story, the two women were no longer paddling anywhere. They were out in the deep part of the lake holding on to each other's boat, almost in a trance.

"Oh My God." said Quinn, smiling over at her friend.

Lisbet smiled too, and shook her head back and forth. "I can't believe it finally happened, but it was so good, just so really good that it was really worth waiting for..."

"I can't tell you how happy I am for you," said Quinn. "Are you all right?"

"I don't know. Yes, I'm all right, but no, I'm not. I am changed and different now – and I don't know what to think."

"Why do you have to think?" her friend asked her. "Just be with the wonder of it and enjoy it!"

"I don't know what will happen now," said Lisbet, almost in a whisper.

"Lisbet, we can never know what's going to happen. Every moment of our lives is kind of a surprise, isn't it? You're gonna have to find a way to be comfortable with not knowing."

"I'm trying, but I'm afraid he might regret what happened and then I'll lose the friendship. I couldn't bear that."

"What did he say when he got into bed with you?"

"He said 'You are my best friend.'"

"Well, I think it must have been pretty important to him that you know that, don't you?"

"Yes, I believe that."

"That friendship is just as much at stake for him as it is for you, Lisbet. Slowly but surely, he has come to depend on your acceptance, support and the love you have for him. I think he was really hesitant to risk that, but finally he took the chance, and now you two will have to see if you can bring that lovely friendship into another realm."

Lisbet nodded her head in agreement, but Quinn could see that she was still worried. She lifted her paddle from her lap and dipped it into the water. "Let's go over to the sunny spot by the island and eat some lunch," she said, sliding off in that direction.

She could hear Lisbet say softly, "Yeah, I guess I'm hungry..."

Quinn smiled to herself, knowing what it was like to lose your appetite and your mind at the same time. There was nothing to be done but await the passage of time to get over this kind of ailment.

A few minutes later Lisbet handed Quinn a sandwich and the two boats floated together silently, rocking a little from the slight wave that came into the sunny cove now and then. There was nothing they needed to say. Quinn didn't want to give her friend any further advice, knowing that Lisbet needed the quiet to let her thoughts swirl all over in her head. Neither of them had the answers Lisbet wanted. Only time would reveal them.

Chapter 22

As August progressed, it got hotter. The water in the lake warmed considerably, and felt like a bathtub instead of a glacial lake. Since there was no air conditioning in the camps and homes, it was hot inside unless there was some sort of breeze to bring relief, and those seemed to be too few and far between. Everywhere you went someone was going to ask, "Hot enough for ya?" It was beginning to get old.

The attic in the old camp was just about unbearable because the sun beat down on the metal roof, which was uninsulated. The attic just heated up like an oven. Windows were open in all of the rooms to bring in whatever cool night air there might be, but it didn't seem to help much. Quinn tried to sleep by tossing her blankets over the foot of the bed, and just using a thin sheet to cover her, but even when she sat there completely still to read, sweat dribbled down her back and dampened her cotton gown. It was annoying, uncomfortable and hard to get to sleep when you were that hot.

She remembered that there was a futon under one of the beds up there, so one morning after a restless night she went to search for it. When she found it, she dragged it out. The kids had used it only a couple of times for extra space when there were overflow sleepovers, so it was still in good condition, just very dusty. She pulled it down the stairs and through the front room to the porch, trying not to get dust all over herself in the process.

With difficultly, she lifted it over the porch rail, and went about shaking it out one half at a time, then turning it over to start the process again. She brought the vacuum cleaner out and turned the suction hose onto it too.

Meanwhile, thinking of how hard the porch floor was going to be, she remembered that there were two foam pads that the boys used to use under their sleeping bags, still rolled up and stashed in one of the mudroom closets. She took the vacuum cleaner back in and came out with the two rolls. Setting them on the floor almost up against the wall of the house on the opposite side of the door from the rocking chairs, she unrolled them and set the futon down on top. The fit was amazingly just right.

Quinn went to the unbearably hot tin closet upstairs to find a fitted bed pad, a white fitted percale sheet, and a flat one with four clean pillowcases. She took four pillows from the extra attic bedrooms and brought all of it down to the porch.

When the makeshift bed was made, it was looking pretty comfortable! To top it off, Quinn found an old mosquito netting that the boys had used on their travels, and screwed a hook into the ceiling above to hang it from. She draped it gracefully over the sides. It looked like a scene from Out of Africa.

By the time she was done, Quinn felt like she was *in* Africa, she was so sweaty, so she peeled off her clothes and slipped into her suit in the mudroom, grabbed a towel and went down for a swim.

The water was like velvet on her skin, cool and dreamy. She rested on her back and looked up at the sky, blue as a morning glory above her, with her arms out to her sides like a water angel. She took some deep cleansing breaths, and before long her body was completely cooled down to an ideal temperature. She was so comfortable she might have fallen asleep had she not been afraid that if she drifted off her body would forget to float and sink to the bottom.

After she dried off and pulled a light shirt on, she walked slowly up the hill so as not to get overheated all over again. She ate cold peaches and yogurt for her lunch, then got dressed again and determined to try to stay slow and quiet for the rest of the afternoon. Not too hard a task...

There was no activity at the boathouse that day. The stonemasons had finished and had done a terrific job. Thank goodness the heat had held off until after Quinn had thoroughly cleaned out the dust and debris they'd left behind.

A few days after she'd cleaned, the new fir floor was laid, and they were all trying to keep off it while they awaited the particular floor finisher they wanted to do the work of sanding and putting several coats of clear finish on it. He was expected right after he completed the project he was currently on, in a day or two.

Meanwhile, the plumber found a break in his schedule and came to install the bathroom vanity top with faucets for the sink, the shower fittings and the kitchen sink, and made the connections to the washing machine. He padded around on the new floor in his socks, rather than scuff it. Quinn went down while he was there to watch everything and it was really exciting when he turned the water on. Everything seemed to work perfectly and there were no apparent leaks.

Will had come by at the end of the day to wire the new exterior lights. Thank goodness that job wouldn't cause him to work up too much of a sweat, because he was probably feeling the intense heat and trying to stay cool too. Quinn had driven into town to get the mail and a few grocery items, and she'd missed him, but she saw the pretty lights by her new back door later when she came home and happened to look down there.

Thinking about the night to come, she located a Coleman battery lantern and a little flashlight to set beside the bed. The lantern had lit when she switched it on, but she had no faith in the age of the batteries, so she found some new ones she could use if some emergency occurred, and brought those out too.

It was too hot for an appetite, so she pared some fresh tomatoes, cucumber, onion and cilantro, and ate the cold salad for dinner. One of the best things about August was homegrown tomatoes, and she enjoyed them every day while they were in season, some from Lisbet's garden and others from the farm market in town. It was going to be salad of some sort for dinner every night until the heat broke.

Quinn was relieved to take off her clothes and underwear in exchange for the light white gown she loved, with nothing under it, so she took her second shower of the day under some cool water and slipped the loose gown on, barely buttoning it. As long as the sleeves were pushed up and she stayed relatively still, she could keep fairly cool, so she made herself as comfortable as possible in the front room with a book, not wanting to go near the attic. She didn't even turn on the lights, but for the one she was reading with. The air barely moved.

When it was completely dark, she got a tall glass of ice water and went out to the interesting little bed on the porch and climbed through the opening between the folds of the netting. She pulled them back closed again and sat against the pillows for a few minutes getting at least a little bit accustomed to the place. She could hear the people in camp on both sides, talking and slamming screened doors behind them going in and out. She could smell the scent of campfires either nearby or down the lake. People were probably sitting around them trying to stay outside as long as they could.

After a while she felt her body sink with relaxation, and she sat listening to the sounds of the night and the distant calls of the loons. For sure, they weren't hot.

There was no point in trying to read anymore only to attract the bugs with the slightest light. She was tired of reading anyway, so she slid down onto the cottony sheet that was fresh with the smell of having been dried on the line. The entire little nest smelled of late summer.

She lay there thinking of how great the summer had been, and how near the boathouse was to her moving into it. She wondered, when that day came would she no longer see Will? He had lots of other work all over the area to get to and he wouldn't be coming by to work anymore unless something came up to necessitate that. She knew that she would miss seeing him for even brief moments in the day. Now was the time she was going to have to take a spoonful of her own medicine and be with a huge level of uncertainty.

With that thought she felt herself begin to drift off to that sweet place that was almost sleep. The little shuffles and stirrings in the woods kept her just on the edge of falling asleep, but the air was ever so much cooler than that of the intolerable attic. She was so glad she'd made up the bed outside.

Just then she thought she heard very soft footfalls on the porch steps. Was it her imagination, or was something coming up onto the porch? Maybe it was a cat or a raccoon. Her body alerted with attention, but she didn't move.

The netting separated slightly, and Will whispered to her, "Move over, I'm comin' in…"

"What are you doing here?" she whispered back.

"It's too hot in my bed. I saw this sweet little arrangement you have and I thought I'd be cooler over here."

"Is that so?"

"Yep." He said, sitting down on the mattress after pulling off his jeans and boxers. He tossed them aside, took off his tee shirt, and pulled the net curtain closed as he rolled into the little tent.

Then he leaned on one elbow and looked at her with a grin. "Aren't you happy to see me?"

"I'm always happy to see you," she said quietly.

"I think you're too hot in that thing," he said pulling at her gown. "Come on, let's get this off."

"I'm not really too h…"

"Well if you're not now you're gonna be," he said, lifting it over her head as she leaned forward. He pushed it to the side and put his mouth to her breast, caressing the other one gently.

Quinn's head tilted back and she was suddenly taken away to the wondrous world where she couldn't talk, speak, or even think anymore. Her body immediately responded to his touch and his mouth and readied itself for all the magnificent things he had to offer.

As he kissed her he caressed her intimately, and she reached for him too, stroking him insistently. He moaned at her touch and rose above her on his knees, barely touching her but just enough to make her rise in the struggle to get closer beneath him, and then he lingered there watching for the intense anticipation in her eyes before he pressed down ever so slowly into all of her.

Quinn did not think that their lovemaking could get any more intense, but he always surprised her with something more and something unexpected. Her desire for him was uncontrollable once he started with her, and this seemed to fire his own. They made love with no regard for being outside where their sounds could be heard by the entire world.

Will was right when he predicted their heat. They were dripping with moisture as they pulled apart to lie on their backs, catch their breath and find some air.

"So, you don't mind if I'm here then?" he chuckled to her.

She needn't answer, obviously, so she just smiled over at him.

He took a drink from her tall glass of water, the ice almost melted, and handed it to her. She drank from it greedily.

They lay for a long time listening to the night and their own breathing, till their bodies cooled off. Just as Quinn was about to drift off to sleep Will pushed into her again and wrapped himself around her, rocking her slowly back and forth until she lost herself with him once more, and then they finally slept in each other's arms, the sheet in a tangle around them.

Chapter 23

The next night Will came at dark to sleep again in the outdoor bed, this time bringing ice cream in big cups for them from the stand in town. Quinn had no idea how he knew what her favorite flavor was, maybe he'd guessed it, but she was so thrilled to have a cup of Rocky Mountain Raspberry she savored every spoonful. He had a chocolate sundae.

Her reaction to the treat was so enthusiastic that Will repeated the offering the next night while the heat continued to bear down on them. It was like camping out with benefits, and Quinn was afraid she was getting spoiled.

But that night the atmosphere changed, and after a period of silence in the air they heard the rolling of thunder in the distance. Lightening followed, and a breeze rolled up the hill from the lake. The two of them were already cooled off from their ice cream, so they laid back together against the pile of pillows, listening to it come from far away rumbling towards them with loud claps of thunder and startling flashes of lightening. The mosquito netting fluttered about them. Without saying, they were both glad to have the porch roof over their heads. They laid still with awe as the storm moved in, booming and flashing in its fury, rain beginning with gusts, then pouring down in sheets. Cooler air came with it, and they snuggled close with their arms around each other under the sheet. When it began to slowly move away, the rain kept coming, and Will got up to retrieve a couple of blankets from the front room inside. They hated to leave the nest they'd become accustomed to, and wanted to stay there for at least one more night listening to the rain.

The next morning was clear, a beautiful late summer day. Since things had cooled off considerably Quinn knew that she would now probably return to her bedroom upstairs, so she pulled the bedding up, holding it to her face for a moment to take in Will's animal scent. The nights she had spent there with him were like a taste of living in the wild, and she didn't want to go back to civilization. Reluctantly, she took the sheets to the mudroom and pushed them into the washer. The day was so nice that she could hang them outside that afternoon instead of using the dryer.

In the ensuing days the floor finisher came to complete the boathouse floor, and it was gorgeous. The finish brought out the light red color of the fir, though it would gradually darken with age and show light spots wherever carpets were laid or furniture placed. Will put some paper from a large roll down to protect it for as long as possible, but it was bound to take scratches and dings from everyday life as soon as anyone began moving around up there with shoes on.

With everything just about done, Quinn was forced to realize that moving in was imminent. She had even paid Will the final check due from his agreement. The crew was doing the very last tasks, coating the trim with finish, hanging the few light fixtures, installing closet shelves and screwing the outlet and switch plates into place. The tiny house was just about ready for her.

The furniture and belongings she'd kept from her old house, along with some of Kole and Jackson's things that they might want to keep for later, were in the local warehouse storage facility in town. In an attempt to live minimally, Quinn had given away almost everything from tables, sofas and dressers to dishware. All she needed was a seating arrangement for in front of the fireplace, her beautiful bed with a few small tables, the drawing board, and a combination dining and work table with chairs. She had brought a couple of her favorite rugs, but they were already in camp away from the threat of damaging moisture. All she had to do was bring them down.

Now when she went to the boathouse in the late afternoons, she carried a box or two with her. It was fun to unwrap the dishes, bowls and covered glass canisters that would store dry foods in view on the new shelves. She had planned carefully when she packed the boxes so there were only the bare minimum of necessary things she would need, and no duplicates. One set of old blue willow china, a few white coffee cups, a cook pan of each size, and of course a tray for bread baking were just about all that had made the cut.

Quinn reserved a day for a small moving company to bring the things from storage over to their new home, set them in place and put the bed together for her. They were able to fit her in the following week. Meanwhile she ordered wood to heat with and had it delivered to a spot under the covered back porch right next to the door. The phone and electrical service were already in place, but she needed to have propane for the furnace that would provide radiant heating, so she set up the delivery time for the new tank and told them where she wanted it, hidden as much a possible from view in the woods.

Her sisters had not let her know if they were coming up for Labor Day, and she probably wouldn't hear till the last minute, so she kept the camp in readiness for their possible arrival just in case. It appeared that Jackson and Kole were going to be too busy to be able to take any more time off.

Back in her attic bedroom, she spent more time at night thinking than reading. She had a list of everything she wanted to do to settle into her new place, but she had mixed feelings about leaving the security of all the familiar surroundings and routines of the old camp, and this surprised her. Hadn't she dreamed for so long of living in the floating world over the water? Now that it was becoming a reality, she thought she would be jumping for joy, but instead she was hesitant, even reluctant.

Her book in her lap and cozy covers around her, she found herself looking out into the starry night that twinkled between the trees through the little window. This was the place that Will had come to find her, bringing with him a spark that melded her body and soul together in a way that made her feel newly whole. He showed her the way of letting go of every thought to let the sensual body take over. The remarkable gift of his loving had engendered her love for him. It was a generous, unselfish love that she knew would never make demands upon him or call for the sacrifice of his freedom or self-determination. She would never want to dampen the ferocious spirit she saw in him that she so loved.

She would now embrace the new way of being that he had brought her, taking it wherever she went. The thought of his gift settled her in a veil of peace and contentment that she never could have before imagined.

The morning of her moving day Quinn was so wakeful that she barely slept at all. Though she went to bed at her regular time, she woke just after midnight and found herself looking out the window most of the rest of the predawn hours despite her struggles to get some sleep before the long day ahead of her. Finally she gave up further attempts, and sat up to meditate in the darkness, warm covers over her shoulders.

The meditation calmed her. Her breathing slowed and her body finally relaxed. When she opened her eyes, she stretched, took the robe from the bottom of her bed and swirled it around her as she went down the hall and stairs to the kitchen for some hot tea. There was a definite chill to the air.

When the tea was ready to brew she brought the painted teapot back up to her room with her cup, and set it on the chest to steep, turning on the lamp to read. She picked up John Donahue's Anam Cara from the bookshelf against the wall, because though she had read it many times, it always seemed to have the exact words of wisdom she needed.

She opened the familiar book and read from words she had already underlined,

"When love comes in to your life, unrecognized dimensions of your destiny awaken and blossom and grow."

Her heart skipped a beat and she felt a slight tingle at her back as she read the words again. She was growing and realizing and recognizing herself at this very moment, even though she had thought she had already done that, and it was behind her. But no, it was a process of continual unfolding even now, and for the rest of her life.

The awakening that Will had brought her had touched every part of her body and soul. A new energy had been brought mysteriously to life with his physical love. It had stirred all the cells of her body into motion with a keen sense of awareness, not only of what was happening to her, but of everything around her. Instead of following the path of aging, and the contemplation of life's end, she was looking forward to all the new things that life could offer her — things she couldn't even imagine yet.

Maybe that was why she felt so shaken with the idea of moving into her new home. Her intuition told her that this was yet another step toward finding the true place of her belonging. It would be a new chapter in the story of her life, and she didn't know what she would find there.

When the early dawn just began to break with a dim light, she finished her tea and headed for the comfort of the shower with the feeling that the day was about to bring beautiful things. She stood beneath the water for a long time and let it cleanse the skin of her old life away – readying her for rebirth.

Quinn dried herself and her hair and dressed in her clean but raggedy jeans and a faded blue chambray shirt with pearled buttons, keeping in mind that she'd be helping all day with the moving. She put on hanging cultured pearl earrings and fluffed her hair back from her face. All of a sudden she was excited.

Down in the kitchen, she heard Will open the door and step in. Just as the microwave pinged, she came into the kitchen and smiled at him as he turned towards her with his cup in his hand.

"You look all pretty and ready for the day..." he said.

"Well thank you. Not too bad yourself," she answered, looking into his penetrating blue eyes. She went to him and kissed him sweetly on the neck.

"What was that for?" he asked with a little smile.

"Just cause you're you..." she said. "Did you know the movers are coming today?"

"As a matter of fact I did," he said. "Everybody knows everything in this town, you know." He started towards the door. "I just wanna go down to check to see if everything's in order down there before they get here."

"Oh, everything's fine. They should be here any time now."

"Okay. I'll see ya down there then," he said and with that he was out through the door.

There was no way Quinn was hungry, but she went back upstairs to retrieve the tea things and bring them down to the sink. She tidied what little there was in the kitchen, then went out to the mudroom to find the stack of fresh bedding she'd left piled there. She put on some cotton socks, and just as she reached for her work boots she heard the sound of the small moving truck start down the driveway. She quickly laced her boots up partway and went outside in case they needed any help backing the truck. They seemed to have everything under control and knew where to go so Quinn grabbed the big stack of bedding and headed on down the hill.

Will was standing at one of the long windows looking out at the lake when she got to the top of the boathouse stairs. The sun was slowly rising, reflecting in a shimmering light over the smooth and motionless water. The ethereal light softly penetrated the whole room from all three sides making feel as if it was floating cloud.

"You have a beautiful place here," he said quietly.

"Thanks to you, Will, and everything you did to make it possible."

"It's your design."

"I'd like to think we did it together. The design is nothing until it's brought to life."

Will continued looking out the window. "Is there anything you need me to do today?"

"No. The movers will bring everything and set up the bed. There's not even really that much. They should be done before lunchtime."

"Okay," Will said with a sigh, touching her arm with his finger. "See you later then."

He tossed his empty cup into the trash pail as he passed it and went for the stairs. Quinn watched him go, and then turned to open a carton waiting on the counter and started to unpack it.

The movers were well organized, and sure enough they were finished bringing everything from the truck well before noon. They took a short break to catch their breath and then began putting Quinn's bed together, setting it in the alcove with its headboard against the back wall, and the foot facing the lake. The view to one side took in the eastern sun and the Forever Wild end of the lake, and the other side led to the bathroom and closet. There was room for a table on each side.

By the time the four post bed was assembled Quinn had already covered the mattress with its pad and the freshly washed sheet, so they tipped it into place for her, making sure all the cross boards and supports were firmly in place with the frame. While the men brought a few more things up the stairs she added the top sheet, a cotton blanket and quilt, anxious to see if it would look as she had imagined it would. She covered the pillows with the fragrant cases and placed them up against the curved white wooden headboard. The pretty bed certainly looked welcoming. She moved a table into place on either side and wondered where the lamps for them had been packed.

The men seemed ready to leave, so she followed them up to the truck so she could pay them, and take a short break for a bit of lunch.

After they left with their check, Quinn went to the kitchen for a long drink of water and made a cucumber tomato sandwich. She took it out to the porch to her rocker and started to eat it slowly, looking down onto the scene of her new home. While she sat in a bit of a reverie, the screened door creaked open and Lisbet burst out with a huge bouquet of flowers.

"Here!" she said thrusting them toward Quinn. "These are for your new place!"

"Oh, those are beautiful!" cried Quinn. "Thank you so much for thinking of that – they're exactly what the place needs…"

"I knew that," said Lisbet. "That sandwich looks terrific. Got any more?"

"Of course I do," said Quinn quickly rising from the chair. She handed the plate to Lisbet.

"Here, you sit and eat this half, and I'll make us another one." She took the bouquet and headed in for the kitchen. "Want some tea?"

"Sounds good, long as you've got some cookies," Lisbet answered, sitting in another rocker. Thank goodness she knew where they would be hiding. "How's the moving coming?"

"All the furniture is already down there. Can you believe it? They came early this morning and we've been working since," she called from the kitchen.

Lisbet began to eat while Quinn set the kettle to boil and filled a glass vase for the flowers. She would arrange them later. The food was still on the cutting board, so she quickly put another sandwich together and brought it out to the porch, handing a half to Lisbet for her plate. She set her own plate on the bench and went back in for their tea.

"It's hard to believe you're moving in already. Seems like you just got here, but it's been six months!"

"Tell me about it," said Quinn with food in her mouth. "The time has just flown by. Are you having company for the holiday?"

"Oh yeah, all the kids are coming with their significant others. The old camp and my house will be full, with people coming and going all over the place. The only thing I can do is run away to the cabin." She reached for her sandwich.

"I figured as much. I didn't expect to see you over here today, with all you must have to do."

"I wouldn't have missed it for the world," Lisbet told her, smiling.

"What's happening with Ben?" Quinn asked.

"Oh we've been on the phone every day as usual. I think he's coming out to the cabin this weekend to avoid the crowds in town, at least I hope he is. He knows I'll be out there where it's quiet."

"So you've found your peace with the change in events?" Quinn asked.

"Well, he's acting exactly like he used to, nothings seems to have changed. He still calls and texts all the time. I just don't know when we're going to have intimate time, but I'm prepared to adjust to letting him take that lead."

"I'm so happy for you, Lisbet. I hope you two find everything you both need."

"Me too. I sure did find one thing I really needed..." she said, raising her eyebrows.

Quinn laughed. "Yep. And that's a good thing."

The two friends finished their lunch, and Quinn took their dishes into the kitchen as Lisbet started down the hill with another box. Quinn grabbed one too and followed her, leaving the clean up for later.

"This looks really wonderful," Lisbet said when she got to the top of the stairs and scanned the big room. "Ooh, the kitchen is great...and your bed looks adorable over there."

"Thank you," said Quinn quietly. "I love it too."

The two women unpacked the boxes they'd brought, and a few others. Lisbet found the two lamps Quinn was looking for, set one on each side of the bed, and turned them on, creating a warm glow. She loved the welcoming look of lights everywhere. She set two others on the kitchen counter and lit them too.

"Now the place looks like home," she said.

Quinn smiled. "Can you help me get this sofa centered in front of the fireplace?"

They maneuvered a big rug into place first, then positioned the sofa with a chair on either side, and a big square wooden coffee table in the center. Lisbet couldn't resist laying a fire in the fireplace, but she didn't light it. Quinn set some small twig tables about strategically, for lamps and books.

"That looks just right," she said.

The dining table was already where she wanted it, as was the drawing table. She had given the movers specific directions with those, so that the floor wouldn't get scratched adjusting them later. The women placed the chairs carefully around the table, which already had the vase full of flowers on it. Quinn took them to the sink and trimmed each of them, placing them each back carefully into the vase so they looked like they had just been picked, and set them in the center of the table. She'd pulled a couple of stems out to put by her bed in a small china pitcher.

Lisbet went to sit in one of the armchairs, leaning back and crossing her legs. "I think you're gonna be happy here," she said.

"Me too," said Quinn.

Chapter 24

After Lisbet left, Quinn prepared some bread dough and put it into the oven to proof. She didn't want to cook the first night so she'd taken out some homemade cream of chicken noodle soup from the freezer to warm if she got hungry. The whole boathouse smelled of the various species of wood, and a bit like some of the finishes, so she wanted to add the familiar scent of something baking in the oven. A slice of fresh toasted bread would be good with the soup too.

There would be plenty of time to unpack boxes because though Labor Day was upon them, she had no one to prepare for this year. Maybe she would get some company for Columbus Day, the last holiday of the season, but she doubted it. The whole weekend would be hers to unpack and adjust to the new space, so the main thing she wanted to do for now was to make the place ready for her first night.

She unpacked a large stack of towels, putting some in the bathroom and the rest in the walk in closet on the shelf right by the door, along with toilet tissue, soap, toothpaste and the rest of the small toiletries she had brought in a box marked "bathroom". There were shower rings in there, so she snapped the fabric shower curtain onto them and threaded them onto the rod. She twisted the curtain rod to fit tightly just high enough for the curtain to overlap the edge of the shower curb. Her bag from up in the camp was already there with her gown, robe, brushes, shampoos and moisturizer - everything she needed for the night and mornings - even a few changes of clothes. She set all these where they belonged and took the bag to the top of the stairs in case she needed it later.

She set her clock with the stack of books she'd been reading on the table at the window side of the bed where she'd be able to look out to the sunrise every morning. She hung her gown and robe behind the bathroom door.

Later that afternoon in the old camp kitchen, she filled a box of necessities - her teapot and cup, teabags, half and half, and butter in its covered dish. She put a bottle of wine in the corner of the box and some wine glasses carefully folded into dishtowels on top. She added some matches and the bread knife Kole had given her long ago.

Since the afternoon was becoming chilly, she ran up to get a flannel gown too, in case it got even colder that night. She remembered her journal, and got that from the front room along with some writing pens and pillar candles. Was that everything? She hoped so, because she wasn't going to go running up the hill for something in the middle of the night. She shut the back door tightly, turned out the lights and pulled the front door closed behind her as she balanced the heavy box awkwardly.

When she got back to the boathouse, she set the box heavily down on the counter, a little out of breath. The sun was lowering, but not yet setting. She could see it all the way down the west end of the lake in a way she never could from camp because of the distance from the lake and the dense woods. The sun was evolving into a multitude of horizontal colors – a sight that was so amazing you had to be there to believe it, she thought. The view was more beautiful than any picture, right through her kitchen windows.

She didn't plan to wear shoes in the house, so she pulled off her boots and set them on the top step. There was a shoe shelf at the base of the staircase, but she didn't want to go back down. The floor was a bit gritty from the movers, so she quickly swept it clean, removing the paper and rolling it up as she went. The new floor felt smooth and soft on her bare feet.

When that was done she looked around approvingly at the space. The pretty floor made everything flow together. She turned to the sink to wash her hands, then kneaded the bread on some flour spread on the big table, and set it into the oven to bake. Within moments the delicious aroma pervaded the entire space. She poured the soup into a pot, covered it and put it on warm, to finish defrosting. Then she opened the wine and poured some into her glass.

Taking the glass to the coffee table with her journal, she bent down to light the fire Lisbet had so thoughtfully laid for her. This was to be the very first fire in the fireplace, so she watched it intently in case there were any problems. It caught immediately, and the smoke drew up through the flue just as it was supposed to. She took her glass up, and raised it to the air before taking a sip as a toast to the new fireplace and to the house itself.

Curling into her favorite old chair, she realized how much she'd missed it while it was in storage. She tucked her legs under and pulled a pillow onto her lap to set the journal on, then sat for a long time without writing a thing, just gazing out the long windows at the lake, and the fire between them crackling and popping as if it had done so for a million years. Before she wrote the first line the bread was ready and she had to go to take it out. While she was up, she saw that the sun was indeed sinking at the horizon, its colors still reflecting up into what was becoming the night sky. In the other direction, she could already see the moon.

It was time to take off her clothes, so she slipped them all off and pulled the time worn flannel gown over her head, buttons open at the front. Its softness was like an ancient baby blanket. Rather than her robe, she placed a lacy cream blanket over her shoulders and arms like a long shawl, and returned to her chair.

She had just begun to write when Will's voice came up from the base of the stairs. "You home?" he called.

"Yes. I'm home," she said happily. "Come up and get a beer to celebrate."

He did just that. His favorite Stella was already in the refrigerator when he opened it, so he grabbed one, popped the top off and came over to where Quinn was sitting, grinning up at him. He smiled down at her and wandered around the room, looking out all of the windows and at everything in the room that had already been put into place.

"Not too bad up here," he said.

"I'm pretty pleased," Quinn answered, "and I feel comfortable already."

"The fireplace seems to be working," he observed.

"Yep, the oven too."

"It smells terrific in here. Is that fresh bread already?"

"There's nothing like something from the oven to christen a new house," she said.

Will went to the other armchair and sat down in it, taking a drink of beer. "Well, I guess that about covers everything," he said, tilting his head with a small smile. "Are you getting company in for the weekend?"

"Not this time," she answered. "Nobody seems to be able to get off work, and I'm just as glad. It'll give me some time to adjust to this place without having to be up at camp entertaining. You?"

"I think my son's gonna be in and out, but he really hasn't let me know for sure what his plans are. Fortunately, I don't have to take care of him."

"That's good," said Quinn. "So you'll be free to do whatever you want."

"Yep," he said. He looked out at the darkening lake, back to the fire and then over to her.

"There's something I want to tell you."

Quinn felt a tinge of fear arise in her. *Oh, what could this be*, she wondered. She didn't like the sound of those words. She looked intently over at him and waited.

"I'm going away," he said.

"You are?" she answered ever so quietly.

"Yeah. I'm gonna be gone about a month out west." He paused, but Quinn remained silent, to let him finish. "I usually try to go every year at the end of the summer, but I have an opportunity to hunt with a special guide I found, if I go early this time."

Quinn began to remember that Will went hunting every fall, but she had never paid much attention to when, or for how long. She was usually gone from camp by Labor Day, maybe with a quick trip up in October to close everything up.

"When are you leaving?" she asked.

"This weekend." he said. "I'm gonna be putting my gear together and flying out Sunday morning. I have to make a couple of connections to get where I'm going. I'll be out in the wild, where there's no phone service, probably. I'll be camping, up way before dawn and bedded down by dark."

"I bet you're looking forward to that, " Quinn offered, though she felt a sinking feeling herself.

"I think this is going to be a pretty good trip. We'll be hunting elk."

"Is anyone going with you — your family or anyone?"

"Nope. Just me and the guide." He took a pull from the beer bottle.

Quinn took a sip of her wine and looked thoughtfully into the fire, taking it in. She wondered if this was a goodbye, too. There was a silence between them.

"Can have some of that soup I saw over there?" he asked her. "I had a long day and didn't get much to eat."

"Of course you can," said Quinn, getting up to serve him some. She sliced the warm bread on a cutting board and brought that over first, setting it before him on the table with some butter.

"This smells great," he said, taking a piece and buttering it. He leaned back in the chair and ate while she poured soup into two large cups and brought them over with spoons. She had lost her appetite but ate a small portion, while Will drained his fairly quickly and went to the stove for some more. He ate some more bread too.

"Don't you want some of this?" he asked her, pointing to the loaf.

"Not right now," she said. "I had a sandwich for lunch."

"That was probably hours ago, right?"

He got up with his cup, taking her empty one from her, and the breadboard to the sink. She followed him with the butter dish, and began putting the food away.

He put his hands on her shoulders, turning her to him. "I'd like to sleep with you now, if that's okay," he said. "I wanted to be here for your first night."

She leaned into his chest and tried to push her fear away. She knew that Will had to be free to do everything his passion led him to do. She couldn't stand in the way no matter how she felt. "Let's go to bed then," she said.

Will went downstairs to close the door, taking off his boots and leaving them, and then came back up to the fire and closed the glass doors there. Quinn turned out the lamps as she moved toward the bed alcove, slipping into the bathroom first.

She got into the bed, turned out the light beside her and waited for him. In a few moments he sat on the bedside, turned out the light there, took everything off and turned into the bed towards her beneath the covers.

"Can we take off that gown? I want to be close to you."

Quinn lifted it over her head, and pulled the covers up to keep warm. She laid back into the pillows. Will moved over to her, turning onto his stomach and placing one arm on the other side of her so he could lean into her on his elbows. Looking at her closely in the dim moonlight, he smoothed her mouth with his fingers, pulling her bottom lip down slightly so that he could kiss her there tenderly.

Quinn could feel her body respond immediately, as it subtly drifted out of her control and into his. She was sure that he knew of his power over her because of the deft effective way he used it. As she willingly gave in to him, he always guided them exactly where he wanted them to go. It was a slow beautiful dance.

Her legs fell apart as they kissed each other, and he in turn moved between them. He kept kissing her deeply until they were both completely taken into their own world, the bed and the new surroundings fading away as in a dream.

Then he moved his mouth to her ear and whispered, "I'm coming back..."

She looked into his eyes as he leaned his head back just enough to see hers. "I'll be here when you do," she answered softly.

He kissed her some more and she pushed herself up to meet him as he came down into her. They moved together in each other's arms in the finely tuned lovemaking that had become theirs until they reached the intimate place they wanted to go together. Then they held each other until sleep overcame them both, the moon now high in the sky shining through the windows on them.

Will left her before the dawn came. She did not go back to sleep, but laid on her side looking out to the water and the light as it finally emerged first as a glow and then as the orange crescent of the morning sun.

Chapter 25

*Q*uinn spent the weekend days gradually opening all the boxes the movers had brought in, placing her well loved belongings on the shelves and in drawers. She stacked her folded clothes in the closet, and hung a few long garments behind the door. All the kitchen things were either stowed away or attractively in plain view on the open shelves above the workspace.

When she needed a break, she went down the stairs to her kayak, slipped it into the water, and floated around with no particular destination. In the evenings she rested before the fire and contemplated the beautiful views that surrounded her and the familiar things she'd set about that made her begin to feel at home.

She thought about Will, planning what he would need for a month in a different kind of wilderness, and getting it all packed effectively to take on a plane. He had gone out west to hunt before, so he probably knew just what kind of environment and conditions to expect. He would be packing, while she was unpacking.

That he had come to share her first night there in the boathouse made her even more grateful for his presence and influence on her life. Everything seemed altered, because of him. She had planned to do all of this alone, and had not had any trepidation about it. But now everything took on a different light – a more distinctly radiant light.

She could feel this invigorating life giving light deep inside her, pervading and renewing her as *chi*, life force. The I Ching had taught her that when one was in alignment with inner truth, one was also connected with cosmic harmony, which activated *chi*. This transformation was becoming a reality for her – she could sense an enhanced harmony with everything, and now it all became so simple to her. There was no effort required. In fact, it was happening on its own accord. It was all about letting go - for in ceasing to try to make things happen, one allowed the cosmos to step in to attain its natural state of harmony, and this was what she was experiencing now.

She saw for the first time that Will was not a distracting interruption, but a life giving force brought to her as a cosmic gift. His vitality was the essential element she had needed to guide her in correcting her course. His was the energy that had initiated a physical and psychological transformation that had revolutionized her very being.

She didn't dwell on these realizations. As she saw and recognized them, she knew to let them too drop away. It was not necessary to keep thinking, she just needed to learn more about how to feel — to let herself go thoroughly into her senses and embrace them.

Late Sunday afternoon the phone rang, startling her. It was her first call in the new place and she had no idea who it was.

"I'm calling from the airport while I wait for the guide to pick me up," said Will. "After today I'll be out in the bush, somewhere. I don't even know where he's taking me but I'm pretty sure my phone won't be working."

"Oh I'm so glad to hear your voice," she said. "How is everything going?"

"Just fine. As soon as he gets here we'll be going in his truck to the campsite. I hope we get there before dark to set up. Then we'll get up in the dark to see if we can find elk at their dawn feeding time."

"That sounds pretty exciting. I hope you find them."

"It would be nice, but we'll just have to see what happens."

There was a silence then. Quinn wasn't sure what to say.

"There's no Stella out here," he said.

"Well, can you find a substitute, maybe a bottle of Jack to take with you?"

"Maybe. But it's not the same," he said quietly.

"No. It isn't," she answered.

There was a moment of silence, but she could hear him breathing.

"There'll be some here for you though, when you come back."

"Good."

After another silence, he added, "Well, gotta go."

"See ya," she said, but he had already gone.

Quinn sank into the chair with the phone in her hand. She closed her eyes, breathed deeply, and immersed herself in the sound of Will's voice as it penetrated her heart.

Made in the USA
Charleston, SC
29 July 2015